G000162116

Who's Who in Women's Historical Fiction

Who's Who in Women's Historical Fiction

Kathy Martin

First published in Great Britain in 2012 by
Remember When
An imprint of
Pen & Sword Books Ltd
47 Church Street
Barnsley
South Yorkshire
S70 2AS

Copyright © Kathy Martin 2012

ISBN 978 1 84468 081 8

The right of Kathy Martin to be identified as author of this work has
been asserted by her in accordance with the Copyright, Designs and Patents
Act 1988.

A CIP catalogue record for this book is
available from the British Library.

All rights reserved. No part of this book may be reproduced or transmitted in
any form or by any means, electronic or mechanical including photocopying,
recording or by any information storage and retrieval system, without
permission from the Publisher in writing.

Typeset in 11pt Minion by Mac Style, Beverley, East Yorkshire
Printed and bound by CPI Group (UK) Ltd, Croydon, CRO 4YY

Pen & Sword Books Ltd incorporates the Imprints of Pen & Sword Aviation,
Pen & Sword Family History, Pen & Sword Maritime, Pen & Sword Military,
Pen & Sword Discovery, Wharncliffe Local History, Wharncliffe True Crime,
Wharncliffe Transport, Pen & Sword Select, Pen & Sword Military Classics, Leo
Cooper, The Praetorian Press, Remember When, Seaforth Publishing and
Frontline Publishing.

For a complete list of Pen & Sword titles please contact
PEN & SWORD BOOKS LIMITED
47 Church Street, Barnsley, South Yorkshire, S70 2AS, England
E-mail: enquiries@pen-and-sword.co.uk
Website: www.pen-and-sword.co.uk

Contents

Dedication

In memory of my truly wonderful mother, Ingeborg Fitzgeorge-Parker, whose life deserves a book of its own.

Acknowledgements

Whilst writing this book I have received an inordinate amount of encouragement and support from a number of special people. I should like to thank them all for being there for me. In particular I want to thank my sisters for reminding me of favourite books we all read long ago. It was fun to cast our minds back, recalling and then discussing books we hadn't thought about for over thirty years. Even though in the end it wasn't possible to use all their suggestions, I very much enjoyed revisiting our shared past. I would also like to thank Anita Lee and Monica Webb, wonderful friends who have been extremely supportive throughout the book's long gestation period and I must thank Anita McGee, another special friend, for the invaluable role she played in helping me source essential books. Gratitude is due, too, to Fiona Shoop for coming up with the idea for the book in the first place and for her continued interest and encouragement. On the home front, I must thank my husband Alastair and daughter Amy, both of whom are a constant support and inspiration to me. Finally, I must pay tribute to the extraordinarily talented women, past and present, whose works of historical fiction continue to enchant me and countless likeminded souls. I extend a heartfelt *thank you* to them all.

Introduction

A S A self-confessed addict of the genre, I am delighted to present this Who's Who of Women's Historical Fiction. Over the years I have spent countless happy hours immersed in historical novels and it is my hope that this book will encourage others to do likewise. For each featured character, I have endeavoured to give enough background information to arouse interest without disclosing crucial plot elements. The need to avoid spoilers has always been uppermost in my mind, but if some have escaped my vigilance I hope I can be forgiven.

I grew up on a diet of women's historical fiction – by which I mean historical novels written by women – and it is a habit I have never outgrown. My mother invariably had a paperback stuffed into her handbag and when she had finished with it she would pass it on to one of my older sisters until eventually it filtered down to me, the youngest girl in a family of five. By this time it would be dog-eared and very possibly coffee stained, but what mattered was that now it was my turn to be transported to another time and place where I would meet an endlessly fascinating cast of characters.

Through my teen years I must have read the complete works of Norah Lofts, Jean Plaidy, Anya Seton and Mary Renault, interspersing them with brief encounters with Margaret Campbell Barnes, Rosemary Hawley Jarman, Georgette Heyer, Catherine Cookson and others. Through these books I encountered historical characters as diverse as Alexander the Great and Geoffrey Chaucer, and ventured into eras uncharted by my school's history department. At the time I was dimly aware that men also wrote historical novels, but for me, the only books worth reading were those penned by the brilliant, prolific women who often wrote under a dizzying number of aliases.

When my reading horizons were finally widened to include male-generated historical fiction, I discovered many superb authors. In particular, I loved R.F. Delderfield and Winston Graham, and appreciated the comic value of George MacDonald Fraser's Flashman series. Today I am a great admirer of C.J. Sansom and his memorable Tudor sleuth, Matthew Shardlake. Yet women's historical novels remain my number one fiction choice, perhaps because at their best they deliver just the right blend of well-researched period detail and nuanced emotional impact.

Defining women's historical fiction

The A to Z section of this book introduces many of the most memorable protagonists from women's historical fiction, as well as characters which are less famous, but equally interesting. Waiting to make your acquaintance is a diverse ensemble that includes virtuous maidens, flawed temptresses, vapid ninnies, arrogant noblemen, steadfast heroes, obsessive loners, sinister villains, heartless cads, comedic relatives, garrulous spinsters, faithful friends, unrequited lovers and obstinate fools.

Before you meet them, I should state my personal definition of women's historical fiction which as a genre can be difficult to pin down. For me, it includes everything from great literary works such as Hilary Mantel's Booker prize-winning *Wolf Hall* to popular, romance-led tales like Catherine Cookson's *Tilly Trotter*, taking in along the way the brooding mysteries of Daphne du Maurier, the Ancient Rome crime romps of Lindsey Davis, and fictionalised accounts of real events as epitomised by Philippa Gregory's *The Other Boleyn Girl*. Different as these novel types may be, they all fall under the historical fiction umbrella and, crucially from the point of view of this book, all are the work of female authors.

It has not been my intention to create an encyclopaedic guide to women's historical fiction. Such a work would run to multiple volumes and would take years, if not decades, to write. Instead, I have attempted to give a representative sample of what is available, concentrating on books that cover the broadest possible historical landscape. Thus we start in Ancient Greece and come to a close in the Second World War. (As it was necessary to choose a cut-off date for the historical fiction featured in this guide, I opted for the end of the war on the grounds that many historians date the birth of modern society from 1945.) Over 430 major, or otherwise interesting, characters from in excess of fifty novels are, featured in what I hope is a fairly representative sample of the genre.

After much consideration I decided to omit 'time-slip' novels in which people from the present interact with characters from the past. Hugely enjoyable as these books often are, I did not include them because I could find no place for their

contemporary protagonists in a guide devoted to historical characters. Regrettably this means leaving out little gems such as Barbara Erskine's *Lady of Hay* – a book I love and have no hesitation in recommending. With less regret I have omitted any frothy, formulaic romantic novels that purport to be historical but, allowing for a quick costume change, could just as easily be set in a modern hospital or school environment. This means you'll look in vain for characters from Barbara Cartland, Mills and Boon, and others of that ilk.

Another self-imposed control has been to restrict the scope of this book to British authors, since there are so many talented home-grown authors, past and present, on which to focus. I have allowed myself three exceptions to this rule. Anya Seton, a superb American writer who published twelve historical novels between 1941 and 1975, can be included because she had an English father. The work of another gifted American-born author, Tracy Chevalier, is featured because she has lived and worked in England since 1984. There is no such justification for Margaret Mitchell, the third and final exception; she is included simply because it would be unthinkable to compile an A to Z of characters from women's historical fiction without mentioning figures as iconic as Scarlett O'Hara and Rhett Butler.

Having discussed omissions, I also need to explain why characters from certain classic works of literature are featured. According to The Historical Novel Society's definition of historical fiction, a novel must have been written at least fifty years after the events it describes, or have been written by someone who was not alive at the time of those events. It is a good definition, but abiding by it here would mean leaving out some of the best-loved novels of all time, including everything written by Jane Austen and the Brontë sisters (even Wuthering Heights misses out; published in 1847, it is mostly set in the eighteenth century, but concludes in 1803).

While this may in itself seem insufficient reason to include these nineteenth century classics, there is no denying that the world inhabited by, say, the Bennets of Longbourn, has long been consigned to history. Therefore, while I recognise that *Pride and Prejudice* would have been thought of as a contemporary work when it was published in 1813, for the purposes of this book it is regarded as a historical novel. The same applies to all inclusions that were contemporary when written, but are now appreciated not just for their characters and plots, but also for evoking the period in which they are set.

Chapter One

Painting the Past

We can never go back again,that much is certain …
Rebbecca, Daphne du Maurier

In which we consider the merits of creating a rich period landscape.

ONE OF the most compelling kinds of historical fiction is that which vividly recreates the everyday life of the era and location in which it is set. A novel may have an intriguing plot and be peopled with the most fascinating array of characters, but without a convincing portrayal of the period's sights, sounds and smells, it might just as well be set in modern times. To please discerning readers of the genre, it's not enough for authors to stick their characters in fancy dress and toss in the odd reference to a barouche. They need to capture the myriad little details that bring their segment of the past alive and delicately weave them into the narrative flow.

The canon of women's historical fiction is particularly rich in works that skilfully evoke the past. Certain passages from *Larksleve*, the first volume in Patricia Wendorf's Patteran trilogy, describe life in nineteenth century rural Somerset in sentences of lyrical prose that verge on the mesmerizing. Based on Wendorf's own family history, the book tells the story of two very different young women whose lives become linked when they swap gifts. Red-headed Eliza Greypaull, the daughter of solid farming stock, reluctantly accepts marriage to a cousin she doesn't love in exchange for possession of the pretty, productive Larksleve farm. Such a bargain has no appeal for her friend, Meridiana Loveridge, whose Romany blood demands she lives free and unfettered, making her own choice when it comes to marriage.

With consummate skill Wendorf contrasts the lives of the hard-working, materialistic Greypaulls with the communal itinerant lifestyle of the gypsy clan to which Meri belongs, at the same time imbuing each way of life with its own unique sense of beauty. Meri's free spirit is evoked by the gaily coloured ribbons that fly loose about her plaited hair, and her disdainful refusal to wear Eliza's cast-off boots. We glimpse her life as she walks alongside sweating horses which work in traces as they haul heavy wagons up a steep hill; their brief intervals of respite coming when Meri blocks the wheels with a chunk of wood chosen for the purpose. Or when she sits with her people around the campfire, blue flames leaping and smoke wreathing upwards, drinking hot, dark tea sweetened with honey, listening as the menfolk talk about 'Beng', their version of the devil.

Greypaull males, we discover, don't waste words on subjects that can't show a profit. They talk about crops and stock, while their women are concerned solely with child-rearing and food preparation. Eliza's happiness comes from counting the cheeses standing in rows in her pristine dairy, or admiring the elegance of her rarely used blue parlour. In a spirit of optimism she spells out 'Larksleve' in flowers at the front of the house. Her existence is dominated by the seasonal activities of the farm – wheat drilling in February, oats and barley in April, and sowing mangold and turnip in May. In June there is haymaking, and late summer brings the harvest. All the while Eliza milks her cows, makes her cheeses, preserves fruit, pickles vegetables, and salts down meat so her family will eat during the lean months of winter.

Even without its engrossing storyline, *Larksleve* would be worth reading for its spellbinding recreation of two contrasting ways of life in Victorian Somerset. As it is, Patricia Wendorf has crafted a magical novel that stays with the reader long after the last page has been turned. The remaining books in the trilogy, *Blanche* and *Bye Bye Blackbird* are also thoroughly readable, but the hypnotic power of the first novel is never surpassed.

As *Larksleve* shows, the successful evocation of domestic life in a historical setting can help elevate a novel from good to great. With *Girl with a Pearl Earring*, Tracy Chevalier beguiles readers with the minutiae of existence in seventeenth-century Delft. Whether Griet, the central protagonist who works as a maid for the

Vermeer family, is doing the laundry, going to market or dusting Vermeer's studio, each routine activity is set before the reader in vivid detail, allowing it to be seen as clearly as if it appeared in one of her employer's paintings. Similar skill is shown by Lindsey Davis throughout her long-running series of novels about Falco, a private informer living and working in the Rome of Vespasian. Within the first three pages of the first novel (*The Silver Pigs*), Davis manages to convey the heat, noise, colour and tension of Ancient Rome, while at the same time sketching out the character of her hero, Marcus Didius Falco, with a few deft strokes. A triumphant piece of scene setting, it seizes the reader's attention until there is no question of stopping until the story has run its course.

While good historical fiction succeeds in layering small, well-chosen nuggets of information to form an understanding of a bygone way of life, it can also create awareness of specific events and topics with which readers may not be familiar. In *The Winthrop Woman*, Anya Seton's remarkable novel about the early New England settlers, she touches on subjects as diverse as the British and Dutch colonisation of America's east coast, Puritan persecution of religious dissidents, and the massacre of Siwanoy Indians at Strickland Plains, Connecticut. All these events – and more – unfold within the framework of a story about Bess Winthrop, a spirited woman struggling to gain control of her own life at a time when female

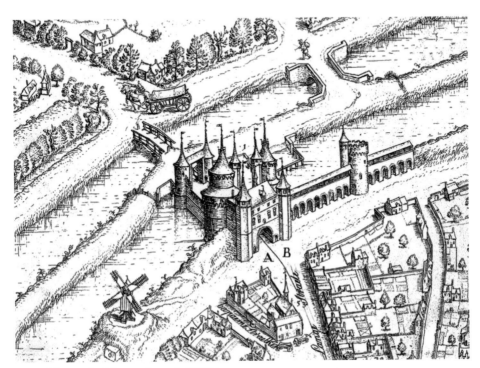

Map of Bruges by Marcus Gerards (1562).

subservience to men was the norm. The fact that Bess Winthrop really existed, and that much of Seton's narrative is rooted in fact, makes the book as fascinating as it is entertaining.

Also shining a light on areas of the past less well-trodden in fiction is Dorothy Dunnett with her brilliant House of Niccolò series, set in the fifteenth-century European Renaissance. In *Niccolò Rising*, the first novel in the series of eight, much of the action takes place in Bruges, and Dunnett manages to impart a convincing flavour of what life would have been like in such a thriving centre of trade. Today Bruges is known to be a pretty tourist destination much-favoured for romantic weekend getaways, but visitors familiar with Dunnett's book cannot fail to search for the Bruges that was once described as the chief commercial city of the world.

Bringing to life a believable version of the far distant past can be no easy task as it calls for careful research, together with considered interpretation and dissemination of facts, but setting a story in much more recent times presents its own challenges. The Second World War, for example, is rich territory for fiction, but because it is still within living memory for many people, authors need to tread carefully when portraying the social history of the period. In a novel set in medieval times, few readers would notice if a character was said to be wearing a garment that wasn't in reality worn for another twenty-five years, but jaws would drop if an author dressed a Second World War heroine in a mini skirt. It could be said that the closer the period setting to the present day, the more intense the scrutiny under which the everyday details are examined.

Yet there can be no denying the advantage to a good writer of familiarity with their subject matter. The personal knowledge and experience Elizabeth Jane Howard brought to the *Cazalet Chronicles*, her brilliant quartet of novels following

the fortunes of a prosperous English family just before, during and after the Second World War, imbues them with the unmistakable ring of authenticity. Her characters have salmon croquettes and Charlotte Russe for dinner, wash with Vinolia soap, and shop at Ponting's in Kensington. Children wear Aertex shirts and sand shoes, their mothers use eau-de-Cologne and swansdown powder puffs, and the men smoke non-stop and drink whisky before dinner. Period details such as these could, of course, be gleaned second-hand, but Howard's use of them is effortless; she speaks the language of the era with the fluency of a native. On its own, this fluency is admirable but unremarkable; when married to Howard's perceptive and human storytelling, the result is little short of perfection.

Chapter Two

Heroes and Villains: The Good, the Bad and the Morally Ambiguous

'…but his friend Mr Darcy soon drew the attention of the room by his fine, tall person, handsome features, noble mien; and the report of which was in general circulation within five minutes after his entrance, of his having ten thousand a year.'

Jane Austen, *Pride and Prejudice*

In which we learn to steer clear of bounders and wastrels.

THE PAGES of a particular kind of women's historical fiction are populated by a regiment of handsome, eligible bachelors. Fair or dark, sincere or sardonic, gentleman or cleric, what they all have in common is that from the moment they appear in the narrative, the reader is mentally marrying them off to the heroine. So too, most likely, are the heroine's mother and friends – think of Mrs Bennet in *Pride and Prejudice* with her five daughters to settle, or Mrs Jennings in *Sense and Sensibility,* whose unsubtle enthusiasm for marrying off her young female friends offends Marianne Dashwood. Such dedication to matchmaking is not surprising given that until the end of the nineteenth century and even beyond, marriage was the only real career option for middle and upper-class girls. (See The Importance of Being Married.)

With finding Mr Right high on the agenda of every self-respecting heroine (and her mamma), the intense level of scrutiny to which potential suitors' incomes and prospects are subjected becomes entirely understandable. Interest is piqued when a good-looking bachelor is introduced, and hopes are raised when it becomes known that he is a man of means. Whether he knows it or not, he is now the legitimate prey of mothers with unmarried daughters, and can expect no peace until he becomes engaged or leaves the neighbourhood. Jane Austen expressed it beautifully when she wrote in the opening paragraph of *Pride and Prejudice*: 'It is a truth universally acknowledged that a single man in possession of a good fortune, must be in want of a wife.'

Note that it is the state of being single and in possession of a good fortune that establishes the gentleman as suitable for marriage. His character and personal appearance do not come into it. When Mrs Bennet implores her teasing husband to call on the newly-arrived Mr Bingley at Netherfield, she knows nothing about him save that he has four or five thousand a year. Fortunately for Mrs Bennet, Charles Bingley is a pleasant young man of blameless character, and is more than ready to oblige her by falling in love with a sweet, pretty girl. Not all heroines fare so well. The hapless young woman who loses her heart to Arthur Huntingdon, the debauched anti-hero from *The Tenant of Wildfell Hall*, is blessed with beauty, brains and a more than adequate fortune, yet none of this saves her from a miserable marriage. Unlike Bingley, Huntingdon drinks and gambles to excess, and to his wife he is cruel, abusive and unfaithful. Yet on the surface he is just as eligible as Bingley since he has good looks, charm and money – exactly the kind of man, in fact, to set Mrs Bennet dreaming of wedding bells.

It could be said that Charles Bingley is historical fiction's archetypal decent, steady type, while Huntingdon represents the ultimate bad boy. Allowing for variations in fortune and circumstance, their counterparts appear several times in the A to Z section of this book. Henry Tilney from *Northanger Abbey* is a brighter, less wealthy Bingley, although his brother Frederick exhibits the callous cruelty of a fledgling Huntingdon. Edmund Bertram (*Mansfield Park*) is a more pious Bingley, and diffident Edward Ferrars (*Sense and Sensibility*) is cut from the same cloth, while both Colonel Brandon (*Sense and Sensibility*) and George Knightley (*Emma*) are older, wiser variants. On the opposite side of the spectrum, Captain Francis Levison from *East Lynne* would give Huntingdon a run for his money in the reprehensible stakes, with *Persuasion's* William Elliot not far behind. Meanwhile, leading the field in a class all his own, is Heathcliff, Emily Bronte's magnificently monstrous creation, who dominates *Wuthering Heights* with his glowering presence.

While there's no denying that the decent Bingley types are perfect husband material in that they will never be unfaithful, risk all on the throw of a dice or drink themselves into oblivion, there is a chance that a lively heroine might find life with them just the tiniest bit dull once the honeymoon is over. That could never be said about historical fiction's wicked charmers; the bad lads who temper their rotten behaviour with charisma, wit and good humour. George Wickham from *Pride and Prejudice* exemplifies the breed; he may be an incorrigible rogue, but his character fairly sparkles off the page, making him hard to truly dislike. Henry Crawford (*Mansfield Park*) is also a thoroughly charming bounder, and Frank Churchill (*Emma*) has the potential to become disarmingly bad although the love of a good woman might save him. Willoughby from *Sense and Sensibility* has elements of Wickham-ism in his personality, but the genuine attachment he feels to the girl he hurts, marks him out in a curious way as both better and worse than his brother blackguards – better because he is capable of real love, and worse because regardless of that, he breaks his loved one's heart.

The essential difference between the Huntingdons and the Wickhams is that the former want to hurt and therefore deliberately inflict wounds, while the latter do it unconsciously as a by-product of their irresponsible lifestyle. While every sensible heroine should pick up her hem and run as fast as she can from a predatory Huntingdon, she would also be well advised to steer clear of Wickhams. To marry one would be to condemn oneself to a miserably unsettled life, moving continually from one dreary lodging to another in an attempt to dodge creditors, and perpetually cadging money or favours from reluctant relatives. Then there would be the nights when her husband would not come home, and she'd know he was lying in the arms of some hussy. No, Wickhams are singularly unfit for marriage, but there can be no denying that their presence in a novel adds an enjoyable frisson to the narrative.

Choosy heroines, those looking for someone more exciting than a good, but potentially dull Bingley, and less unreliable than a Wickham, could do no better than to set their cap at a hero who is nearly, but not quite, perfect. Admittedly this is a high risk strategy since these characters always have a cluster of other young ladies vying for their attention, and it is axiomatic that the girl who does finally win his love will have to endure bitter heartache before reaching the altar. Yet the prize of living happily ever after with Mr Not-Quite-Perfect renders all such considerations inconsequential.

Fitzwilliam Darcy from *Pride and Prejudice* must be the most famous example of the 'nearly but not-quite-perfect' breed. He has everything any heroine could

C.E. Brock illustration of Mr Bingley with Jane Bennet.

C.E. Brock illustration of Mr Denny introducing Mr Wickham to the Bennet girls.

F.H. Townsend illustration of Mr Rochester with Jane Eyre.

possibly want – good looks, nobility, intelligence, a large fortune, and a beautiful home – but set against this are his arrogance, a deep-seated belief in the superiority of his opinions, and apparent disdain for his social inferiors. Plus, to some extent he is already spoken for, at least in the mind of his overbearing aunt who has determined that he must marry her daughter, and not forgetting his best friend's sister who is also making every effort to land him. It takes a very special type of heroine to navigate those obstacles, overcoming along the way her own prejudice against the man, and make it to the finishing line with a smile on her face.

While Darcy is the benchmark for all not-quite-perfect heroes, women's historical fiction has other noteworthy examples to offer. There is handsome, successful Captain Wentworth (*Persuasion*) who wallows in hurt pride, and Gilbert Markham (*The Tenant of Wildfell Hall*), an amiable and intelligent young farmer cursed with an extremely suspicious mind. Or even, from a very recent historical novel, Ivo Maltravers (*My Last Duchess*) who combines the desirable attributes of a dukedom and ancient castle with good looks and charm, yet conceals deep sadness behind his polished façade.

The important point to remember about not-quite-perfect heroes is that their flaws are only ever superficial. There's nothing that can't be put right by a well-written letter and an act of selfless generosity, or an impassioned tête-à-tête with the beloved, preferably involving tears and handkerchiefs. Mr Not-Quite-Perfect has no skeleton lurking in his closet, no shady secret that will shock a respectable heroine to her core, no regrettable penchant for dishonesty and no reputation for scandalous behaviour. Heroes of this nature do exist in women's historical fiction but they fall squarely into the morally ambiguous category.

It is interesting to note that some of the most memorable male characters in women's historical fiction have pasts that don't bear close scrutiny. Daphne du Maurier excelled at creating heroes of this type. In *Rebecca*, Maxim de Winter is so busy hiding something from his naïve second wife that he fails to realise how much damage his lack of candour is doing to their relationship. In contrast, the leading men in two other du Maurier bestsellers are completely open with the women they love, but their honesty does not extend into their everyday activities. Jean-Benoit Aubéry (*Frenchman's Creek*) relieves ennui by committing acts of piracy on the Cornish coast, while Jem Merlyn (*Jamaica Inn*) is an unrepentant horse thief. Piracy and theft are unlikely to feature high on a list of desirable occupations for the ideal man but remarkably, Du Maurier helps us understand the romantic appeal of this unpromising gallows fodder.

While Aubéry and Merlyn relish their existence on the wrong side of the law and choose quite deliberately to stay there, de Winter has a more conventional nature. In the ordinary course of events he would live and die a thoroughly respectable man, but the shape of his life is altered by one phenomenally bad decision. When fate leads him into a shabby world of pretence and dishonesty, he chooses to lose his integrity rather than let society see his shame. Ultimately, however, the strain of leading such a sham life causes him to snap, with cataclysmic consequences. Comparisons between de Winter and Edward Rochester, the morally ambiguous hero of *Jane Eyre*, are inevitable given that both characters have paid dearly for an early mistake, and conceal secrets which have the potential to wreak irrevocable damage on their lives. Of the two, de Winter is perhaps less culpable for the predicament in which he finds himself, and therefore more to be pitied, yet it is Rochester who wrings the heart most successfully. He can be moody, abrupt and even cruel, but he is always compelling and passionate, and in his hour of need not even the most flint-hearted heroine would turn from him.

Arguably the most appealing, morally ambiguous character to emerge from the pages of women's historical fiction is Rhett Butler, the handsome, debonair hero from *Gone With the Wind*. He delights in scandalising genteel Southern society with his outrageous behaviour, while at the same time venerating a gentle lady who embodies the very values he affects to scorn. His highly-complex character is further demonstrated by the fact that he lives recklessly but loves cautiously, forever concealing the true depth of his feelings from the woman he loves. As a prototype for the ultimate swoon-worthy hero his status is rivalled only by Mr Darcy, yet in many ways he has more in common with Wickham than with Darcy. Wickham, though, would never risk his skin for a way of life he knew to be doomed, but Darcy almost certainly would. Perhaps that is the key to Butler's appeal – he is a tantalising blend of the nearly but not-quite-perfect-hero with the wicked charmer. He is passionate and caring, and life with him will never be dull. The woman he loves is a very lucky girl, if she only has the sense to realise it.

Chapter Three

Historical People in Fiction

'There is a history in all men's lives.'
William Shakespeare, Henry IV Part 2

In which we examine the fictionalisation of real characters from the past.

MANY WOULD agree that the proper function of historical fiction is to entertain rather than educate, yet it is inevitable that people will pick up nuggets of information when reading books set in the past. It follows that authors have a duty to strive for accuracy when describing real events or, if altering events to fit a storyline, acknowledge that they have done so. At the end of Daisy Goodwin's *My Last Duchess*, the author acknowledges that she has 'taken one deliberate liberty with chronology' for the purposes of her plot. Even though the liberty referred to is very small, Goodwin is right to draw attention to it because otherwise readers would be left with an inaccurate version of events.

I have good reason to be thankful for authorial accuracy. When I read *Gone with the Wind* at the age of sixteen I picked up enough detail about the American Civil War, a topic my school didn't cover, to help me pass an important history exam. I was supposed to answer a question on Britain's nineteenth century Corn Laws but didn't want to, partly because I found the subject deathly dull, but mainly because I hadn't bothered to revise. In desperation I scanned the paper for a more favourable question and to my relief found one on the American Civil War, a subject I knew a little about having paid closer attention to *Gone with the Wind* than to my infinitely dreary history text book. Had Margaret Mitchell played fast and loose with the facts in her epic novel, my cheeky ploy would have backfired. Instead, thanks to Mitchell's skilful interweaving of history into her romantic narrative, my skin was saved. While no rational person would recommend studying for exams by reading nothing but historical fiction, the anecdote demonstrates that useful knowledge can be acquired from well-researched novels.

Had I chanced, prior to that exam, to read a novel set in the era before the repeal of the Corn Laws, I might have had more enthusiasm for the subject, since good historical novelists bring the past alive. They familiarise us with different periods by showing where people lived, what they wore and ate, how they spoke, and how they interacted with one another. Great events are shown through the eyes of characters we have come to care about and this helps us understand the impact these events had on the lives of ordinary people. However, when it comes to portraying real people from history, authors are often unable to rely on 'facts' because contemporary descriptions of prominent figures are frequently contradictory, depending on the bias of the chronicler. During the Wars of the Roses, for example, pro-Lancastrian scribes would have described Henry VI as pious and gentle, whereas to Yorkist supporters he was feeble-minded and pathetic.

This unreliability worsens when people are written about after their death, particularly if the chronicler is hostile to them. Before he died at the Battle, of Bosworth, Richard III enjoyed a reasonable reputation. Whatever the rights and wrongs of his claim to the throne, he was known by his actions to be courageous and skilful in battle and a gifted administrator with a respect for justice. Moreover, nothing about his physical appearance was thought sufficiently unusual to be recorded by the chroniclers of the day. Yet after his death, Tudor propagandists such as John Morton and Polydore Vergil annihilated his reputation and turned him into the deformed, nephew-murdering monster some still believe in today. Fortunately for Richard, many writers have taken up their cudgels on his behalf, including a fair number of novelists. One of the most sympathetic and memorable fictional portraits of Richard III was that created by Rosemary Hawley Jarman in *We Speak No Treason*. The entire book is devoted to the rehabilitation of his reputation and is written with such passion that once read it is virtually impossible to ever again think ill of Richard.

When Hawley Jarman set out to challenge the preconceptions surrounding Richard III she was lucky enough to have a wealth of source material, even if much of it was inimical to her hero. About certain historical figures, however, precious little contemporary information exists beyond their name and their place in history. In such cases the author has to flesh the character out using their own imagination, their knowledge of the period, and any small clues that can be gleaned from the negligible information that does exist. Anya Seton's *Katherine* (voted 95th in the BBC's 2003 search for the nation's best-loved novel) tells the

story of Katherine Swynford, a relatively lowborn fourteenth century woman who became the ancestress of a long line of sovereigns stretching from Yorkist times to the present day. The novel brilliantly recreates the era of Edward III, Chaucer, and the Black Death, while telling a passionate love story that is as convincing as it is memorable. Yet as Alison Weir's 2007 biography of Katherine Swynford demonstrates, virtually nothing is known about her; so scanty are contemporary references to her that we don't know where or when she was born, what she looked like or when she first became John of Gaunt's mistress. For a biographer such dearth of information presents a major stumbling block, but for an imaginative fiction writer it can be a blessing. Instead of being shackled by detail, a blank canvass exists on which to create a vibrant portrait. When Seton wrote *Katherine* she took full advantage of her blank canvass to paint a protagonist as vivid and believable as any entirely fictitious heroine.

The popularity of historical fiction means that novels can have a widespread influence on how we perceive well-known figures from the past. Authors, whether working within a framework of facts or conjuring a portrayal from imagination alone, have to make a decision as to whether their depiction is going to be sympathetic or unfavourable. A sympathetic characterisation from a bestseller can stimulate interest in the real person and encourage readers to learn more about them by reading biographies and other relevant non-fiction. By contrast, unfavourable characterisations often set a precedent for portraying figures in a similar light in subsequent novels. There is, for example, a long tradition of presenting Jane Boleyn, sister-in-law of Anne, as dangerously malevolent, and until Hilary Mantel's Booker-prizewinning *Wolf Hall* came along, Thomas

Cromwell was almost always cast in the role of unmitigated villain. Comfortingly familiar as these portraits may be, it comes as a refreshing change when they are challenged. Mantel's Cromwell can be ruthless, yes, but he is also touched with an emotional vulnerability that makes him surprisingly likeable. He is shown to be, like most of us, a complex human being, capable equally of great kindness and studied vengeance. By laying bare the man behind Cromwell's notorious reputation, Mantel reminds us to look beneath the surface before forming our judgements.

Ultimately, we need to accept that many of history's questions will never be answered to our satisfaction. We may never know whether Richard III did or

Engraving of Richard III.

didn't murder his nephews, or whether John of Gaunt's decision to marry his long-term mistress was prompted by his love for her or by the desire to legitimise their children. We can never be certain that Jane Boleyn's decision to testify against her husband and sister-in-law was prompted by malice rather than fear for her own safety, or that Thomas Cromwell engineered the downfall of his rivals. It is the function of biographies and history books to try and throw some light on these and other questions, but they can never supply definitive answers. Neither can historical novels, but they do present a version of events that can kindle our interest in the periods they relate to, and make us question our preconceived notions about the fascinating cast of characters who made our history.

Chapter Four

The Importance of Being Married

'A single woman, with a very narrow income, must be a ridiculous, disagreeable old maid!'

Emma by Jane Austen

In which we assess the prospects for single ladies of limited means.

IN MUCH female-penned historical fiction the topic of marriage is ever present in the plot. It may not be referred to outright, but the reader knows, and the author knows that the reader knows, that any pretty young girl heading out to a ball isn't going purely for the love of dancing or to show off a new gown. Enjoyable as she may find both activities, her real object in attending the ball is to attract an eligible suitor. In novels with a medieval or Tudor setting, appearing at Court serves the same purpose as being seen at a ball. Since a degree of social standing is required for entrée to balls and Court, girls from less-privileged backgrounds have to make do with meeting men at church, occasional country dances or even, in the case of working class heroines, at their place of work.

The frequency with which finding a husband recurs as a theme in good-quality historical fiction is indicative of the overwhelming importance matrimony played in women's lives, rather than any authorial obsession with weddings and happy-ever-afters. Up until fairly recent times gently-reared daughters were expected to become wives and mothers; it was the only career option open to them that combined respectability with the possibility of happiness and fulfilment. The future could be decidedly grim for girls who failed in the marriage market, especially if their parents were short of funds. In Jane Austen's *Emma*, the eponymous

'GIVING HER AWAY.'

Youthfully made-up Spinster, over forty, just engaged, proudly introduces her Young Betrothed to the Family Gardener.
Family Gardener. "Ah, Miss Letty, I'm that glad! I've been waiting for this day for the last twenty years!"

Dating from 1905, this humorous sketch by C. Shepperson demonstrates that even into the Twentieth century women were under pressure to marry

heroine is sanguine about her decision never to marry because she has sufficient money to live comfortably as an unmarried woman. At the same time she spells out, with greater clarity than sympathy, the unpleasant prospect awaiting impoverished spinsters:

> 'Never mind, Harriet, I shall not be a poor old maid; and it is poverty only which makes celibacy contemptible to a generous public! A single woman, with a very narrow income, must be a ridiculous, disagreeable old maid! – the proper sport of boys and girls – but a single woman, of good fortune, is always respectable, and may be as sensible and pleasant as anybody else.'

Girls less fortunate than Emma, whose parents could not afford to keep them at home, recognised that matrimony was the only way to avoid seeking work as a governess or paid companion. These were the limited occupations open to a well-bred young woman if she wanted to retain her status as a lady. Working in a shop or as a lady's maid – even if she could find such positions – would rob her once and for all of her claim to gentility. In theory, working as a governess or companion maintained a woman's status as a lady, although in practice she held an ambiguous position in which she was neither fish nor fowl. Her birth, upbringing and education identified her as a lady, yet her dependence on an earned income placed her on the same footing as a servant. This was not the only drawback to becoming a governess. Pay was rarely generous and employers could be cold and unduly demanding. The governess might have to travel far from familiar territory to find a post and she might find the children in her care unruly or spiteful. Even with a decent, well-meaning employer, the life of a governess could be lonely, but with a bad one it was utterly miserable. In *Jane Eyre*, sisters Diana and Mary Rivers have to work as governesses because there is not enough money for them to live at home with their clergyman brother. Charlotte Brontë leaves the reader in no doubt about the unpleasantness of their predicament:

> 'Diana and Mary were soon to leave Moor House, and return to the far different life and scene which awaited them, as governesses in a large, fashionable, south-of-England city, where each held a situation in families by whose wealthy and haughty members they were regarded only as humble dependants, and who neither knew nor sought out their innate excellences, and appreciated only their acquired accomplishments as they appreciated the skill of their cook or the taste of their waiting-woman.'

In *Emma*, meanwhile, the genteel but impoverished Jane Fairfax faces the very real prospect of becoming a governess. Emma, as we have seen, declares her intention never to marry, safe in the knowledge that she will never lack for money, but Jane is not so fortunate. Her view of the profession she is about to join is made clear when she compares it to the slave trade: '... but as to the greater misery of the victims, I do not know where it lies.'

Yet while contemplating the potential unhappiness of her future role, she has only to look at her aunt, the voluble Miss Bates, to know that when she is too old or too frail to continue working, she faces an even bleaker prospect. Once a highly-respected clergyman's daughter, Miss Bates now scrimps and saves to make ends meet, relying on invitations from kind friends to enliven her days and inevitably attracting ridicule from the less charitably inclined.

Cranford's spinsters and widows enjoy a society almost entirely devoid of a masculine presence (illustration by Hugh Thomson, 1892).

Mrs Ferrars, one of a trio of widows from Sense and Sensibility; illustration by C.E. Brock.

Even when unmarried daughters were able to stay at home, the stigma attached to their old maid status meant they could expect to be treated with indifference at best, and at worst, with contempt. In Anne Brontë's *The Tenant of Wildfell Hall*, Mary Millward, oldest daughter of a widowed clergyman, is a decent, hardworking woman who is 'trusted and valued by her father, loved and courted by all dogs, cats, children, and poor people, and slighted and neglected by everyone else.'

The irony of Mary's situation is that as 'housekeeper and family drudge' she is of far more use than Eliza, her flirtatious younger sister, but because Eliza is pretty and has every chance of making a good match, society holds her in higher regard. At least Mary has the comfort of being appreciated by her father.

The convention of unmarried daughters devoting the best years of their lives to caring for elderly parents continued well into the twentieth century, and if literature is to be believed it was often a thankless task. Poor Miss Milliment from Elizabeth Jane Howard's Cazalet Chronicles has spent years looking after her tyrannical old father and when he dies is left so hard up that she is obliged to find work as a governess. At least Sybil Beddows, the spinster daughter of Alderman Mrs Beddows and her auctioneer husband from Winifred Holtby's *South Riding* has a comfortable home, but in some ways she is no more her own person than Miss Milliment. She fetches her father's slippers when he returns from work, and accepts without quibble her duty to look after her dead brother's daughter.

With the alternatives to marriage appearing so manifestly unattractive, it is scarcely surprising that young women frequently agreed to bind themselves to men they didn't love, and in some cases, positively disliked. When plain Charlotte Lucas in Jane Austen's *Pride and Prejudice* agrees to marry the silly, pompous man her best friend Lizzie has only just rejected, the reader feels as appalled as Lizzie. Yet Charlotte is marrying him with her eyes wide open; her acceptance of his proposal has been made 'solely from the pure and disinterested desire of an establishment'. For the Charlottes of the world, escaping spinsterhood is all that matters. The three unmarried sisters from Tracy Chevalier's *Remarkable Creatures* may not entirely agree. While not embracing their single state with unbridled enthusiasm, they become accustomed to their lot and Elizabeth, the middle sister, wryly acknowledges that there are worse fates. Nevertheless, there is pathos in her relief that their lack of husbands is not openly mocked – although there may be smirking behind their backs.

For a refreshingly different stance on the desirability or otherwise of matrimony, it is necessary to visit Cranford, the fictitious northern town invented by Elizabeth Gaskell in her novel of the same name. Led by the indomitable Miss Jenkyns, the town's old maids and widows choose to regard the absence of men in their lives as desirable, not regrettable. The most upliftingly defiant comment on the single state, however, must come from Sarah Burton, Winifred Holtby's head teacher heroine from *South Riding*. Energetic, ambitious and keen to inspire young minds, Sarah has quite deliberately chosen spinsterhood over marriage to a man whose views she cannot respect. Instead of moping, she throws herself into leading a full and useful life. 'I was born to be a spinster,' she proclaims, 'and by God I'm going to spin.' Charlotte Lucas might shudder at such a sentiment, but the ladies of Cranford, while regretting Miss Burton's vehement language, would wholeheartedly approve.

A widow's lot

As we have seen, there is a tendency for life to treat cruelly spinsters in women's historical fiction, but in general widows have a happier time. It is true that there are examples of widows in desperate circumstances – the semi-invalid Mrs Smith from *Persuasion* springs immediately to mind – but there are also plenty of widows who live comfortably, enter into a busy social life, and enjoy meddling in the lives of their friends and acquaintances. The novels of Jane Austen offer up a particularly rich assortment of memorable widows. In *Pride and Prejudice* Lady Catherine de Bourgh comports herself with a degree of imperiousness more fitting to a reigning monarch in the apparent assumption that her wealth and privilege command deference and obedience from all lesser personages. Her behaviour simply serves to make her a figure of fun to anyone with a sense of the ridiculous (not Mr Collins, then) but in terms of character and integrity, she is streets ahead of Mrs Norris from *Mansfield Park*. This odious woman ruins two nieces with her unbridled sycophancy, while making another thoroughly miserable with spiteful barbs about her inferior status. For sheer well-meaning jollity, on the other hand, *Sense and Sensibility*'s Mrs Jennings is hard to beat while from the same book, Mrs Dashwood is a rare portrait of a woman grieving sincerely for her late husband and Mrs Ferrars gives us a woman abusing the influence of her position to control her son's life. In *Persuasion*, meanwhile, we encounter a completely different type of widow. Mrs Clay is still young and she wants to find a new husband, preferably one with sufficient income to keep her in comfort, so she is circling her friend's father with predatory intent.

A different predatory widow plays a prominent role in *We Speak No Treason*, a wonderful novel set in the Wars of the Roses. Dame Elizabeth Grey is beautiful but poor and she has two young sons to bring up; it is easy to understand why she decides to use her looks to ensnare a powerful protector but her actions are to have grave repercussions for the entire country. In contrast Katherine Parr, another historical figure, was anything but predatory when she attracted the attention of Henry VIII. Already twice-widowed, she was hoping finally to marry a man of her own choice when the king's lustful eye fell on her.

This brings us to the subject of remarriage. As with old maids, money makes all the difference as to how a widow is treated by society in historical fiction. A rich widow will be welcome everywhere, whereas one struggling to stay afloat financially may find her invitations from former friends are few and far between. Yet the lot of the poor widow is still preferable to that of the poor spinster because she has evaded the stigma of being left 'on the shelf'. She may be pitied for losing her husband, but if she has inherited a fortune the pity will be tempered with a new respect for her as an independently wealthy woman, and as soon as decency allows she will have suitors knocking at her door. Even if she has been left with little to live on, the very fact of having 'Mrs' in front of her name will earn her a degree of goodwill and will protect her forever from being considered 'a ridiculous, disagreeable old maid'.

A to Z of Selected Characters from Women's Historical Fiction

Using the A to Z

A symbol appears beside each character's name, denoting the setting of the novel in which they appear. For example, a fan denotes Regency society while a Tudor rose signifies the Tudor era. More than one symbol indicates that the book spans several eras, except the cow which indicates that whatever the era, the setting is rural.

Symbols

 Ancient Greece

 Stuart

 Ancient Rome

 English Civil War

 Medieval

 17th century Netherlands

 Wars of the Roses

 17th century England

 15th century European Renaissance

 New England settlers

 Tudor

 French Revolution

 Georgian

 Late Victorian

 Regency

 World War I

 Late Georgian Cornwall

 20th century pre-World War I

 1830s provincial England

 World War 11

 Mid Victorian

 Rural setting

 American Civil War

The letters **RP** alongside a character indicate a fictionalised portrait of a real historical character. Some characters appear in more than one book featured in the guide, but to avoid confusion they are only listed once. So, for example, Henry VIII appears in *The Other Boleyn Girl*, *The Lady Elizabeth* and *Wolf Hall*, but the description given for him refers only to his characterisation in *The Other Boleyn Girl*.

A note about names

Characters are generally listed under the surname by which they are known at the start of the book. For example, Lydia Bennet is listed under B for Bennet even though her name changes later in the book. This is done partly for simplicity, since many characters change their surname more than once, but also so that important plot developments are not given away. However, relatively minor characters that change name early in a novel are listed under the surname by which they are known for the majority of the book.

When characters are referred to in a book by two names, one formal and the other a family name, I have in most cases listed them under their formal name with their family name in brackets alongside. Thus, Lady Alconleigh from Nancy Mitford's *Pursuit of Love* and *Love in a Cold Climate* is under A for Alconleigh with Aunt Sadie, the name by which the narrator refers to her throughout, in brackets. However, when a character's formal name is never given, they are listed under their family name; thus, Lady Alconleigh's unmarried sister is listed under A for Aunt Emily.

Members of the nobility are frequently known by more than one name and this makes it difficult to determine the name under which they should be listed. With John of Gaunt, for example, I had to decide between listing him under G for Gaunt or L for Lancaster (Duke of). I opted to list him under G for Gaunt because there have been many other Dukes of Lancaster over the years, but history knows only one John of Gaunt.

Roman names present a particular problem since male characters may have up to three names – a personal one, a family name and another which may or may not have been a nickname. An argument could be made for listing Roman characters under their family name, but as this comes second in a string of three names, I have listed them under their last name in order to make them easier to find in the A-Z.

A is for Alconleigh, Anning, Aubéry and more

Acciajuoli, Nicholai Giorgio de   **RP**
From *Niccolò Rising* by Dorothy Dunnett

An elegant Greek nobleman with an impeccable background, Acciajuoli arrives in Bruges in the company of a group of Scottish lords at the start of the book. He is returning from a visit to Scotland which was driven by the need to raise a ransom for his brother who has been captured by the Turks at Constantinople. This part of his mission has been successful, but he has another, more secret agenda, which is to mobilise Christendom to launch a new crusade against the Turks.

Acciajuoli is a finely dressed individual with a dark olive complexion, close-set dark eyes, combed black beard, fine teeth and manicured hands. His Florentine robes help conceal the fact that he has a wooden leg. Astute, observant and civilized, he is good at spotting potential and early on takes a close interest in a character most others regard as a doltish nuisance.

Aigeus (King)
From *The King Must Die* by Mary Renault

The King of Athens, Aigeus is a troubled man as he has no direct heir, his two marriages having failed to produce any children. His brother, on the other hand, has numerous sons, most of whom now have children of their own. Aigeus fears that once he dies, his nephews will rip Athens asunder in bloody civil war as they vie for ultimate power. What he needs more than anything else is a strong heir of his own to hold the city together. Eighteen years before the book begins, he consulted the Oracle at Delphi for a solution to his problem but was unable to interpret the answer.

Aithra
From *The King Must Die* by Mary Renault

Daughter of King Pittheus of Troizen, a small city southwest of Athens, Aithra is the Chief Priestess of the cult of Mother Dia, the goddess believed by the people to be the wife of Poseidon. Aged about 23 when the book starts she has one child, a boy called Theseus, whose paternity is shrouded in mystery. Aithra is a loving mother to whom her son is very attached.

Alconleigh, Lady (Aunt Sadie)
From *The Pursuit of Love* and *Love in a Cold Climate* by Nancy Mitford

Believed to have been inspired by Nancy Mitford's own
mother, Lady Redesdale, Lady Alconleigh is beautiful,
dreamy and vague. It is implied that she is worn out
with childbirth having produced seven children, three
boys and four girls, most of whom are exceptionally
high-spirited. However, her children have learned to be
wary of her as she can unexpectedly snap out of her
reveries and catch them in some misdemeanour.
Although a caring mother, she is largely ineffectual
when it comes to understanding her mercurial offspring
and protecting them from their own impetuosity. She
finds talking about health and religion distasteful.

The Pursuit of Love,
collectable Folio Society
edition.

Alconleigh, Lord (Uncle Matthew)
From *The Pursuit of Love* and *Love in a Cold Climate* by Nancy Mitford

One of the great comic characters of twentieth-century literature, Lord Alconleigh
(aka Fa or Uncle Matthew) is a brilliant, albeit unkind, caricature of Nancy
Mitford's father, Lord Redesdale. A large, handsome man who grinds his teeth
when angered, Lord Alconleigh proudly displays the entrenching tool with which
he whacked to death eight Germans during the Great War. Violent, uncontrolled
and prone to rages of epic proportion, he is a wildly eccentric individual who
cracks whips on the lawn at five in the morning and hunts his children with blood
hounds. A mass of contradictions, he is terrifying, intolerant and bullying, but
also sentimental and capable of immense charm. Narrating the book, his niece
Fanny (whom he loathes) describes his bark as worse than his bite, although the
numerous thrashings and whackings administered to his children might suggest
otherwise. He is an unforgettable character, a great hater, frequently cruel and
occasionally kind, who dazzles on every page on which he appears.

Allandale, Jeremy
From *April Lady* by Georgette Heyer

A respectable young man of modest means, Jeremy Allandale is employed at the Foreign Office and expects soon to receive an overseas posting that will alter his circumstances for the better. This will be a blessing since his widowed mother has little money of her own and needs his help to finance the education of his brothers and sisters. Allandale is in love with Lady Letitia Merion, a 17-year-old heiress, and wants to marry her, but will not do so without the blessing of her guardian, Lord Cardross, even though his rather flighty beloved does not share his scruples. Those that know the young couple are mystified as to why Lady Letitia has lost her heart to Allandale because although he is reasonably good-looking he is also rather dull – his manners are very formal and his conversation is tortuous rather than amusing. In short, he is not at all the kind of young man likely to win the affection of a giddy young girl and yet that is exactly what he has done.

Allen, Mr
From *Northanger Abbey* by Jane Austen

Mr Allen is a childless, wealthy gentleman who owns the principal property in the rural community of Fullerton, home town of Catherine Morland, the book's heroine. A kind, gouty, card-playing gentleman, he keeps a distant eye on Catherine when she accompanies him and his wife on a visit to Bath.

Allen, Mrs
From *Northanger Abbey* by Jane Austen

Wife of Mr Allen (see above), Mrs Allen is a well-meaning but vapid older woman whose abiding interest in life is fashion. Passive and mild-tempered, she is not bright enough to protect her inexperienced young friend, Catherine Morland from making mistakes when she enters into Bath society.

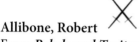

Allibone, Robert
From *Rebels and Traitors* by Lindsey Davis

A London printer with seditious leanings, Allibone is a compact, sandy-haired man who risks punishment by selling inflammatory material. He is a lenient master to his young apprentice, Gideon Jukes, and is in love with Margery, his wife, a woman some years older than he. When Margery dies around the same time that Jukes completes his apprenticeship, he goes into business with him in new premises which are situated in a part of London at the centre of the movement against the King. He fights with the London Trained Bands' Green Regiment when the tension between crown and Parliament descends into armed conflict.

Anacrites
From the *Falco Series* by Lindsey Davis

Although he doesn't make an appearance until *Shadows in Bronze*, the second Falco novel, thereafter Anacrites is a regular character in these mysteries set in Ancient Rome. A former slave who has been given his freedom and has now amassed considerable wealth, he works at the Palace as Emperor Vespasian's Chief Spy. He has a compact frame, bland face, unusual grey eyes and eyebrows so pale they are scarcely visible. Not afraid to use unscrupulous methods in the course of his work, he is clever, capable and thorough. He is also ready to make an enemy of Marcus Didius Falco who is encroaching on territory he regards as his own.

Anning, Joseph   RP
From *Remarkable Creatures* by Tracy Chevalier

The son of Richard and Molly Anning from Lyme Regis, Joseph – or Joe as he is more commonly known – is older than his sister Mary by three years. Like Mary and his father he has a gift for finding fossils on the beaches between Lyme and Charmouth, but unlike them he does not enjoy the pursuit, preferring to stay warm and dry indoors rather than spending hours outside in all weather. He also dislikes the fact that the majority of Lyme residents regard fossil hunting as peculiar. Joe wants nothing more than to conform, to be like everyone else, and therefore he abandons fossil hunting in favour of a more conventional occupation.

Anning, Mary **RP**
From *Remarkable Creatures* by Tracy Chevalier

Having survived a lightning strike that ought to have killed her when she was a baby, Mary Anning grows up with the awareness that she is somehow different. Born into a working class, chapel-going family living close to Gun Cliff in Lyme Regis, Mary regards life's hardships as inevitable and accepts family deaths with sad composure. Her father is a cabinet maker with a sideline in selling fossils to rich tourists, and her mother is a shrewd, capable woman made weary by constant child-bearing. Despite the many pregnancies, the only children to survive are Mary and her older brother, Joe.

Portrait of Mary Anning reproduced by permission of the Geographical Society of London.

When the narrative begins Mary is a tall, lean, self-possessed child with a plain face and bold brown eyes that seem always to be searching for something. She has a gift for fossil hunting, almost knowing instinctively where to find them, and having lived all her life by the sea she has a natural feel for the tides. Her skill in finding fossils brings in much-needed income for the Anning family, although for Mary it is about more than money as she is fascinated by her prehistoric discoveries. This enthusiasm makes her careless of her appearance as she grubs about in the dirt looking for 'curies', her word for curiosities, and marks her out as something of an oddity in her community. Although her brother shares her gift for fossil hunting he dislikes doing it, so Mary has no one with whom to share her passion. Until, that is, she is befriended by Elizabeth Philpot, a middle-class spinster who arrives in Lyme Regis when Mary is still a girl. Elizabeth's friendship sustains Mary through bereavement, danger and epic discovery, but is eventually severely tested by jealousy.

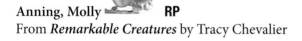

Anning, Molly **RP**
From *Remarkable Creatures* by Tracy Chevalier

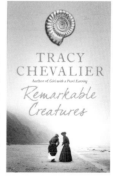

A tall, gaunt woman who has borne ten children and watched most of them die in infancy, Molly is forever occupied in some kind of back-breaking work. She is uncomfortable with the unusual fascination her husband and children feel for fossils, but is forced to accept it because it brings in much-needed income. Towards Elizabeth Philpot she is at first slightly hostile and suspicious because she knows that Elizabeth encourages Mary's fossil obsession. Eventually, however, she comes to trust her. Beneath Molly's normally cautious and taciturn exterior there is a surprisingly shrewd brain, and when occasion demands she is capable of conducting negotiations with her social superiors with cunning and confidence.

Anning, Richard   **RP**
From *Remarkable Creatures* by Tracy Chevalier

The father of Mary and Joe Anning, Richard is a good-looking, lithe man of medium height with a strong jaw, dark blue eyes and dark lustrous eyes. He earns his living as a cabinet maker, but to his wife's annoyance prefers going out onto the beach at Lyme Regis in search of 'curies' – fossils in other words – to sell to affluent visitors. Regardless of how much he earns, however, the family always seems to be in debt. He passes his talent for fossil hunting on to his son and daughter. His work as a cabinet maker is acceptable but not exceptional, and his workshop is chaotic, revealing a disorganised mind. His personality is harshly teasing and his manners are occasionally rough.

Ariadne
From *The King Must Die* by Mary Renault

The daughter of Minos, King of Crete, Ariadne is a beautiful young woman who represents the Goddess-on-Earth in the Cretan religion. She is small and slender, with pale golden skin, burnished bronze hair and a cool clear voice.

Illustration of the statue *Ariadne on the Panther* by Johann Heinrich von Dannecker, 1824. Frankfurt.

Armstrong, David
From *The House at Sunset* by Norah Lofts

The son of kind-hearted shopkeepers from the (fictitious) town of Baildon in Suffolk, David is at first glance a decent, God-fearing young man who helps his parents run their grocery business and delivers charitable gifts to old ladies. Yet appearances can be deceptive; in reality David is a selfish, cold-hearted character with dangerously sociopathic tendencies.

Astell, Joe
From *South Riding* by Winifred Holtby

A dedicated Socialist who clawed his way from abject poverty to become a schoolmaster, Astell wants nothing more than to spend his life fighting for the cause he believes in with all his heart. During the war his stance as a conscientious objector earned him a prison sentence; when he was released he worked first as a printer and then travelled to South Africa to help organise trade unions for the black miners. Returning from the Transvaal with tuberculosis, he moved to the South Riding for the sea air and quiet life that his doctors ordered, but as soon as his health improved just a little he threw himself once again into the political fray by getting elected to the County Council.

At the start of the book he has just been elected Alderman, not because his Socialist views are shared by his council colleagues, but because his election denies Robert Carne, a reactionary South Riding farmer, the honour of Alderman status. Serving in local government is not what Astell really wants to do. He knows there are much bigger battles to be fought and he is deeply frustrated by the limitations imposed on him by his frail health. A tall, thin man with curly red hair and a delicate complexion, Astell is said to have a harsh, unpleasant voice. He has previously been married, to a Jewish woman as dedicated as he to the Socialist cause, but since her death from influenza in 1924 he has been a single man.

Asterion
From *The King Must Die* by Mary Renault

Supposedly the son of Minos, the King of Crete, Asterion is widely rumoured to be the result of an elicit liaison between Pasiphae, Minos's dead queen and an Assyrian bull leaper. He is a short man with a monstrously thickset body, coarse curly black hair and a bestial face. As heir to Minos his official title is Minotaurus.

Astorre
From *Niccolò Rising* by Dorothy Dunnett

A mercenary captain working for the Charetty company of Bruges and Louvain, Astorre – real name Syrus de Astarii – is a hard, fighting man who leads the band of bodyguards that protect Charetty goods and employees from attack when they are on the road. Although bow-legged and small in stature, Astorre is a skilled fighter and is as fit as a twenty-year-old. The puckered scar over one eye and scarlet frill (all that remains of one ear) bear witness to the many battles he has survived. His manners are coarse, but Astorre is valued by his employer, Marian de Charetty, because he is astute and experienced. Some of his actions are driven by his deep enmity for a rival mercenary captain called Lionetto.

Atkyns, Sir Edward  **RP**
From *Milady Charlotte* by Jean Plaidy

A very wealthy man in his early thirties, Sir Edward owns a large Tudor manor house in the Norfolk countryside. He is a tall, well-built man with sparkling eyes set in a fleshy face which promises to run to fat if he is not careful. Generally genial and amusing, he is an inveterate philanderer who is used to getting his way with women. Even when he marries he finds he is unable to resist a pretty face, however unwelcome his attentions prove to be.

Aubéry, Jean-Benoit
From *Frenchman's Creek* by Daphne du Maurier

A cultivated Frenchman with estates in Brittany, Aubéry has tired of respectability and turned to a life of piracy aboard his ship, *La Mouette* (The Seagull). Enjoying the intricate plotting almost as much as the dangerous action, he leads his band of trusted Breton companions in increasingly audacious acts of piracy against the rich Cornish landowners. When he needs to lie low, he sails *La Mouette* into a concealed creek on the Navron estate which has a conveniently absent owner, Sir Harry St. Columb. Here Aubéry relaxes by fishing or observing, and sketching the diverse birdlife of the Helston River. Occasionally he wanders up to the house at Navron where he is given good food and a comfortable bed by his former servant, William, who now works at Navron with the express purpose of being useful to the Frenchman.

Collectable 1959 edition of Frenchman's Creek.

Tall and dark, Aubéry has a slow, mocking smile and he eschews the seventeenth century fashion for elaborate wigs in favour of wearing his own hair. His personality has an interesting duality: on the one hand he is a contemplative and philosophical individual looking for peace and serenity, on the other he is a reckless thrill-seeker craving excitement and danger. This enigmatic nature is what makes him so attractive to the woman drawn into his life as if by an irresistible force.

Aunt Emily
From *The Pursuit of Love* by Nancy Mitford

Surrogate mother to Fanny Logan who narrates The Pursuit of Love, Aunt Emily elects to bring up her dissolute youngest sister's baby because, unlike her other sister, Lady Alconleigh, she is unmarried and has no children of her own. She is less beautiful than her siblings, but has more strength of character than Lady Alconleigh and is far more respectable than Fanny's mother. Aged 40 at the start of the book, she is kind, calm and sensible and has devoted her life to creating a stable home for Fanny. As is soon revealed, however, she is capable of springing a dramatic surprise on her unsuspecting niece.

B is for Bennet, Burton, Butler and more

Barker, Miss Betty
From *Cranford* by Elizabeth Gaskell

An elderly lady living in Cranford, a quiet northern town, Miss Barker is the daughter of the former town clerk. As a young woman she found employment as a lady's maid before opening a millinery shop in Cranford with her sister, serving the town's genteel population. The shop was closed when her sister died and now Miss Barker lives in retirement, dressing exceedingly well in the bonnets and ribbons left over from her stock, and behaving with excessive politeness and gentility. She owns a fine Alderney cow to which she is deeply attached.

Basset, Squire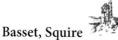

From *Jamaica Inn* by Daphne du Maurier

A Cornish landowner and magistrate who was tricked some years ago into selling Jamaica Inn to the odious Josh Merlyn, Basset is a bluff, hearty fellow who knows Merlyn is up to no good and means to catch him out. Aged about 50, he is a big, burly man with a heavily lined and weather-beaten face.

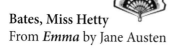

Bates, Miss Hetty

From *Emma* by Jane Austen

A middle-aged spinster living in reduced circumstances with her elderly mother – the widow of a former Highbury vicar - Miss Bates is short, neat and extremely garrulous. A harmless and generally popular soul, her great pleasures in life are socialising with village friends and reading letters sent by her niece, Jane Fairfax. Although she has been used to better things, she now exists on very little, but manages to remain cheerful in the face of adversity. Her conversation is neither witty nor intelligent, but she is liked by many for her simple good nature.

C.E. Brock illustration of Miss Bates.

de Bayonne, Nirac

From *Katherine* by Anya Seton

One of the few entirely fictitious characters in the book, Nirac comes from Gascony, a part of France that belonged to England in the mid-fourteenth century, the period in which the novel is set. Small, dark and wiry, he is nimble, quick-witted and capable, but he has a violent streak and a primitive cast of mind that thinks in terms of love and hate, with no nuances in between. Having had his life saved in battle by John of Gaunt, Duke of Lancaster, he is now devoted to the noble lord and is prepared to carry out his wishes whatever they may be. Given his volatile temperament, this is potentially a recipe for disaster.

Beauchamp, Lady
From *My Last Duchess* by Daisy Goodwin

Charlotte Beauchamp is a classically beautiful young woman with blonde hair, a high forehead, wide-set blue eyes and a chilly demeanour. She dresses exquisitely and always looks the very essence of cool elegance. With her husband Sir Odo she maintains an overtly civil relationship, but the tension between them is palpable. Early on it is revealed that she once was great friends with Ivo Maltravers, the Duke of Wareham.

Beauchamp, Sir Odo
From *My Last Duchess* by Daisy Goodwin

Odo by name, odious by nature – Sir Odo is a rich man who hides his malicious nature behind a veneer of elegance. The nephew of Lord Bridport with whom the wealthy American Cash family stay when they visit Dorset, he is married to the icily beautiful Charlotte. A big man, he has blond hair, limpid blue eyes and an oddly high-pitched voice.

Beddows, Alderman Mrs
From *South Riding* by Winifred Holtby

A farmer's daughter who has spent her entire life in the (fictional) South Riding of Yorkshire, Emma Beddows is 72-years old at the start of the novel, but she has the energy and mental prowess of a much younger woman. A plump, sturdy little body with bright, spaniel-coloured eyes, she loves to be busy and useful and finds great satisfaction serving her community as a local government officer. Good-humoured, shrewd and sensible with a no-nonsense manner and a strong belief in her own sound judgement, she is well-liked by most people and can be relied on to lend a sympathetic ear to their troubles.

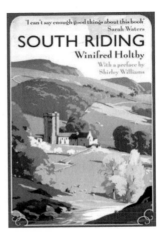

'I can't say enough good things about this book'
Sarah Waters

SOUTH RIDING
Winifred Holtby
With a preface by
Shirley Williams

Mrs Beddows' current state of contentment has been hard won. Her husband Jim, a penny-pinching auctioneer and corn merchant ten years her junior, turned out not to be the man she thought he was, she lost two babies in infancy, and her son Willy died after being gassed in the Great War. Yet over time she has come to terms with grief and disappointment and is grateful for what life has given her including two grown up daughters – Chloe, a lecturer at the Sorbonne and Sybil who is unmarried and lives at home – and a granddaughter, Wendy, who is Willy's child. More than this, she is a South Riding Alderman with the respect and confidence of the local populace, and a governor of the local girls' High School to boot. Most of all, perhaps, she relishes being the close confidante of Robert Carne, a handsome middle-aged farmer with whom she is more than a little in love, albeit in a maternal way. When Carne brings his problems to her she feels entirely happy.

Bedford, Jacquetta, Dowager Duchess of **RP**
From *We Speak No Treason* by Rosemary Hawley Jarman

Once married to the Duke of Bedford, Jacquetta has for many years now been the wife of Sir Richard Woodville, a relatively unimportant Lancastrian knight. Together they have produced a large family which includes the beautiful Elizabeth who was widowed when her husband, Sir John Grey, died of wounds sustained fighting for the Lancastrians in the on-going power struggle between the warring houses of York and Lancaster. Once as lovely to look at as her daughter, Jacquetta is now a wrinkled old woman who spends her time devising herbal remedies to revive her looks. She also brews potions for more sinister purposes, and anyone inadvertently stumbling onto her secrets places themselves in danger, especially as Jacquetta is using her unusual talents to help her daughter snare a very important suitor.

Benedict, Ethelreda
From *The House at Old Vine* by Norah Lofts

A girl of 15 when her isolated Fenland home is flooded, Ethelreda is rescued by a passing boat and taken to the Suffolk port of Bywater. As she is now an orphan - her mother has been dead for some time and her father died of sickness just before the flooding – she takes a skivvying job at an inn. Having lived all her life in a tiny, remote community with its own archaic traditions, she has problems adjusting to her new environment. Her unusual appearance – long white-blonde hair worn in a braid, and thin, nut-brown face with jutting cheekbones – does little to help her fit in and neither does her strange accent which makes her native English sound like a foreign language. Thus her life is miserable for a time until she is offered a better situation by a kind schoolmaster staying at the inn as a guest. Although she is completely uneducated, Ethelreda is extremely intelligent and resourceful. At the earliest opportunity she learns to read and write, at the same time doing the work of three people so that she soon becomes indispensable to her new employers. She also discovers that although she has always thought herself plain, there are those that find her extremely desirable.

Bennet, Elizabeth
From *Pride and Prejudice* by Jane Austen

The heroine of Pride and Prejudice, Elizabeth – also known sometimes as Lizzy or Eliza - is an intelligent, spirited and intensely moral young woman of 20. Her parents, Mr and Mrs Bennet of Longbourn in Hertfordshire, have five children – all daughters – of whom she is the second oldest. Her older sister Jane is generally considered the beauty of the family, but Elizabeth is very pretty, with fine eyes and a figure that is 'light and pleasing'. Thanks to her lively wit she is her father's favourite but her mother loves her least of all her children.

Elizabeth Bennet and Mr Bennet, Pickering and Greatbatch, 1833.

Always ready to laugh, especially at the absurd, she is capable of strong affection, as evidenced by her devotion to Jane and her friendship with her neighbour, Charlotte Lucas. She is, however, far from perfect, showing little tolerance for her mother's foibles and judging Charlotte severely for accepting a marriage proposal from a man she does not love. More crucially, when she meets, separately, Mr Darcy and Mr Wickham, she allows her pride to influence her opinion of them. Later, though, she realises that her judgement is flawed and has the grace to feel deeply ashamed. Jane Austen thought Elizabeth Bennet 'as delightful a character as ever appeared in print', an opinion shared by countless readers down the years.

Bennet, Jane
From *Pride and Prejudice* by Jane Austen

Oldest of the Bennet girls, 22-year-old Jane is gentle, sweet-tempered and forgiving. Although she lacks Elizabeth's vivacity and wit, she has a quiet intelligence which enables her to hold her own when the sisters engage in good natured disagreements. She is a pleasing character with a tendency to see good in even the most disagreeable characters because her own kind nature finds it impossible to think ill of her acquaintances. Balanced against these admirable qualities is her tendency to conceal her innermost emotions, a characteristic that leads Mr Darcy to conclude that she does not feel deeply. He is mistaken in this and when her romance takes a wrong turn, Jane suffers profoundly, albeit mostly in silence.

Bennet, Lydia
From *Pride and Prejudice* by Jane Austen

Aged 15 when Pride and Prejudice begins, Lydia is the youngest Bennet daughter. A tall, well-built girl with a fine complexion and good-natured face, she has been introduced into society early because she is her mother's favourite child. Sociable and lively, she is also frivolous, ignorant, self-willed and far too pleased with herself for her own good. Interested solely in the pursuit of pleasure, her reckless action plunges herself and her family into a potentially disastrous situation. When she is saved from the social oblivion that is the anticipated consequence of her ill-considered act, she demonstrates neither remorse for her behaviour nor gratitude for her rescuer. The worst of Lydia's faults can be attributed to too much spoiling from her mother and too little guidance from her father; in different circumstances, she could have developed better characteristics although her lack of intellect would have precluded her becoming another Elizabeth or Jane.

She went after dinner to show her ring, and boast of being married, to Mrs. Hill and the two housemaids

Lydia Bennet displaying her ring, C.E. Brock, 1895.

Bennet, Mr

From *Pride and Prejudice* by Jane Austen

Mr Bennet is a minor member of the landed gentry. He lives at Longbourn House, a small manor set within its own grounds situated near the fictional town of Meryton in Hertfordshire. Although not rich, his estate produces a comfortable income of about £2,000 a year, enough to allow him to keep a butler, cook, housekeeper and several other domestic servants. However, Longbourn is entailed, meaning it can only pass to a male heir. This presents a problem since the 23-year marriage of Mr and Mrs Bennet has produced five daughters and no sons. As further children are not anticipated, it seems certain Longbourn will pass to a distant cousin, Mr Collins, when Mr Bennet dies.

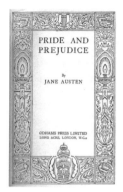

Title page of Pride and Prejudice, Odhams Press Limited.

The tragedy of Mr Bennet's life is that he allowed his bride-to-be's youth, beauty and good humour to blind him to her manifold faults. Having discovered her true character soon after their marriage, his affection swiftly dissipated. He does, however, derive amusement from her foolishness, a fact he does not trouble to hide from his children. He is a clever, cynical man who has become indolent through disappointment. Spending much of his time closeted in the library with his books, he has neglected his daughters' education and, inexcusably, has failed to make provision for their financial security after his death. Although he generally has a low opinion of his youngest daughters, he values Jane and is especially fond of Elizabeth.

Bennet, Mrs
From *Pride and Prejudice* by Jane Austen

A handsome woman in her mid-to-late forties, Mrs Bennet is vastly inferior to her husband in intellect and refinement. Narrow minded, foolish and self-pitying, she lives for socialising and exchanging gossip. When life thwarts her, she develops nervous complaints which vanish as soon as things go her way again. Her overriding obsession is to make good matches for her five daughters and with marriage the only respectable career option for women of their class, her concern is understandable, particularly since Mr Bennet has neglected to make adequate provision for their future. However, her unsubtle match-making attempts embarrass and distress her older daughters, and generally make her a target for ridicule.

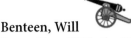

Benteen, Will
From *Gone With the Wind* by Margaret Mitchell

Formerly a 'cracker', i.e. a poor white man scratching a living from the land in Georgia in circumstances far removed from the lavish ostentation of the plantation owning families, Will Benteen returns to his home state after fighting for the Confederacy in the American Civil War. On his long way home he passes through Tara and is given food and shelter by the O'Hara family. As his journey has been arduous, not least because he has lost part of one leg, he is invited to stay at Tara while he recuperates. With his background in farming he soon makes himself useful, and it is decided that he will stay on permanently to help run the place. Honest, capable and hardworking, Will is a valuable asset, but the fact that in due course he pays court to one of the O'Hara girls, indicates how much times have changed, because before the war a man from his background would never have been able to socialise with an O'Hara daughter, much less consider marrying her.

Bentwood, Simon
From *Tilly Trotter* and *Tilly Trotter Wed* by Catherine Cookson

A prosperous tenant farmer on the Sopwith estate in County Durham, Simon is a well-built young man of 24, broad-chested and reasonably tall at an inch-and-a-half under six feet. He has thick chestnut-coloured hair and a strong, if not entirely handsome, face. Bentwood is good friends with Tilly Trotter's grandparents with whom he shares a weighty secret. He has known Tilly since she was a child of 5 and has developed strong feelings for her, although he fails to realise just how strong until it is too late. Basically a decent man, his judgement can be poor when it comes to the important things in life, and his strong sense of self-worth makes him unwilling to show the expected degree of subservience to his social superiors.

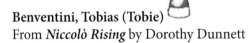

Benventini, Tobias (Tobie)
From *Niccolò Rising* by Dorothy Dunnett

When Tobie, a hard-drinking doctor, makes his first appearance in this complex novel he is in Bruges, working with the mercenary army led by a strutting Frenchman called Lionetto. He has been with Lionetto's band for a year, but dislikes the man and is therefore likely to leave if another opportunity presents itself. Extremely well-qualified, skilled and with an influential uncle, he could easily find a comfortable position tending the ailments of noblemen, but he prefers to work with fighting men.

Physically, Tobie's defining feature is his bald head which is crowned by a fuzz of pale hair. He has eyes that reveal his drinking tendency, pale skin and a small, mobile mouth. Occasionally gruff, he is a compassionate and intelligent man who develops an interest in Claes, an intriguing dye shop apprentice working with the Charetty company in Bruges.

Bertha
From *My Last Duchess* by Daisy Goodwin

The illegitimate daughter of a black South Carolina laundry maid and a white man who has long since vanished, Bertha works as the personal maid of Miss Cora Cash, a young society heiress. She hasn't seen her mother for ten years and is beginning to forget what she looks like. Although Bertha is homesick, she likes her position which brings her a life far more comfortable than she would have had at home in South Carolina. Bertha sometimes dislikes her spoilt mistress, but is nonetheless loyal to her and even pities her to some extent for living under the thumb of her overpowering mother. A pretty girl with very light skin and smooth hair, Bertha keeps herself neat and takes as much pride in her appearance as her mistress. In her own way she is every bit as socially ambitious as her employers.

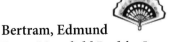

Bertram, Edmund
From *Mansfield Park* by Jane Austen

Aged about twenty-four at the start of the novel, Edmund is the youngest son of Sir Thomas and Lady Bertram of Mansfield Park. Although his father is rich, his older brother is destined to inherit everything and therefore Edmund must choose a profession. He opts for the church as he is a genuinely pious young man with good morals. That he is also kind and compassionate is evidenced by the trouble he takes to befriend and mentor his shy young cousin when she comes to live at Mansfield Park. Nevertheless, his good heart and steady head are no protection when he finds himself falling for the attractive and worldly Mary Crawford. He turns a blind eye to her faults, on one

Edmund Bertram with his cousin Fanny Price, C.E. Brock, 1908.

notable occasion bending to her wishes at the expense of his own instincts. His character is put under further scrutiny when he urges his cousin Fanny to accept a marriage proposal from a man he knows she does not love. Although his motives are blemish-free, in this instance his judgment is not. Ultimately, however, Edmund has enough good sense to realise where his future happiness lies.

Bertram, Julia
From **Mansfield *Park*** by Jane Austen

The youngest daughter of Sir Thomas and Lady Bertram, Julia Bertram is a good-looking girl of about nineteen when the main action of the novel begins. Although generally good-humoured and lively, her character has been spoilt by her aunt's indulgence and her mother's indolence. She is neglectful and sometimes unkind to her young cousin Fanny, but her character is more foolish than bad, and had she been taught generosity and humility as a child, she might have become a better person. As it is, Julia is slightly more likeable than her older and more beautiful sister, and though her behaviour is extremely rash towards the end of the story, her fate is happier than it might have been.

Mansfield Park title page, 1908 edition.

Bertram, Lady
From *Mansfield Park* by Jane Austen

Wife of Sir Thomas Bertram of Mansfield Park, Lady Bertram is an amiable, yet woefully inert character whose vapidity allows her daughters to fall under the malign influence of their aunt, Mrs Norris. Shallow and lazy, she is practically sofa-bound and thinks solely of her own comforts, which is why she doesn't hesitate to make a virtual servant of her young niece, Fanny Price.

Bertram, Maria
From *Mansfield Park* by Jane Austen

Aged about twenty when the story begins, Maria (to rhyme with *pariah*) is the beautiful, but thoroughly spoilt, oldest daughter of Sir Thomas and Lady Bertram of Mansfield Park. Encouraged by her aunt Mrs Norris to harbour inflated opinions of her own importance, Maria is vain, flighty, self-indulgent, ungenerous and entirely lacking in moral backbone. She accepts a marriage proposal from a rich man she doesn't care for in order to escape the frigid atmosphere of Mansfield Park. Then, when a more exciting prospect presents itself, she behaves extremely badly in full view of her hapless fiancé. Although it is made clear that Maria has been ruined by the obsequious attentions of her aunt, it is also apparent that her personality was deficient in the first place. Maria Bertram careers through the narrative on a self-destructive trajectory, but she is such an unsympathetic character that her dismal fate brings the reader nothing but satisfaction.

Bertram, Sir Thomas
From *Mansfield Park* by Jane Austen

The owner of Mansfield Park, Sir Thomas is a wealthy landowner with interests in the West Indies. Respectable and rather stern, he has a strong sense of duty and responsibility which is why he is willing to give a home to his young niece, Fanny Price. For all his good intentions, however, he is a cold, aloof man, so preoccupied with status and money that he fails to notice the damaging effect his unpleasant sister-in-law is having on his daughters' development. Sadly, three of his four children find his company oppressive and are relieved when business matters take him from home for a prolonged period. Nevertheless, Sir Thomas is a decent man and ultimately he has enough self-knowledge to see where he has gone wrong and learn from his mistakes.

Sir Thomas Bertram with Fanny Price, C.E. Brock, 1908.

Bertram, Tom
From *Mansfield Park* by Jane Austen

A careless young man of about twenty-five, Tom Bertram is destined to inherit Mansfield Park when his father dies. Much less serious than his younger brother Edmund, Tom leads the typically dissolute life of an oldest son, drinking to excess, gambling and generally over-indulging. His fondness for theatricals is indirectly responsible for his sister Maria's disgraceful behaviour towards her fiancé, and for the general lapse in standards that affect most of the young people at Mansfield Park during Sir Thomas Bertram's absence. Tom is not wholly bad, though, and is not beyond redemption.

Bevan, Bevan
From *Rebels and Traitors* by Lindsey Davis

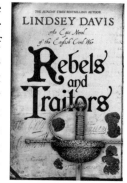

The great-uncle of Gideon Jukes, the book's central male
protagonist, Bevan has married late in life but made up for
it by producing many children with his wife, the widow of
a printer. His marriage has dashed the expectations of his
niece who hoped he would leave his wealth to her youngest
son, Gideon. Instead, Bevan procures an apprenticeship for
the boy with a London printer, a decent man called Robert
Allibone. Although he is outwardly on good terms with the
Jukes family, gouty, hard-drinking Bevan is frequently at
odds with them especially when it comes to politics – the
Jukes are for Parliament while Bevan is a Royalist.

Bingley, Charles
From *Pride and Prejudice* by Jane Austen

Aged 22, Charles Bingley is a good-looking young man,
with a gentlemanly appearance and good manners. Not
especially clever, he is easy going, unaffected and
pleasant. He has inherited a large fortune of £100,000 and
an annual income of between £4,000 and £5,000 a year,
making him a prime target for mothers like Mrs Bennet
with daughters to settle. If he has a fault, it is that he is
too easily persuaded by his friend Fitzwilliam Darcy to
distrust his own judgement in affairs of the heart. His
arrival at Netherfield Park, an estate situated about three
miles from Longbourn, sets in motion a chain of events
that have a far-reaching impact both on himself, his
friend and his neighbours, the Bennet family.

Mr Bingley riding with
Mr Darcy, Hugh Thomson,
1894.

Birch, Lieutenant-Colonel Thomas   **RP**
From *Remarkable Creatures* by Tracy Chevalier

Aged about fifty, Birch is a tall, erect former solider in the Life Guard regiment
who arrives in Lyme Regis in search of fascinating geological finds. With a
handsome, weather-beaten face, upright military bearing and bushy black hair
streaked with grey, he makes a striking figure, striding confidently about in his

long red soldier's coat. He soon captivates the impressionable Mary Anning and even manages to charm her mother who is normally immune to flattery. Only Elizabeth Philpot, Mary's spinster friend, is sceptical about Birch, disliking the way he basks in the Life Guards' recent glory at Waterloo even though he was not there, having long since retired from the army. She also suspects that he cheats at fossil hunting by studying Mary's face for signs that she has discovered something, then pouncing and claiming her find as his own. Worse than this, Elizabeth believes that Mary is complicit in Birch's false discoveries because she is infatuated with him. Birch is aware of Mary's infatuation and far from discouraging it, shows great irresponsibility in allowing it to grow until their intimacy is the talk of the town. When he leaves Lyme quite suddenly, Mary is left with a damaged reputation and unrealistic hopes of becoming his wife, yet although Birch is selfish and thoughtless, he is not quite the heartless scoundrel Elizabeth takes him for.

Blanche, Duchess of Lancaster RP
From *Katherine* by Anya Seton

Born into the highest echelons of English fourteenth-century nobility, Blanche is accustomed to wealth and privilege, but unlike some of the high-ranking court ladies, she has not been spoilt by her position. Sweet, serene, devout and compassionate, she genuinely loves her husband, John of Gaunt, and is very content to be his wife and the mother of his children. Although she is not desperately keen on the physical side of their relationship, she submits to his advances with tolerant goodwill and he in return accepts her submission with gratitude.

There is an almost holy quality to Blanche's beauty that inspires reverent awe in most that know her. She has long, silver-blonde hair, blue eyes and a pale oval face. In repose her expression is calm and passionless, but it is transformed by her smile which is of piercing sweetness. Lovely, shining and good, Blanche is considered by Geoffrey Chaucer to be the most gracious lady in the land.

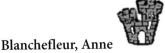

Blanchefleur, Anne
From *The Town House* by Norah Lofts

Born into impoverished nobility, 16-year-old Anne lives with her eternally optimistic parents at Old Minsham Hall, an ancient and somewhat dilapidated fortified house not far from the Suffolk town of Baildon. What little money they have is spent equipping Anne's brother Godfrey to become a page at the home of wealthy relatives. Anne herself is passed around from one great house to another in the hope that she will find a rich husband, but although she is a good-looking girl, her shabby clothes and lack of dowry deter noble suitors who value money over a comely wife. Sick of the perpetual round of humiliating visits to aristocratic aunts and uncles, she is willing to consider a marriage proposal which arrives from an unexpected quarter.

Boleyn, Anne   **RP**
From *The Other Boleyn Girl* by Philippa Gregory

The oldest daughter of courtier Thomas Boleyn and his wife (the daughter of the Duke of Norfolk) Anne is just 15-years old when the novel begins. When she returns to England after a spell in France, she is already a stylish and self-assured young woman imbued with the fashions and mannerisms of the French court. As beautiful as her younger sister Mary, she is all dark hair and dark eyes, in contrast to the golden-haired, grey-eyed Mary. Anne comes to court just as King Henry VIII begins his flirtation with Mary and she is instructed by her power-hungry family, led by her Howard uncle, to help her sister become the King's mistress. This she does willingly and skilfully, although resentment that she has been passed over in preference for Mary causes her to treat her sister with casual cruelty.

Far more sophisticated and cultured than Mary, Anne is fluent in French and Latin, and she is comfortable discussing philosophical and theological matters. She also composes music, sings prettily, dances gracefully and converses wittily. Beneath the fascinating polish, however, Anne is calculating, cynical, spiteful and ambitious to a dangerous degree. In spite of herself she falls in love with someone, but when that relationship fails, she hardens her heart and determines to reach for the ultimate prize. Where Mary is a helpless pawn, to be used and then discarded when no longer useful, Anne is a bold queen, making her own moves, taking calculated risks and aiming straight for the king. Skilled in making men desire her, she is ruthless and clever enough to get what she wants whatever the cost to anyone else. Her only real weakness is her vicious, ungovernable temper. Initially she manages to keep it hidden from the court, but as time progresses she lets her guard down and allows her rage free rein. This reckless lapse will cost her dear.

Boleyn, Lady Elizabeth **RP**
From *The Other Boleyn Girl* by Philippa Gregory

Daughter of the powerful Duke of Norfolk, Elizabeth married beneath her station when she wed Sir Thomas Boleyn of Hever Castle in Kent. Perhaps because of this, she is every bit as ambitious as her husband to see the Boleyn family rise at court and she does not scruple to use her children to achieve her aim, even when it means the virtual prostitution of first one daughter, and then another, to the king. Having had her daughters raised by strangers, first by a wet nurse and then in France at the court of the

Hever Castle, the Boleyn family's Kent residence.

French king, she has no maternal feelings for them. Neither does she show much affection for her son George. To Elizabeth, all her children are assets to be placed strategically for the greater good of the Boleyn and Howard families. Whenever they are ill, in distress or in danger, she distances herself from them and stays away until she deems it safe to return. Noble by birth, Elizabeth is very far from noble by nature.

Boleyn, George **RP**
From *The Other Boleyn Girl* by Philippa Gregory

Smooth and handsome, young George Boleyn is an elegant courtier, as at home making gallant but insincere speeches to Queen Katherine as he is hunting, hawking and gaming with King Henry. Thanks to his charm, wit and good spirits he stands in high favour with Henry and he uses his position to place his beautiful sisters in front of the amorous monarch. George is every bit as committed to the advancement of the Boleyn and Howard clan as the rest of his grasping relatives, but he plays his part with subtlety and intelligence. He helps soothe and cajole his sister Mary into becoming the king's mistress and throws her crumbs of comfort when she is ignored or slighted by the rest of her family. With Anne, his self-assured, worldly-wise sister, he is on more equal terms as both have a sharp intelligence and share a lust for power. When Anne wants advice or needs to control her temper, George is always at hand with the right word or gesture. With both sisters he is perhaps too affectionately familiar, often kissing them on the lips, stroking their hair and even falling asleep on their beds. Despite this, he seems to be attracted more to men than to women. As he is a dutiful son, his actions are frequently at variance with his personal preferences, even to the extent of marrying Jane Parker, one of Queen Katherine's ladies-in-waiting, to whom he has a strong aversion which cannot be entirely accounted for by his sexual orientation. Using his natural gifts, George is able to climb high in his pursuit of power, but the ascent takes him to some dark places that he would rather not visit. And like many high climbers, he comes to realise that should he put a foot wrong, there is a long, long way to fall.

Boleyn, Sir Thomas   **RP**
From *The Other Boleyn Girl* by Philippa Gregory

The grandson of a self-made man, Sir Thomas is a courtier in the service of Henry VIII, with houses and land holdings in Kent and Essex. Despite the humble origins of his forebears, he has considerably improved his standing by marrying Elizabeth Howard, the daughter of the Duke of Norfolk, and is now firmly allied to their faction at court. He has three children – George, Anne and Mary – all of whom he regards as no more than useful commodities to be traded for favours and advancement. He is a cold, unnatural father, bestowing approval on his children only when they succeed in gaining the favour of the king. By his actions he is shown to be completely amoral, as when he bullies his youngest daughter into becoming the king's mistress, despite the fact that she is already married to a young man he himself has chosen for her. He never shows the slightest affection for any of his children and is quick to distance himself from them whenever they are in trouble. He is, in short, a vile man.

Bolter, The
From *The Pursuit of Love* by Nancy Mitford

Mother of Fanny Logan who narrates *The Pursuit of Love,* this much-married social butterfly is nicknamed 'The Bolter' on account of her habit of bolting from one man to another. Her original bolt was from her first husband, Lord Logan, whom she deserted soon after Fanny's birth, pausing just long enough to deposit her baby with an unmarried sister. The Bolter – who is never referred to by a first name – is absent throughout most of the book, appearing towards the end having escaped from 'a ghastly prison camp in Spain'. Living up to her reputation of always having a man in tow, she arrives at Alconleigh with a rough-looking Spaniard called Juan. Foolish and feckless, she is permanently rooted in the styles and mannerisms of her youth. Though described by her daughter as 'silliness personified', she is redeemed by her frankness, high spirits and abundant good nature, and because of her rackety lifestyle she is a memorable and amusing character.

Borselen, Katelina van
From *Niccolò Rising* by Dorothy Dunnett

The daughter of a well-connected Fleming called Florence van Borselen, Katelina is a fine-looking young woman of 19 when the book begins. She has just arrived in Bruges in the company of some Scottish nobles, having spent the last three years in Scotland as maid of honour to the Scottish queen. Although she is glad to be back, her homecoming is tinged with disgrace, since she has returned single, having refused to accept the much older Scottish man her father had selected for her. Now her only option is to find another husband if she doesn't want to be packed off to a convent for the rest of her life. Luckily there is one potential suitor at hand, Simon de St Pol, who is young, good-looking and nobly born. Yet even though he seems the perfect solution to her dilemma, Katelina has reservations about Simon and is not at all sure that she likes him.

Katelina is a proud, spirited young woman who sometimes allows her temper to gain control of her tongue and her actions. She dresses in narrow, plain gowns 'in the Scottish fashion' and wears the sort of pointed headdresses often found in fairy tale illustrations. She has fine skin which colours when she is angry or embarrassed, well-defined dark eyebrows and an athletic figure.

de Bourgh, Lady Catherine
From *Pride and Prejudice* by Jane Austen

Lady Catherine de Bourgh is a tall, large woman with strong features which hint at former good looks. The widow of Sir Lewis de Bourgh of Rosings in Kent, Lady Catherine never forgets for a minute that she is the daughter of an Earl. She is the aunt of Fitzwilliam Darcy, his mother having been Lady Catherine's sister. Arrogant, conceited and dictatorial, she is not accustomed to being crossed and sees nothing wrong in imposing her will on those she considers her social inferiors. She is, in fact, a decidedly formidable character.

Lady Catherine de Bourgh, C.E. Brock, 1895.

Brandon, Colonel
From *Sense and Sensibility* by Jane Austen

Friend and neighbour of Sir John Middleton, a distant
relative who provides a refuge for the homeless Dashwood
women, Colonel Brandon is a rich, unmarried gentleman
aged 35. Although not handsome he has a 'sensible' face
and very gentlemanly appearance. His age and serious
nature incline Marianne Dashwood, with whom he falls
in love almost immediately, to consider him old, stuffy and
rather ridiculous, but her sister Elinor is wise enough to
recognise that he is a thoroughly decent man and she likes
him very much, a feeling that is reciprocated. As the sisters
later discover, a tragic event from his past is responsible
for his grave demeanour.

C.E. Brock illustration of
Colonel Brandon with
Elinor Dashwood, 1908.

Brimsley, Mrs
From *South Riding* by Winifred Holtby

A good-looking middle-aged widow, Mrs Brimsley runs a smallholding with her
sons on the bleak Cold Harbour Colony in the South Riding of Yorkshire. She is
a capable housekeeper and an excellent cook, and now that her sons are grown
up and thinking about finding wives, she could do with another interest in life.
With her maternal nature and strong domestic skills, she would make an ideal
stepmother for a large, motherless family.

Brocklehurst, Mr
From *Jane Eyre* by Charlotte Brontë

A large, forbidding clergyman, bushy-browed and dressed in
sombre clothes, Mr Brocklehurst oversees the running of
Lowood Institute, a charity school for orphaned children to
which Jane Eyre is sent. Wealthy and narrow-minded, he allows
the girls in his care to shiver in insubstantial clothing and subsist
on a semi-starvation diet, while his own well-fed daughters
dress in velvet, silk and furs. A cruel hypocrite, he is responsible
for the ill-treatment of the pupils and therefore for the deaths
of those unable to withstand such awful conditions.

Jane Eyre, slip-cased
Heritage Press
edition, 1942.

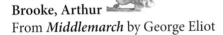

Brooke, Arthur
From *Middlemarch* by George Eliot

A wealthy bachelor from a good family, Brooke shares his home, Tipton Grange, with his two nieces, Dorothea and Celia Brooke. An irresolute, dim-witted and essentially incompetent man, he lacks the ability to manage his estate efficiently. As a result his tenants live in abject squalor. This does not prevent him from running for Parliament on a reforming manifesto.

Brooke, Celia
From *Middlemarch* by George Eliot

Celia is a genteel, conventional young woman who lives with her older sister at Tipton Grange, the home of her bachelor uncle Arthur Brooke. With no original ideas of her own, she is happy to take on the comfortable and undemanding role of wife to a local baronet that her sister unexpectedly rejects.

Brooke, Dorothea
From *Middlemarch* by George Eliot

Young, intelligent and well-to-do, Dorothea Brooke lives with her bachelor uncle and her younger sister, Celia at Tipton Grange in the environs of the (fictitious) Midlands town of Middlemarch. Although she has the means to attire herself in the latest fashions, Dorothea is not remotely interested in pretty gowns and fancy hairstyles, choosing to wear plain, simple dresses which are well-suited to her pure, dignified beauty. Unlike most young women in her position, Dorothea has a social conscience and she wishes to use her life to improve the lot of others. This impulse induces her to spurn a comfortable, conventional life as wife of a prosperous baronet in favour of marriage to a dry, pedantic clergyman many years her senior who is engaged in writing a work which is, in his

Dorothea Brooke from The Works of George Eliot, Vol 11, Middlemarch part 3 published by The Jenson Society, NY, 1910

opinion, of great importance. Dorothea elects to become his wife because she mistakenly believes that she will find fulfilment helping him complete his work. Essentially generous and warm-hearted, she makes the error of misjudging her own character, believing she is capable of greater self-sacrifice and acquiescence than is really the case.

Brown, Captain
From *Cranford* by Elizabeth Gaskell

A retired naval officer aged sixty-something, Captain Brown takes a small house in the quiet northern town of Cranford when he is employed locally on railway business. A wiry man with a military bearing, he dresses in a padded coat which is more often than not threadbare. Living with him are his two unmarried daughters, Mary and Jessie, to whom he shows immense consideration and affection. Once he was unwise enough to mention his straitened financial circumstances in public, thereby breaking one of the unwritten Cranford rules of polite behaviour. Despite being shunned for this offence he remained ignorant of his faux pas, and with his frank and friendly manner, was soon forgiven and welcomed back into Cranford society where his resourcefulness and masculinity are something of a novelty.

Brown, Miss Jessie
From *Cranford* by Elizabeth Gaskell

Miss Jessie Brown is the youngest daughter of Captain Brown (see above). Aged about twenty-eight, she is a pretty woman with a rounded face and dimples. Her pleasant manner and smiling face make her popular enough with the ladies of Cranford for them to overlook unfortunate gaffes about an uncle in trade and an out-of-tune singing voice. She is devoted to her father and her irritable, ailing sister, going to immense pains to make her comfortable.

Brown, Miss
From *Cranford* by Elizabeth Gaskell

Aged about forty, Mary Brown is the oldest daughter of Captain Brown (see above). Plainer and more hard-featured than her sister, she is suffering from a serious illness which adds a sickly pallor to her already deficient appearance and causes her to be peevish and cross.

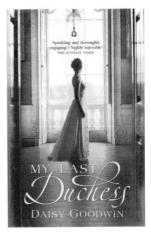

Buckingham, Duchess of
From *My Last Duchess* by Daisy Goodwin

Known as the 'Double Duchess' because she was married first to the Duke of Wareham and then, following his death, to the Duke of Buckingham, Duchess Fanny is skilled at charming influential men. The daughter of a Somerset squire, she used her talents to marry well and then, having presented the Duke with two heirs, proceeded to take a string of lovers including the Prince of Wales and her footman. Her formerly excellent relationship with her son Ivo plummeted when she married the Duke of Buckingham very soon after her first husband's death. Still a very attractive woman, she enjoys being the centre of attention and manipulates people to get what she wants.

Buckland, William   **RP**
From *Remarkable Creatures* by Tracy Chevalier

An educated man who is fascinated by natural history, Buckland knows Lyme Regis well as he grew up in nearby Axminster, Now, however, he has taken holy orders and lives in Oxford where he teaches geology, although he visits Lyme from time to time to search for fossils. Unlike many religious men he has a relatively open mind about geological finds and tries to find ways to reconcile them with his faith. When he is fossil hunting he uses local woman Mary Anning as a guide, but as he isn't a worldly man he doesn't consider the damage he is doing to her reputation, or to her finances come to that as it doesn't occur to him to pay her. It is left to another to suggest that there should always be a chaperone when he and Mary are together.

With a balding head, baby face, big lips, sparkling eyes, sloping shoulders and protruding belly, his appearance is rather comical and he makes a curious sight when he goes onto the beach wearing a top hat and carrying a blue sack to hold his finds. His eating habits are more curious still, for he is attempting to eat his way through the animal kingdom and thinks nothing of picking up dead gulls to cook for supper. For all his peculiarities Buckland is a decent enough man, even though he is so entirely wrapped up in his pursuits that he remains blissfully unaware of the expectations of others.

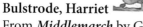

Bulstrode, Harriet
From *Middlemarch* by George Eliot

The wife of Nicholas Bulstrode (see below), Harriet is a good-hearted, honest and devout woman. The sister of Walter Vincy, the mayor of Middlemarch, she has a forgiving nature and remains faithful to her husband when his murky past comes back to haunt them.

Bulstrode, Nicholas
From *Middlemarch* by George Eliot

A respectable and wealthy banker in the Midlands town of Middlemarch, Bulstrode is a deeply-religious figure with a shady past he is eager to hide. A genuine desire to be seen to be good drives him to get involved in philanthropic works, but his essentially selfish natures prevents him from becoming the man he desperately wants to be. When his past catches up with him, Bulstrode's true nature comes to the fore with disastrous consequences.

Burgess, Mr
From *Tilly Trotter* and *Tilly Trotter Wed* by Catherine Cookson

Tutor of the unruly Sopwith children and one of the few people they respect, Mr Burgess is a wise old bachelor who lives for reading. Kind and non-judgemental, he lives in a small cottage which he fills with hundreds of books.

Burns, Helen
From *Jane Eyre* by Charlotte Bronte

Jane Eyre's first friend at the grim charity school to which she is sent at the age of ten, fellow pupil Helen Burns has a thin face and sunken grey eyes, symptoms, no doubt, of the consumption (tuberculosis) from which she suffers. Although she is picked on and treated cruelly by a member of staff, Helen is able to remain passive and calm thanks to her strong faith in God's love and the afterlife. Unlike Jane, she is able to turn the other cheek and refuses to think ill of those who victimise her. If she seems to be too good to be true, it is worth remembering that Charlotte Brontë's sister Maria is thought to have been the inspiration for Helen Burns.

Burton, Sarah
From *South Riding* by Winifred Holtby

A 39-year-old teacher who has returned to her native South Riding after an absence of many years, Miss Burton is full of enthusiasm when she takes up her new position as headmistress of Kiplington Girls' High School. The daughter of a drunken blacksmith who accidentally drowned himself, and a capable District Nurse, she is lively, competent and very forward-thinking. Intelligence and hard work have won her degrees from Leeds and Oxford and now, with wide experience gained in London and South Africa, she is eager to run a school of her own. Modern, enterprising and determined to improve her school, she has an attractive zest for life and a burning desire to equip her

BBC DVD of South Riding starring Anna Maxwell Martin as Sarah Burton.

pupils with the tools they will need to make the best of their lives. A series of disappointing love affairs has persuaded her that she is better off on her own, but instead of regretting her single status she channels all her energy into her work. Yet her warm, passionate nature is not well suited to a celibate life and before long she finds herself unwillingly drawn to a handsome and troubled adversary.

The character and appearance of Sarah Burton are drawn so vividly that she fairly bounces off the pages. She is a small, slight woman with vivid, wiry red hair and slender ankles. Facially she is not pretty – her nose is too large, her mouth too wide and her light green eyes too small – yet people are attracted to her for the neatness of her figure and vitality of her nature. Her expression is candid and her smile both friendly and challenging.

Butler, Rhett
From *Gone With the Wind* by Margaret Mitchell

Dark, handsome and dangerous, Rhett Butler has been disowned by his prominent Charleston family for behaviour ill befitting a gentleman. Without the financial support of his family he is forced to live on his wits, earning his living as a professional gambler.

Flyer for Gone With the Wind the musical.

Now he is shunned by most respectable members of society, but those that do know him are unable to resist his debonair charm and wit. When war breaks out between the Confederacy and the Union States in 1861, Rhett declines to join the army, instead becoming a blockade runner, dodging enemy ships to take cotton to England and bring back much needed supplies. His opportunistic escapades earn him a hero's reputation as well as a considerable fortune.

The persona Rhett shows to the world is that of a cynical, immoral individual who cares nothing for honour and who despises the old Southern values. To some extent this portrait is true, yet time and again his actions demonstrate a romantic attachment to the ideals he affects to scorn. That he attempts to camouflage his occasional acts of gallantry with self-deprecating irony is indicative of the complex contradictions of Rhett's character; put simply, he simultaneously loathes and loves the society he grew up in. This paradigm is best demonstrated by his contempt for Ashley Wilkes, the living embodiment of noble Southern manhood, and his almost reverential affection for Ashley's wife, who is the very personification of a gracious Southern lady.

While Rhett is prepared to laugh at himself for his attachment to an outmoded way of life that has, moreover, already rejected him, he is less happy for others to perceive his weakness. In particular, he cannot bear for the woman he loves to know the real him, to see the vulnerable man behind the façade of mockery and easy charm. Despite occasional outbursts of violence and brutality, his efforts to maintain the appearance of a hard-hearted rogue would not fool a more perceptive woman, but Rhett has the misfortune to love someone who is singularly obtuse about affairs of the heart. Thus, his chances of happiness in his personal life are severely restricted by his continual denial of emotional dependency and her inability to comprehend his true feelings.

C is for Carew, Cazalet, Cromwell and more

Caesar, Domitian   **RP**
From *The Falco Series* by Lindsey Davis

Youngest son of the Emperor Vespasian, Domitian is an unstable 20-year old at the start of the Falco novels. Physically he is a younger, softer version of his brother Titus (see below) and he shares his intellect and ability, but there is a bad streak running through Domitian that makes him a danger to himself and others.

Caesar, Titus   **RP**
From *The Falco Series* by Lindsey Davis

Aged about thirty at the start of the series, Titus is the oldest son of the Emperor Vespasian. Fit, stockily built and good-looking, he is a skilled general, intelligent, intuitive and trusted completely by his father. Rumoured to have had an affair with beautiful Queen Berenice of Judea, he has the air of a lady's man and is more than a little interested in the noble Helena Justina, a Senator's daughter who plays an important role in the novels.

Cardross, Giles, Earl of
From *April Lady* by Georgette Heyer

Wealthy, charming and handsome, Lord Cardross was able to choose a bride from amongst the most eligible girls in London. His friends were therefore surprised when he opted to marry sweet and innocent Lady Helen Irvine, daughter of the famously profligate Lord Pevensey. Undeterred by their fourteen-year age gap or by the knowledge that his beloved's family is fatally flawed when it comes to managing money, he married her for the very good reason that he had fallen in love with her and hoped the feeling was mutual. Now, nearly a year after their marriage, Cardross is beginning to suspect that Nell, as his wife is widely known, only married him for his money. His doubts are fuelled by her extravagant spending and the emotional distance she maintains from him.

Cardross is a decent man with good manners and a great deal of patience which he needs when dealing with both his young wife and his half-sister and ward, Lady Letitia Merion. He is frustrated by his inability to break through Nell's polite detachment, and he sometimes sounds like a schoolmaster addressing an errant pupil when he confronts her about her debts. None of this bodes well for their future happiness, but as this is a light-hearted romantic novel love, surely, will overcome all difficulties?

Cardross, Helen (Nell), Countess of
From *April Lady* by Georgette Heyer

The daughter of Lord and Lady Pevensey, Nell is a lovely, innocent girl of 18 who has done rather well for herself by marrying Lord Cardross, a wealthy Earl. Her family are delighted by the match because the Earl has provided his profligate and financially embarrassed in-laws with a generous, but unspecified, amount of money. When the book starts, she has been married to Cardross for not quite a year. Although Nell genuinely loves him, their relationship is already floundering because, in accordance with some bad advice provided by her mother, she refuses to let her husband know how she feels about him. Things are not helped by her discovery that he had a mistress prior to their marriage, or by her extravagance and her insistence on giving money to her wastrel brother.

A conventionally pretty girl with blue eyes and fair hair, Nell is sweet-natured and affectionate. If left alone to be guided by her own heart she would make a success of her marriage in no time but, beset by relatives and friends who do her no service, she persists in withholding her true feelings from her husband.

Carew, Jye
From *Larksleve* and *Blanche* by Patricia Wendorf

Adored son of Somerset mason Luke Carew and the proud gypsy, Meridiana Loveridge, Jye is a beautiful child who strongly resembles his handsome father. Early in his childhood it becomes apparent that his hearing is impaired, and by, the age of 10 he has become completely deaf. His deafness gives him a sense of isolation which is exacerbated by the strangeness of his mother compared to the other village women. Although he loves her, he is made uneasy by her gypsy ways. Jye has natural intelligence and he learns to read and write before losing his hearing, but his deafness affects his speech, causing those who don't know him well to think him slow. When he is old enough he follows in his father's footsteps and becomes an apprentice stone mason.

Montacute village, home of the Carew family.

Big, strong and handsome, he could have women running after him, but Jye is shy so he keeps himself to himself, rarely entering into conversation or volunteering an opinion. His consuming passion is a precious damask rose bush which he nurtures in his free time, but he discovers a different, unwelcome kind of passion when he encounters a beautiful, seductive and determined young woman who appals and attracts him in equal measure.

Carew, Luke
From *Larksleve* and *Blanche* by Patricia Wendorf

Nineteen-year-old Luke is a skilled stone mason living in the Somerset village of Montacute. The oldest of nine children, he is the main support of his widowed mother, Charity Carew. Taller and broader than most in his community, his thick black curls and swarthy complexion suggest there is gypsy blood somewhere in his ancestry, although this is strenuously denied by Charity. A reserved, God-fearing young man who speaks only when necessary, Luke loves his work and is proud of his skill as a mason. Steady and ambitious, he is ill-equipped to resist the determined onslaught of Meridiana Loveridge, a young gypsy girl who has set her heart on him.

Carey, Mary   **RP**
From *The Other Boleyn Girl* by Philippa Gregory

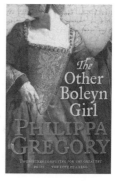

Married at the tender age of 12 to William Carey, a minor courtier in the service of Henry VIII, Mary is the youngest daughter of Thomas Boleyn and his wife, the nobly born Lady Elizabeth Howard. (Most historians believe that Mary was in fact the oldest Boleyn daughter but it is open to debate and anyway in a work of fiction it is not uncommon for facts to be altered to suit the plot). She is very beautiful with abundant golden hair and a milk and honey complexion. Her father is a rising man, using his wits and his alliance with the powerful Howard family to become a major player at the court of Henry VIII. When the story begins in earnest, Mary is just 14 and the favourite lady-in-waiting of Henry's wife, Katherine of Aragon. However, the queen's favour evaporates when the king casts lustful eyes at Mary and her unscrupulous family, seizing this chance to further their ambitions by pushing her into the royal bed. At first Mary is unwilling, partly because she reveres the Queen and doesn't wish to hurt her, and partly because she believes she should stay faithful to her husband. Soon, though, intense pressure from her family, her own flattered vanity, and a genuine admiration for the king, combine to persuade her to do all she can to ensnare Henry.

Although she has her faults, unlike the rest of her family Mary is not venal and she has a faithful, loving nature. She adores George, her handsome brother, but has a tricky relationship with her sister, Anne. Mary admires Anne's beauty, grace, wit and style but there is a sizeable dollop of sibling rivalry between the two which is why Mary feels triumphant when she, rather than her sophisticated sister, captures the king's fancy. Ultimately, however, Mary is insufficiently scheming and manipulative to successfully play such high-stake games, and experience teaches her that she is happiest leading a simple life away from the machinations of the court.

Carey, William **RP**
From *The Other Boleyn Girl* by Philippa Gregory

A gentleman in the service of Henry VIII, Carey is married to Mary Boleyn, the beautiful youngest daughter of Sir Thomas Boleyn. The marriage was arranged for mutual advantage, but all the same, he has feelings for his innocent young wife. However, they have not long been married before he is forced to stand aside and allow Mary to become the king's mistress. He resents being cuckolded so publicly, but is rewarded handsomely with gifts of land and money. Nevertheless, he keeps a watchful eye on Mary and looks forward to the day when she can return to him.

Carlill, Juliana
From *Rebels and Traitors* by Lindsey Davis

When she makes her first appearance in the novel Juliana is 17 and has been living for three months with her elderly guardian in a rented house in Wallingford. The age of her guardian, coupled with her belief that he might make a pass at her before too long, convinces Juliana of the pressing need to find a well-to-do husband. To this end, her guardian has been putting about a tale that she is a land-owning heiress with friends in high places. Although it is a wild exaggeration, the story does contain a grain of truth and in any case, before too long, a couple of young gentlemen come calling.

Brought up by her granddaughter, a French adventuress, Juliana is a pleasant, intelligent girl with a mind of her own. She is not beautiful, but her appearance is pleasing all the same; she has brown hair, worn in a bun with long ringlets either side, grey eyes, a small nose and a 'medium figure'. She loves to read and has a tough, practical side to her personality that enables her to survive many ordeals.

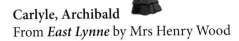

Carlyle, Archibald
From *East Lynne* by Mrs Henry Wood

A respectable lawyer with a house and successful practice in the town of West Lynne, Archibald Carlyle, 27, is a very tall man with an appearance that is pleasing and distinguished rather than handsome. He has a clear, pale complexion, dark hair and deep grey eyes under drooping eyelids. Having been educated at Rugby and Oxford, he has acquired gentlemanly manners and is thus more comfortable associating with members of the aristocracy than is the norm for country lawyers.

Kind, generous and entirely honourable, Carlyle means well, but his actions are too often determined by two women who have undue influence in his life. One, his half-sister Cornelia, took charge of his upbringing when his own mother died at his birth, and although he is now a grown man, he has not lost the habit of acquiescing to her wishes. The other female who involves herself in his life is Barbara Hare, a pretty young woman he has known all his life and for whom he feels a brotherly affection, never suspecting that Barbara's love for him is anything but sisterly. While helping Barbara with a secret matter that affects her family, Carlyle spends a lot of time talking to her privately and comforting her when she is distressed. The controlling nature of his sister and the enforced intimacy of his meetings with Barbara are to cause problems when Carlyle falls in love and marries a naïve and sensitive young girl.

Carlyle, Cornelia (Miss)
From *East Lynne* by Mrs Henry Wood

Tall, bony and angular, Cornelia Carlyle is the unmarried daughter of the late Mr Carlyle, respected law practitioner in the country town of West Lynne. Her mother died when she was a child, but it was not until Cornelia was a grown woman that her father remarried. This time his wife died in childbirth and Cornelia took on responsibility for the baby, a boy called Archibald. When he was a child she loved him fiercely, but ruled him with an iron hand, and even now, when he is fully grown and in charge of his own law firm, she continues in her attempts to control his every deed. Strong-minded, forceful and unnecessarily penny-pinching, Miss Carlyle interferes unrepentantly in her brother's life and is sniffily resentful of anyone who threatens her domain.

Carne, Midge
From *South Riding* by Winifred Holtby

The 14-year-old only child of Robert Carne (see below) and his aristocratic wife Muriel, Midge is a thin, bespectacled girl who spends a great deal of time on her own in the crumbling grandeur of Maythorpe Hall. With her mother in a home for the mentally ill and her father busy attempting to save his farm, Midge has been left to her own devices for far too long. Highly strung in the first place, she is driven by a toxic combination of boredom and anxiety into hysterical fits which suggest she may have inherited her mother's mental instability. Yet she might be saved from insanity by attending Kiplington Girls' High School, although there are those that consider the school, habitually frequented by the daughters of small tradesmen, as inappropriate for the granddaughter of a baron.

Carne, Robert
From *South Riding* by Winifred Holtby

A big, handsome gentleman farmer with dark hair and a sensitive mouth, Robert Carne of Maythorpe Hall is a very worried man. His aristocratic wife has gone mad and now lives in an expensive private asylum. His teenage daughter Midge is dangerously highly strung; his heavily mortgaged farm is rapidly losing money and to cap it all he is suffering from angina. As he goes about his daily business he is racked by guilt, believing that marrying him and bearing his child was what broke his unstable wife's fragile grasp on sanity. His only comforts are the fellowship of his farm workers who share his conservative views, and the warm friendship he has formed with Alderman Mrs Beddows, a much older woman to whom he confides his troubles.

Standing for the traditional way of life, Carne is unwilling to adapt to the changing times. His natural allies are ex-servicemen like him who fought in the Great War and want the rhythm of life to continue as it did before they went off to fight for king and country. As a councillor he can be relied upon to oppose innovation and change, not through lack of interest in the welfare of others, but through a genuine conviction that the old ways are better. To strangers he comes across as surly, but he is capable of immense charm and is a decent, honourable man whose only fault is to be hopelessly adrift in modern times.

Casaubon, Rev. Edward
From *Middlemarch* by George Eliot

A rich, scholarly clergyman in late middle age, Edward Casaubon is the owner of Lowick, a considerable estate in the environs of Middlemarch, a town in the Midlands. His defining characteristic is ambition, specifically his desire to write a masterful academic work called *The Key to All Mythologies*. He gives the impression of being erudite and intellectual, but in reality he is riddled with doubt about his abilities. When he attracts the admiration of a good-looking and intelligent young woman, his ego is flattered, but he misinterprets what she wants from him and fails to appreciate both the depth of her intellect and the strength of her character.

 Casaubon is a dry, pedantic character who, although as susceptible as any man to the charms of a beautiful, warm-hearted woman, should really remain a bachelor. His insecurities make him difficult, suspicious and cold, and when he feels threatened by a rival he reveals a thoroughly mean streak.

Cash, Cora
From *My Last Duchess* by Daisy Goodwin

The wealthiest American heiress of her generation, Cora Cash has been brought up to expect the absolute best that life has to offer. Living in ostentatious luxury with her flour magnate father and socially ambitious mother, she has been groomed from birth to marry into the English aristocracy, since it is her mother's fervent desire to have a titled daughter, and Mrs Cash is used to getting what she wants. As the book opens, Cora is preparing for her coming out ball, after which she will be whisked away to England on her father's private yacht so that the search for a blue-blooded, cash-strapped suitor may begin.

 A tall, good-looking girl of 18 with long chestnut hair, a tiny waist, greenish eyes and a face that is strikingly attractive without being beautiful, Cora is clever, spoilt

Consuelo Vanderbilt, on whom Cora Cash is loosely based.

and vain. She revels in the luxurious trappings of her life while resenting the rigid control of her domineering mother. Her privileged upbringing has made her confident and spirited, attributes that will come in handy when she is dropped into the alien milieu of the English upper classes.

Cash, Mr
From *My Last Duchess* by Daisy Goodwin

Winthrop Rutherford Cash II inherited a fortune from his father, a self-made man who started life as a stable boy. Winthrop has increased his company's profitability to such an extent that virtually every loaf in America is now baked with Cash's flour. While his wife spends his millions pursuing her dream of social supremacy, he amuses himself with a series of infidelities.

Cash, Mrs
From *My Last Duchess* by Daisy Goodwin

Nancy Cash is the wife of American flour magnate Winthrop Cash with whom she has one child, Cora. A formidable and ferociously ambitious woman, she has used her husband's immense wealth to propel her family up the social ladder. Yet even though the parties thrown by Mrs Cash are always the most exciting, and her houses are the most opulent, the taint of new money prevents her from attaining the society ascendancy her heart desires. She believes that only by marrying her daughter into the British aristocracy will New York's first families accept her as one of their own. Cora's own wishes do not enter into her plans.

The handsome daughter of a Confederate colonel, Mrs Cash grew up knowing how to command an army of servants and not much else. Aware of the holes in her own education she has taken care that her daughter should be polished and accomplished.

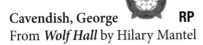

Cavendish, George   **RP**
From *Wolf Hall* by Hilary Mantel

Cardinal Wolsey's gentleman usher when the main narrative of the book begins, Cavendish is 'a sensitive sort of man who talks a lot about table napkins'. Yet he is loyal to the Cardinal, worries about his comfort, and exhibits a degree of backbone in adversity.

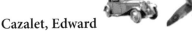

Cazalet, Clary (real name Clarissa)
From *The Cazalet Chronicle* (comprising 4 novels: *The Light Years, Marking Time, Confusion* and *Casting Off*) by Elizabeth Jane Howard

Aged 12 at the start of *The Light Years*, the first book of *The Cazalet Chronicle* which opens in the summer of 1937, Clary is the daughter of Rupert Cazalet and his first wife, Isobel, who died giving birth to a son, Neville. Although she was only five when her mother died, Clary feels the loss, and her unhappiness has been intensified by her father's subsequent marriage to a beautiful but shallow young woman who has no interest in her stepchildren. As a result, Clary is spiky, insecure and prone to nightmares.

Unlike her cousins Polly and Louise to whom she is close in age, Clary is not a pretty child; she has a round, freckled face and is something of a 'dumpling', although she does have lovely eyes. Her lack of conventional prettiness is compounded by a disinterest in her appearance and a tendency to be messy. Beneath the unpromising exterior, however, Clary is a faithful, intelligent and loving child whose awkwardness is a symptom of her struggle to come to terms with her mother's death and her father's remarriage. This struggle isn't helped, initially at least, by the large Cazalet family gathering that takes place at her grandparents' home in the Sussex countryside that summer. Clary is a major figure in *The Cazalet Chronicle*. The story charts her progress from a needy adolescent craving attention and affection, to a teenager steadfastly clinging to hope long after her elders have abandoned it, and concludes with her poised on the brink of professional and personal contentment.

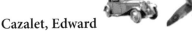

Cazalet, Edward
From *The Cazalet Chronicle* by Elizabeth Jane Howard

Aged 40 at the start of *The Light Years*, Edward is the second son of prosperous, upmarket timber merchant William Cazalet and his wife Kitty. Edward works in the family business and lives in London with his wife Villy and three children, Teddy, Louise and Lydia. He served with

distinction in the First World War and despite the horror of the trenches, came back relatively unscathed, physically and emotionally. Handsome and charming, he expects life to be good to him and is seldom disappointed. He has a roving eye and is serially unfaithful to Villy, although this does not prevent him from claiming his conjugal rights on a regular basis. That she clearly doesn't enjoy his lovemaking bothers him not at all since he considers this quite normal in a respectable wife. His good points are that he is generous, has pleasant manners and is very fond of his family, particularly his older brother Hugh who also saw action in World War I. Apart from his infidelities (of which she is unaware), he is considerate to Villy and is an affectionate, if distant, father to his children. However, his likeability as a character is severely limited by his selfishness and his inability to think very deeply about anything or, indeed, to hold an original opinion. Even more damningly, his uncontrollable sexual instincts drive him to behave in a morally indefensible manner, with long-lasting repercussions.

Cazalet, Hugh
From *The Cazalet Chronicle* by Elizabeth Jane Howard

Eldest child of William and Kitty Cazalet, Hugh is in his early forties in the summer of 1937. Unlike his brother Edward, the awful experiences he underwent in the First World War have left their mark on him. His physical injuries include an amputated hand and shrapnel in his head which causes debilitating headaches. These make him irritable, especially when he knows that people have noticed his pain. Most of the time, however, he is mild mannered, kindly and decent. He is utterly devoted to his wife, Sybil, with whom he finds solace from his nightmarish memories, and is a fond father to his children Polly and Simon. He particularly adores Polly, although he goes out of his way to not let his preference show.

Like Edward, he lives in London and works at the family firm. As *The Cazalet Chronicle* opens he is watching the situation in Germany with trepidation, fearing that another catastrophic war is on its way.

Cazalet, Kitty (the Duchy)
From *The Cazalet Chronicle* by Elizabeth Jane Howard

Benign matriarch of the Cazalet clan, the Duchy (an affectionate nickname based on her Duchess-like demeanour) is 70 at the commencement of *The Cazalet Chronicle*. Married to William, she has four grown up children – Hugh, Edward,

The Duchy is happiest in the Sussex countryside. Image ©Janet Richardson, used under the Creative Commons Attribution-ShareAlike 2.0 license.

Rachel and Rupert – and seven grandchildren with another on the way. Although she has a house in London, the Duchy prefers to spend her time at Home Place, a rambling house in the West Sussex countryside where she is able to indulge her passion for gardening. Although her marriage has been outwardly successful, she has little in common with her husband and is content to manage her household without having much to do with him. Their contact is largely restricted to mealtimes as the rest of the time they use their unmarried daughter Rachel as a go-between.

Very pretty in her youth, in her old age she is still a fine-looking woman, albeit without a scrap of vanity. Kind in a brisk, no nonsense sort of way, she believes firmly in simplicity, so good plain food, open windows and tepid bath water are the order of the day at Home Place. She is a skilled amateur pianist and when not working in her garden is at her happiest playing or listening to classical music.

Cazalet, Louise
From *The Cazalet Chronicle* by Elizabeth Jane Howard

The oldest child of Edward and Villy Cazalet, Louise is 14 when *The Cazalet Chronicle* opens. A lovely looking girl, she is obsessed with Shakespeare and John Gielgud, and dreams of becoming an actress. Teddy, her brother, is away at boarding school, but the Cazalets do not consider their daughters' education a high priority, even though the girls for the most part are brighter than the boys. Thus, Louise makes do with lessons at home given by her mother's former governess, Miss Milliment. She shares these lessons with her cousin Polly.

Louise has a scratchy relationship with her mother. She longs to please her but frequently fails, for reasons that have more to do with Villy's discontent than any real shortcomings of her own. She gets on much better with her father until an unfortunate incident sours the relationship forever.

Louise knows she isn't a particularly good person – she compares herself unfavourably with Polly – and this makes it easy to empathise with, and care about, her without actually liking her very much. Like all the Cazalet girls she is naïve about sex and finds the transition from girlhood to womanhood unbearably tedious. Her character is believed to have much in common with the author as a young woman.

Cazalet, Neville
From *The Cazalet Chronicle* by Elizabeth Jane Howard

The youngest child of Rupert and Isobel Cazalet (who died giving birth to him), Neville is about seven at the start of *The Cazalet Chronicle*. He is resented by his sister Clary for causing her mother's death while his young stepmother, Zoe, resents him simply because she dislikes having to share her husband with his children. Although his devoted nurse (nanny) takes good care of him, he is emotionally vulnerable and is developing a deliberately awkward, couldn't-care-less attitude in an attempt to disguise his insecurities. A funny-looking boy, with sticking up hair and a bumpy forehead, he suffers bad asthma attacks brought on by anxiety. Although he provides moments of high comedy, Neville is a sad little character, struggling to cope in the fairly dysfunctional life of his immediate family, and as the Chronicle progresses, his situation deteriorates quite badly before it begins to improve.

Cazalet, Polly
From *The Cazalet Chronicle* by Elizabeth Jane Howard

The oldest child and only daughter of Hugh and Sybil Cazalet, Polly is approaching her thirteenth birthday at the start of *The Cazalet Chronicle*. A very pretty, honest and kind-hearted girl, she is great friends with her cousin Louise with whom she has lessons, although she soon forms a deeper bond with Clary, another cousin to whom she is closer in age. Polly gets on with both her parents although she suspects, rightly, that her mother favours her brother Simon. She accepts this ungrudgingly, partly because she is good-natured, but also because she has a very close relationship with her father. The knowledge that his experiences in World War I have left him physically and mentally scarred make Polly dread the very real prospect of another war, so much so that she suffers silent agonies during the Munich crisis of 1938 and faints with relief when 'peace with honour' is announced.

Polly is unsure what she wants to do when she grows up, but she does know that she wants a home that she can enjoy decorating and furnishing. She has excellent taste and loves collecting antique knick-knacks which she displays in her bedroom. While unaware that she is extremely pretty – frowning on vanity, the Cazalets never comment on their children's physical appearance - she likes to dress well and is always groomed and tidy. Loyal, open and honest, Polly is probably the nicest of the Cazalet grandchildren and perhaps because of this her story, whilst enjoyable, is not quite as engrossing as some of the others.

Cazalet, Rachel
From *The Cazalet Chronicle* by Elizabeth Jane Howard

An unmarried 38-year-old at the start of *The Cazalet Chronicle*, Rachel is the third child and only daughter of William and Kitty Cazalet. A dutiful and loving daughter, she adores her three brothers equally and is a benevolent aunt to their children. Physically, she is good looking with fine skin, eyes alert with intelligence and humour, and a pleasant, if unremarkable, face. Like her mother she is utterly devoid of personal vanity and does little to enhance her appearance – her hair is worn in a loose bun and she dresses in sensible jersey suits and brown brogues. As she has a naturally self-sacrificing nature she accepts without question that her role is to live with her parents and help with the running of their household. She always puts the needs of her family before her own wishes and in doing so often hurts her great friend Sid (real name Margot Sidney) with whom she is in love. Her family know Sid from her occasional visits to Home Place and they like her, but none of them suspect that the relationship goes beyond friendship. In fact, in one sense it does not, since Rachel is uncomfortable with the physical manifestations of love and naïvely believes that Sid is satisfied with their platonic relationship.

Cazalet, Rupert
From *The Cazalet Chronicle* by Elizabeth Jane Howard

The youngest of William and Kitty Cazalet's children, Rupert is aged 34 when *The Cazalet Chronicle* begins. Unlike his older brothers, he was too young to fight in the First World War and perhaps as a result, he has a lighter, more relaxed personality with none of Hugh's physical and mental scarring, or Edward's woman-chasing tendencies. Not that life has been especially easy for Rupert – his first wife died in childbirth, leaving him with a 5-year old daughter and newborn son to care for, and following his marriage three years ago to Zoe, he now has a very young, selfish and insecure wife to keep happy. Rupert has artistic tendencies and longs to devote his time to painting, but with a family to support, he is obliged to earn his living as an art teacher. Any attempts to paint in his spare time are thwarted by Zoe who resents anything that takes his attention away from her.

Rupert is a likeable character who attempts to be a good father to his children, but sometimes falls short of the mark because he is torn. He fell for Zoe's beauty at a time when he was emotionally vulnerable and now, having married her, is doing his best to suppress the realisation that she is self-obsessed and shallow. Although kind, funny and compassionate, he can be irritatingly irresolute and indecisive.

Cazalet, Simon
From *The Cazalet Chronicle* by Elizabeth Jane Howard

Aged 11 at the start of the saga, Simon is the son of Hugh and Sybil Cazalet. At present he has just one sibling, his older sister Polly, but his mother is heavily pregnant. Simon is her favourite child and unlike her husband, who endeavours to conceal his partiality for Polly, she is none too subtle in disguising it. Simon is away at prep school much of the time and when he returns she fusses over and indulges him. Perhaps because of this, Simon is a sensitive boy who regards the prospect of changing to senior school with horror. At Home Place during the long summer holiday, he spends most of his time doing things with his cousin Teddy whom he admires because he is older and a prefect at his school.

Cazalet, Sybil
From *The Cazalet Chronicle* by Elizabeth Jane Howard

Wife of Hugh and mother of Polly and Simon with another baby or perhaps twins on the way, Sybil is 38 at the start of *The Cazalet Chronicle*. She and Hugh are happily married. He came out of the First World War damaged physically and mentally, but meeting and falling in love with Sybil gave him a new purpose in life. Although they have now been married for seventeen years, they remain devoted to one another, although the possibility of another war is casting clouds over their contentment, as are Sybil's unspoken fears about giving birth. As her pregnancy advances she is becoming increasingly uncomfortable and anxious, although she does everything she can to conceal her feelings from Hugh. This is typical of their relationship; she pretends she is feeling fine and maintains she would like to go out for the evening in the mistaken belief that this is what Hugh wants to do. In fact what he longs to do is have a peaceful evening at home with Sybil, but he unselfishly agrees to go out because he believes her when she says it is what she wants to do.

Normally an attractive woman with long hair the colour of raw mahogany, Sybil is looking tired at the start of *The Light Years* and her body is 'the size of a house'. She is an intelligent, rather serious woman, who reads books for enlightenment and education rather than for pleasure, but she nevertheless enjoys her life as a wife and mother.

Cazalet, Teddy
From *The Cazalet Chronicle* by Elizabeth Jane Howard

The second child of Edward and Villy Cazalet, Teddy is aged 13 when the first novel in *The Cazalet Chronicle* begins. Mad about cricket, tennis, and other sports, he is a robust boy, interested in typically boyish subjects such as submarines and polar expeditions. Oblivious to any tensions within his family, he is mostly concerned with eating vast quantities of food and maintaining the admiration of his younger cousin, Simon. Having spent his formative years in the almost exclusively male environment of his prep school, he has learned to regard females as weak and rather embarrassing, and at the end of term he dreads the thought of his mother collecting him from school in case she commits the ultimate faux pas of hugging him. Although he is not a central figure in *The Cazalet Chronicle* and his personality is never more than sketchily drawn, Teddy's progress from hearty schoolboy to vulnerable young man offers an interesting sidebar to the main plot lines.

Cazalet, Viola (Villy)
From *The Cazalet Chronicle* by Elizabeth Jane Howard

The wife of Edward Cazalet, Villy is by no means the most likeable character in *The Cazalet Chronicle,* but she is certainly one of the best defined, and because the reader understands her so well, it is impossible not to empathise with her at least a little. About forty when the story begins, on the surface she has everything – a handsome husband, comfortable home and three healthy children, Louise, Teddy and Lydia. However, all is not well with her marriage and although Villy is completely unaware of Edward's philandering, she finds herself dissatisfied with her lot without really knowing why. Sex is a chore, a duty to be endured without enthusiasm and Edward's perfunctory lovemaking doesn't encourage her to think it could be more enjoyable. At the heart of Villy's discontent, however, is the fact that she gave up her career as a ballet dancer in order to marry Edward, only to discover that the life she

Villy abandoned her ballet career to marry Edward Cazalet. (Photo by unknown photographer shows 1930s ballerina Tatiana Riabouchinska darning a ballet slipper.)

has chosen does not fulfil her. Even though she is busy enough running her household, caring for her children and keeping an eye on her widowed mother, she feels there is a void in her life which she seeks to fill with an endless succession of activities, none of which give her more than temporary satisfaction. The tendency to discontent is in any case a family one, inherited from her imperious mother, Lady Rydal, the widow of a distinguished composer, and shared by her better-looking sister, Jessica Castle.

Physically, although Villy is not unattractive, she has never been conventionally pretty, and as she ages her claims to good looks are diminishing. She has a slim, boyish figure with small breasts that are sagging prematurely, grey hair, a bony face, heavy eyebrows and thin lips which she attempts to improve by wearing unflattering carmine lipstick.

Cazalet, William (the Brig)
From *The Cazalet Chronicle* by Elizabeth Jane Howard

Known to all his family as 'the Brig' and sometimes to his sons as 'the Old Man', William is the Cazalet family patriarch, calling the shots not just in London where the family's timber business is based, but also at Home Place, the Cazalet house in the West Sussex countryside. Ostensibly his wife, 'the Duchy', is in charge here, and it is true that he is content to leave the mundane details of menus and bedroom allocation to her, while he sits in his study, hogging the telephone and ordering new building projects without stopping to discuss them with his wife. In this, of course, he is simply behaving as any respectable Victorian paterfamilias would. Born the year before Queen Victoria became a widow, he grew up with a nineteenth century attitude towards the proper roles of men (breadwinning and decision making) and women (running a household and bringing up children) and although the old century has passed, his attitudes have not. Now that their four children are grown up, his relationship with his wife is mostly conducted in public across a dining table or via notes carried from study to drawing room by their unmarried daughter, Rachel.

For all his old-fashioned ideas, however, the Brig has an astute mind and he keeps a keen eye on the turbulent European political situation. His eyesight is fading, a fact that troubles him immensely as it means he cannot see to read, but he gets round this by compelling various members of his family to read for him, whether or not they are willing.

Cazalet, Zoe
From *The Cazalet Chronicle* by Elizabeth Jane Howard

Zoe is another important and exceptionally well-defined character in this engrossing series of books. Aged 22 when the story begins, she has for three years been married to Rupert, youngest of the three Cazalet brothers. Exceptionally pretty, she loves nightclubs, dancing and wearing lovely clothes, and although she genuinely loves Rupert she is too immature to understand how her resentment of his children, Clary and Neville, causes him pain. Vain, shallow and egocentric, Zoe is easy to dislike and yet the author skilfully manages to convey that the responsibility for her faults is not entirely her own. Brought up by a mother who doted on her daughter's prettiness and made countless little economies in order that she might be indulged, Zoe was taught to think of nothing but herself and her appearance. Although not lacking in intelligence, all her efforts have gone into making herself as beautiful and well-groomed as possible rather than improving her mind. As a result, she is embarrassingly ignorant.

As a stepmother she is a disaster since, little more than a child herself, she wants Rupert all to herself, sulking or creating scenes whenever she is thwarted. Yet unpromising as she sounds, Zoe is not beyond redemption. She does possess a conscience which is lying dormant at the start of the story, but when it is roused – by an event that shakes Zoe to the core – she begins to grow up and gradually a kinder, more reasonable woman starts to emerge. Whether it happens in time to save her marriage remains to be seen.

Champernowne, Katherine (Kat)   **RP**
From *The Lady Elizabeth* by Alison Weir

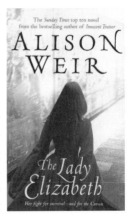

In charge of the household and upbringing of Lady Elizabeth (Henry VIII's daughter by Anne Boleyn) from the age of 4 until she is a grown woman, Kat Champernowne first appears in the book as a fashionably-dressed, energetic middle-aged woman who speaks with a gentle Devon accent. She has dark hair, round cheeks and doe-like eyes which have a mischievous glint. Related to Elizabeth on her mother's side, Kat is warm and reliable and she quickly develops genuine affection for her young charge, becoming a second mother to her in all but name. Yet although she is a permanent and loving presence in Elizabeth's life, someone who is always on her side come what may, Kat does have her faults. In particular she is jealous when other women become close to Elizabeth, and given the predatory ambition of many at Court, she does not always protect her young charge as carefully as she might. On at least one occasion a serious lapse of judgement on her part places Elizabeth and some of her household, Kat herself included, in gravest jeopardy.

Charetty, Felix de
From *Niccolò Rising* by Dorothy Dunnett

A callow youth of 17 when the book begins, Felix is heir to the Charetty dyeing and pawn broking businesses which operate in Bruges and Louvain. He has been educated at the University of Louvain and his widowed mother has attempted to instil in him an understanding of their trade. To her regret Felix at present prefers hunting and larking about with Claes, his apprentice companion, to knuckling down to serious matters. In order to curb his excesses his mother has asked the Charetty company notary, an educated young man called Julius, to keep an eye on him, but although he tries, it isn't always possible to keep Felix out of trouble. When he is caught out in wrongdoing, however, Claes accepts all the responsibility and willingly suffers the punishment in his stead.

Felix has a rat-like nose, brown curled hair and a gaunt frame. A great admirer of fine clothes, he likes to dress modishly and has a penchant for wearing ludicrous hats. He is not a great scholar and cares more about horses and dogs than business, but he occasionally shows glimpses of his late father's shrewdness and this allows his mother to hope that he will eventually mature into a responsible businessman. For the time being, though, he is just a silly, boisterous boy who becomes sullen and red-faced when criticised.

Charetty, Marian de
From *Niccolò Rising* by Dorothy Dunnett

Approaching 40 at the start of the novel, Marian de Charetty is a small, round, active woman with naturally red lips, rosy cheeks and bright blue eyes. A widow, she has been running the moderately prosperous Charetty dyeing and pawn broking business since the death of her husband two years ago. Her brain is sharp and she has a good understanding of both business and human nature. However, her inexperience as a leader has caused her to be overly tough with her employees and her concerns about the immaturity of her son Felix, the heir to the Charetty business, have caused her to drive him too hard as well. Another ever present worry is her apprentice, Claes, who is forever getting himself into scrapes. Marian realises that Claes is far from being the happy moron most people take him for; she knows he is perceptive and gifted, but worries that his talent for trouble will cost him his life. Most of her associates in Bruges consider that remarriage is the obvious answer to her problems and there is at least one suitor eager to become her husband.

Charles I (King)
From *Rebels and Traitors* by Lindsey Davis

A small, dapper man, Charles Stuart is unwavering in his belief that his right to rule the country without interference from anyone descends direct from God. He is brave and honourable, but his inability to see any point of view but his own brings disaster on himself, his family and his people.

Chaucer, Geoffrey   **RP**
From *Katherine* by Anya Seton

The man often referred to as the father of English literature has a legitimate role in this novel since he really was married to Philippa de Roet, the sister of the eponymous heroine. In the book, Chaucer is first encountered as a young man of 26 who is making himself useful at the court of Edward III. Although of fairly humble origins – his father is a vintner - he has, nevertheless, been attached to the royal household since he was a boy, starting as a page in the household of Lionel, Duke of Clarence and in due course becoming a squire in the service of the king. He is valued by his royal master for his trustworthiness and shrewd intelligence and these same qualities have recommended him to Philippa, one of the queen's attendants, as a suitable husband. It is not a love match but they like each other well enough and as the alliance has royal approval everyone is content. In any case, Chaucer's heart secretly belongs to the beautiful Duchess of Lancaster, a gracious lady far above his station. His attachment to her is entirely chaste, he is happy merely to gaze at her from afar.

Anya Seton gives a convincing portrait of Chaucer's appearance. He is described as short and stout with a stubby brown beard and hair cut unfashionably short above his ears. He dresses soberly in clerical garb and his fingers are permanently ink-stained. These unexciting features are lightened by an alert face that reflects sweetness and quiet amusement.

Churchill, Frank
From *Emma* by Jane Austen

Frank Churchill is the only child of Mr Weston, the man who marries Emma Woodhouse's former governess, Miss Taylor at the start of the book. Taken as a small boy to be raised by relatives of his dead mother, Frank has maintained a loving relationship with his father by letter, although he has not seen him for many years. Following Mr Weston's remarriage, Frank, now an adult, promises to make a long overdue visit in order to meet his new stepmother, but due to the demands of his ailing aunt his much anticipated arrival in Highbury is delayed. When he does come he is found to be very handsome, pleasant and sociable and is liked by all apart from the perceptive Mr Knightley who distrusts his easy going charm and regrets that Emma appears to be smitten with him.

Colour illustration by C.E. Brock of Frank Churchill from a 1909 edition of *Emma*.

Clarence, George, Duke of   **RP**
From *We Speak No Treason* by Rosemary Hawley Jarman

The oldest surviving brother of Edward IV, George of Clarence shares many attributes with his regal sibling. Like Edward, Clarence is tall, fair and handsome, but over-indulgence has already started to take its toll on his looks even though he is still young. Again like Edward, Clarence is possessed of an easy charm that helps when he is pursuing women, and he enjoys eating and drinking to excess. Yet the similarities end there because George lacks the depth of intelligence and understanding that makes Edward successful as a monarch. When he is deprived of something that he believes should be his by right he becomes dangerously petulant. Untrustworthy and greedy for money and power, he is susceptible to treachery and should his plans go awry, relies on a combination of fraternal affection and his own persuasive charm to keep him from danger.

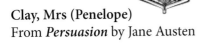

Clay, Mrs (Penelope)
From *Persuasion* by Jane Austen

The widowed daughter of Sir Walter Elliot's lawyer and agent, Mrs Clay is a clever, scheming woman who ingratiates herself with foolish, conceited Elizabeth Elliot in a bid to raise herself far out of her social station by marrying Sir Walter Elliot. With a projecting tooth and heavy freckles, she is not a beauty but, nevertheless, is sufficiently attractive for both Anne Elliot and Anne's godmother Lady Russell to fear that she may one day achieve her aim.

Cleves, Anna (Princess of)   **RP**
From *The Lady Elizabeth* by Alison Weir

The sister of the Duke of Cleves, an influential German Protestant nobleman, Princess Anna is 25 when she becomes betrothed to Henry VIII soon after the death of his third wife. Although he now has his longed for male heir, high infant mortality rates make it advisable for him to try for more sons and therefore he needs to remarry. When Anna arrives in England in 1540 she has never met her future husband and he has only seen her in a miniature portrait. She is a kind, practical woman who is prepared to take a motherly interest in his children. Unfortunately, her angular face, unfashionable clothes, guttural accent and stale smell make a poor impression on the fastidious Henry and he takes an immediate dislike to her. The marriage goes ahead but is dissolved almost immediately afterwards on the dubious grounds that Anna was previously promised to someone else. Gracious now that he is free of her, Henry proclaims Anna his dearest sister and gives her handsome homes to live in including Hever Castle, the childhood home of Anne Boleyn. Happy to have survived a dangerous situation, Anna lives a comfortable life enlivened by occasional visits to court.

Collins, William
From *Pride and Prejudice by* Jane Austen

A tall, heavy-looking young man of 25, Mr Collins is Mr Bennet's cousin and will inherit Longbourn when Mr Bennet dies because it is entailed to the nearest male relative. He is rector of Hunsford in Kent, a position he owes to the patronage of Lady Catherine de Bourgh. When he first appears at Longbourn it is with the intention of securing one of his cousins in marriage. A silly man, Mr Collins is conceited and pompous and his obsequiousness to Lady Catherine and her daughter renders him completely ridiculous. He is, for all that, a delightfully comic character and his speeches are masterpieces of stupidity and self-importance.

Mr Collins from Pride and Prejudice, George Allen, 1894; illustration by Hugh Thomson.

Colly, Stephen
From *I Capture the Castle* by Dodie Smith

Handsome Stephen is an unofficial member of the Mortmain family. Supposedly employed by them, for some time he has received nothing but scanty food and pretty basic lodging in return for his labour. He does not mind, however, as he is hopelessly in love with Cassandra and, knowing how she loves literature, attempts to woo her with poetry he passes off as his own work. Sadly for him, Cassandra is well read and knows he has not written the poems.

I Capture the Castle, Folio Society 1997.

Cotton, Neil
From *I Capture the Castle* by Dodie Smith

Younger of the two wealthy Cotton brothers, Neil is a good-looking, fresh-faced young man who is visiting England with his mother and older brother, Simon, who has just inherited the Scoatney estate to which the Mortmains' leased castle belongs. Neil has been brought up in California and plans in due course to return to the USA to become a rancher. According to Cassandra who narrates the book, he has a pleasant American accent – 'like the nice people in American films, not the gangsters'. He also looks rather like a character from the movies, the heroine's brother, perhaps, rather than the hero.

Cotton, Simon
From *I Capture the Castle* by Dodie Smith

Older brother of Neil Cotton, Simon has come to England to inspect the Scoatney estate that he has inherited from his recently-deceased English grandfather. Brought up in New England (unlike his brother Neil who was raised in California), Simon has the curious English-American hybrid accent of people from the region. Although neatly dressed and generally pleasing in appearance, he has a small, pointed black beard similar to those worn by Elizabethan noblemen. To girls with fanciful imaginations it can look rather devilish. There is, however, nothing devilish about Simon; bookish and serious, he is a kind, considerate man with a gentle sense of humour.

Cozens, Norma
From *Love in a Cold Climate* by Nancy Mitford

The wife of a senior Oxford professor, Norma Cozens comes from a wealthy and respectable country family that involves itself in every aspect of rural life. Permanently annoyed about something and with looks reminiscent of a cross guinea pig, she pretends to be scandalised by Lady Montdore and enjoys exchanging ill-founded gossip about her with fellow university wives. Nevertheless, she is good-natured at heart and manages to be both kind and critical to Fanny, the narrator of *Love in a Cold Climate*.

Cranmer, Dr. Thomas   **RP**
From *Wolf Hall* by Hilary Mantel

The son of a minor landowner, Cranmer is a Cambridge scholar who in the past has worked for Cardinal Wolsey and is now working for the king. He is a sincere man whose air of melancholy is due to the loss of his wife and baby in childbirth. Following their deaths, he made the decision to take holy orders and thus live a life of celibacy. He dislikes monks and is close to the Boleyns who are flirting with Protestantism.

Crawford, Henry
From *Mansfield Park* by Jane Austen

Handsome, wealthy and intelligent, on the face of it Henry Crawford is eminently eligible and has everything going for him. When he is first introduced to the residents of Mansfield Park as the brother-in-law of the local clergyman, he makes a highly favourable impression on everyone except Fanny Price who instinctively distrusts him. Amusing, charming, unscrupulous and flirtatious, Henry enjoys making the Bertram girls fall for him even though he has no intention of marrying either of them. In fact, since Maria is safely engaged to another man she becomes the target of his most pointed attentions. Later on he sets out to win the heart of mousy little Fanny Price purely for his own amusement, but things don't at all go according to plan.

Henry Crawford, *Mansfield Park*, J.M. Dent & Co., illustration by C.E. Brock, 1908.

Crawford, Mary
From *Mansfield Park* by Jane Austen

Mary is the pretty, lively and agreeable sister of Henry Crawford (and Mrs Grant, wife of the new Mansfield Park clergyman). Clever, witty Mary soon becomes as welcome at Mansfield Park as her charming brother, particularly with Edmund Bertram who finds her irresistible. To Mary's considerable annoyance - she would prefer to marry an older son – the attraction is mutual. She is further disturbed when she discovers that Edmund intends to take Holy Orders since she has no desire to become a clergyman's wife. This is just as well because Mary is far too worldly and her morality is too dubious for her to make a success of such a role. But she is an entertaining character and some readers may like her better than the book's intended heroine, Fanny Price.

Mary Crawford playing the harp, *Mansfield Park*, J.M. Dent & Co., illustration by C.E. Brock, 1908.

Crawley, Frank
From *Rebecca* by Daphne du Maurier

The agent at Manderley, an impressive Cornish coastal estate owned by Maxim de Winter, Crawley is a thin, colourless man with a prominent Adam's apple. A bachelor who leads a quiet life, he is considered dull by some people as he is safe, conventional and very correct. However, he is also very kind, tactful and considerate, and he does his best to make life easier for the new Mrs de Winter who he likes very much.

Crisp, Mary
From *The House at Sunset* by Norah Lofts

A tall, angular woman of 30, Mary is the unmarried daughter of Italian immigrant Alfredo Crispi (anglicised to Crisp) and his English wife, Elsie. The couple's other daughters have married and left home but Mary remains with them, helping to run their eating house in Baildon, Suffolk. Aware that although she is elegant and well-dressed she looks sensible rather than pretty, she feels doomed to a life of tedious spinsterhood until a customer is taken ill at the restaurant and she undertakes his nursing. Thereafter, her life takes a very unexpected course and although she is to know great sadness, she finds a fulfilment she never dreamed of when serving meals at Crisp's Eating House.

Cromwell, Anne   **RP**
From *Wolf Hall* by Hilary Mantel

Oldest daughter of Thomas Cromwell and his wife, Liz Wykys, Anne is a plain girl who delights her father with her intelligence and her desire to learn.

Cromwell, Grace   **RP**
From *Wolf Hall* by Hilary Mantel

The youngest child of Thomas Cromwell and Liz Wykys, Grace is a very pretty little girl with golden hair and a sweet face.

SIR THOMAS CROMWELL KNIGHT etc.

Sir Thomas Cromwell (from the University of Toronto Wenceslas Holler Digital Collection).

Cromwell, Gregory **RP**
From *Wolf Hall* by Hilary Mantel

Gregory is Thomas Cromwell's oldest child and only son. He has been well-educated but shows no aptitude or liking for business, preferring gentlemanly pursuits. Luckily, his father has no wish to force him against his will into the family business.

Cromwell, Thomas **RP**
From *Wolf Hall* by Hilary Mantel

Aged a little over 40 when the main narrative begins, Cromwell is working for the powerful Cardinal Wolsey as his trusted 'man of business'. He has done well to achieve this position, having been born the son of a drunken brute from Putney who regularly beat his family. Sometime before his fifteenth birthday Cromwell was subjected by his father to an attack of such violence that he ran away from home, taking a ship to France where he enlisted as a soldier. During the decade or so he spent overseas, first soldiering and then learning about commerce in Italy and Antwerp, he made useful contacts and acquired a great deal of business acumen. On his return to London he found that the prospects were good for a man of his ability, especially one prepared to take risks.

Now, at the start of the book, he is happily married and has two houses of his own, one in Stepney and the other at Austin Friars. His wife has given him three children – Gregory, a boy of nearly 13, and two younger daughters, Anne and Grace - and a comfortable home life, although his work for the Cardinal gives him little enough time to enjoy it. In any case he likes to work long hours, 'first up and last to bed'. He speaks in a low, rapid tone and is equally at ease conversing with all classes. He is cultured, knows the law and can converse fluently in several languages including Latin. With his unusually strong eyesight he misses little that is to be seen and uses his keen intuition to discover much that is hidden. Although he keeps his opinions to himself he is sympathetic to the Protestant cause. Physically, he is well built but not tall, with dark wavy hair and small eyes which light up in conversation. People fear him, sensing that he is capable of violence, but he has learned to keep his emotions in check. The driving forces in his life are his loyalty to Wolsey, his work and his family. Having suffered at the hands of his father he is determined to be kind to his own son.

D is for Danvers, Darcy, Dashwood and more

Danver, Richard
From *Milady Charlotte* by Jean Plaidy

An experienced and resourceful young man in his early twenties, Danver works for the British government in a capacity that involves frequent trips to France, a country teetering on the brink of revolution. A close friend of the actress Charlotte Walpole for whom he has protective feelings, he gives the impression of being arrogant and slightly mocking, but when he chooses he can be excellent company. Tall, with startlingly blue eyes and light brown hair streaked with blond, he dresses like a gentleman in velvet and lace, although his rugged face and tanned skin ensure he is never mistaken for a dandy.

Danvers, Mrs
From *Rebecca* by Daphne du Maurier

The housekeeper at Manderley, a magnificent house on the Cornish coast owned by Maxim de Winter, Mrs Danvers is a tall, gaunt woman who is supremely efficient at her job. Severely dressed in deepest black, she has prominent cheek bones and hollow eyes that give her a sinister death's head appearance.

She was obsessively devoted to Rebecca, de Winter's first wife and is enraged when he marries again within a year of Rebecca's death, and so shows freezing hostility to the new Mrs de Winter. Cold, unsmiling and superior at the best of times, when her guard drops she reveals her unnerving fixation with the dead woman. Intelligent, capable and formidable, Mrs Danvers is also more than a little bit mad.

Darcy, Fitzwilliam
From *Pride and Prejudice* by Jane Austen

Mr Darcy is a tall, handsome man of 28, with a fine figure and noble appearance as befits a gentleman with aristocratic connections (his mother, Lady Anne, was the daughter of an Earl). The owner of Pemberley, a magnificent estate in

Derbyshire, he has an income of £10,000 a year (a very considerable amount in the early nineteenth century). He is also intelligent, has sound judgement, and is a good, reliable friend and a devoted brother to his sister, Georgiana. On the negative side, he is perceived by many as being haughty, reserved and fastidious with disdainful manners and a proud nature that frequently causes offence. As the novel progresses, however, his deeds, letters and speech reveal that a much warmer character is concealed behind his seemingly cold exterior. Mr Darcy has become one of the best known and best loved characters in English literature and this popularity owes a lot to the memorable portrayals of him in film and television adaptations. It owes even more, however, to Jane Austen's genius in understanding the irresistible appeal of a proud hero made humble by love.

Darcy discussing Elizabeth Bennet with Bingley, George Allen, 1894, illustration by Hugh Thomson.

Dashwood, Elinor
From *Sense and Sensibility* by Jane Austen

Nineteen years-old at the start of the book, Elinor is one of its two central characters (the other being her sister Marianne). Elinor, Marianne, and their younger sister Margaret, are the children of Mr Henry Dashwood of Norland Park – a substantial estate in Sussex - by his second wife, the first having produced his only son, John Dashwood, who is the heir to Norland Park. The oldest of the Dashwood girls, Elinor is good-looking rather than beautiful, with a delicate complexion, regular features and a pretty figure. Sensible, intelligent and resilient, she is a very likeable character who endures setbacks, slights and heartbreak with admirable dignity and restraint. A loving daughter and sister, she shoulders much of the responsibility for her family's well-being when their financial circumstances are greatly reduced following Mr Dashwood's death, and despite her young age, is able to give her mother good advice which is not

C.E. Brock illustration of Elinor Dashwood and Edward Ferrars, 1908.

always heeded. Reserved by nature, Elinor conceals her own strong emotions from her family and because of this they mistakenly believe she has none. In fact, she feels and suffers greatly but it is her way to do so without inflicting her pain on others.

Dashwood, Fanny
From *Sense and Sensibility* by Jane Austen

Wife of Elinor and Marianne Dashwood's half-brother, Fanny is a cold, selfish and narrow-minded woman. She dotes on her spoilt son Harry, and with her widowed mother, Mrs Ferrars, is intent on propelling her brother Edward towards a distinguished career in one field or another. When her husband inherits Norland Park on the death of his father, she treats his stepmother and half-sisters with coldness and makes it clear she wants them to leave. Worse still, she dissuades John from giving his sisters a generous settlement even though he has promised to look after them, and even begrudges them the crockery and linen that is theirs by right. When she discovers that Edward has feelings for Elinor she becomes even more spiteful towards her sisters-in-law, missing no opportunity to slight them. In short, she is one of the thoroughly detestable characters Jane Austen excelled in creating, deeply unpleasant and yet fascinating to encounter on the page.

Dashwood, John
From *Sense and Sensibility* by Jane Austen

Henry Dashwood's only child by his first marriage, John is a steady, respectable young man with a tendency to be cold and selfish. However, with his weak character he could have been moulded by a pleasant wife into becoming reasonably kind and affectionate. Instead, he marries Fanny, a woman far more cold, calculating and selfish than himself. When his father dies John is already comfortably off, having inherited a sizable fortune from his mother, and so he intends to honour his father's dying request to look after his half-sisters and their mother. However, his grasping wife persuades him not to settle any money at all on them, and thereafter he allows her to treat them with barely concealed disdain. His one redeeming quality is his genuine affection for his ghastly wife.

Marianne Dashwood saying goodbye to Norland, *Sense and Sensibility*, George Allen 1899, illustration by Chris Hammond.

Dashwood, Marianne
From *Sense and Sensibility* by Jane Austen

Aged 16 at the start of the book, Marianne is the second daughter of Mr and Mrs Henry Dashwood of Norland Park. Although she is as clever and good natured as her sister Elinor, Marianne is entirely governed by her emotions, throwing caution and prudence to the wind when in the grip of strong feeling. She believes this to be the most honest and admirable way of behaving and naïvely disapproves of those who hesitate to express their feelings. When she has to move with her mother and sisters to a cottage in Devon following the death of her father, Marianne finds it impossible to disguise the distaste she feels for the well-meaning but overly familiar, relatives who have provided their new home. At the same time she rushes headlong into a romance with a dashing neighbour, ignoring the conventions in the belief that his feelings for her are as solid as hers are for him. When the romance turns sour she is plunged into the deepest despair, but ultimately emerges wiser and happier.

Dashwood, Mrs
From *Sense and Sensibility* by Jane Austen

Aged about 40 at the start of the book, Mrs Dashwood is warm-hearted, affectionate, impractical and a little unworldly. Grief-stricken when her husband dies, she initially does little to lift herself out of her misery as it is her nature to succumb completely to whatever emotion she is feeling. Moreover, she does not find it easy to adjust to the greatly reduced financial circumstances in which she and her daughters find themselves, relying heavily on the common sense of Elinor, her oldest daughter, whilst placing much store by the passionate nature of Marianne, her middle child whose personality in many ways resembles her own.

Davey, Francis
From *Jamaica Inn* by Daphne Du Maurier

The vicar of Altarnun, a parish not far from Jamaica Inn, Davey is an albino with cropped white hair, and pale eyes that are almost white. He speaks with a soft persuasive voice and despite his odd appearance has a restful, reassuring manner. For a vicar his conversation is remarkably free of Biblical references.

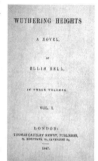

Dean, Ellen (also known as Nelly)
From *Wuthering Heights* by Emily Bronte

The same age as Hindley Earnshaw – in fact she is the daughter of his nurse - Ellen Dean grows up with the Earnshaw children and knows their faults better than most. Although she is a servant, her familiarity with the Earnshaw children allows her

Wuthering Heights original title page, 1847.

an unusual degree of intimacy. When Catherine Earnshaw marries and leaves Wuthering Heights, Ellen goes with her as her maid and is therefore on hand to witness (and later recount) the unfolding events.

Sensible and compassionate, lowborn Ellen is much easier to like than most of the socially superior characters in the book. That's not to say she doesn't have flaws of her own – she allows her own feelings and prejudices to influence her actions, and when she recounts the *Wuthering Heights* story her version of events is inevitably coloured by her personal preferences. Nevertheless, Ellen is a beacon of goodness compared with the many morally unstable characters in the novel.

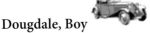

Dougdale, Boy
From *Love in a Cold Climate* by Nancy Mitford

Nicknamed 'the Lecherous Lecturer' by the irreverent Radlett children because of his persistent and unfortunate habit of groping little girls, 'Boy' Dougdale is a minor landowner who is married to Lady Patricia, sister of the grand and stately Lord Montdore. An obsessive snob, he is in awe of the illustrious ancestry of his wife's family and deeply regrets the lack of children in his marriage simply because they would have had noble blood. A past affair with his sister-in-law, the overbearing Lady Montdore, is hinted at, but now his role in her life is more akin to private secretary or lady's companion. Around 50 at the start of the book, he is short, with a jaunty little figure and curly black hair which has started to grey. He is considered good looking by his peers, but Fanny Logan, the book's narrator, finds him creepy and thinks he looks horribly pleased with himself. His mania for the Hampton family leads him to a course of action which has far-reaching consequences for many of the book's characters.

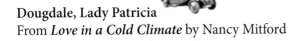

Dougdale, Lady Patricia
From *Love in a Cold Climate* by Nancy Mitford

A few years older than her husband Boy, Lady Patricia is the fragile and long-suffering sister of the illustrious Lord Montdore. A beauty in her day, sadness and suffering has taken its toll on her looks, turning her fair hair white and her white skin yellow. She was passionately in love with Boy for several years before he married her, but the common conception is that he only did so in order to get close to the Hampton family which his snobbish heart adores. She is painfully aware of her husband's infidelities but not of his predilection for little girls.

Drew, Biddy
From *Tilly Trotter* and *Tilly Trotter Wed* by Catherine Cookson

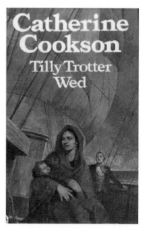

Widowed, capable Biddy is a large, bony woman with a
lot of children, many of whom work at the failing
Sopwith mine in County Durham. Although there is
rarely enough money to go round, Biddy keeps her
family as clean and comfortable as possible, doling out
wholesome food and no-nonsense advice in equal
measures. Having toiled down the mine herself for
fifteen years, she is well aware of the unbearably hard
nature of the work. Although she has had no choice but
to let her older offspring seek employment as pit-
workers, she is determined to spare her youngest two a
similar fate. Motherly and kind, she is the ideal person
for a friendless girl to turn to for comfort and advice.

Drew, Katie
From *Tilly Trotter* and *Tilly Trotter Wed* by Catherine Cookson

Plump, homely and kind, Katie is one of Biddy Drew's many children. She works
long hours at the Sopwith mine, enduring terrible working conditions in order to
scratch a living. In spite of this she is a cheerful, good-natured girl who befriends
Tilly Trotter at a time when she is in dire need of friends.

Drew, Sam
From *Tilly Trotter* by Catherine Cookson

A member of the large Drew family, Sam is a young pit-worker employed initially
at the mine owned by Mr Rosier, a hard man who forbids his workers to learn to
read and write, because he believes educated men will demand better working
conditions. Sam is sacked by Rosier when it is discovered that he has been having
lessons with Mrs Ross, the parson's wife, but he is given a new job and
accommodation by Mark Sopwith, a more enlightened County Durham mine
owner. Sam is a decent, hardworking man and an affectionate brother and son.
He develops feelings for Tilly Trotter and she is fond of him, but only as a friend.

Dysart, Viscount
From *April Lady* by Georgette Heyer

The brother of Lady Cardross, Dysart is heir to an Earldom, but the estate he will inherit is entirely without money since his father has gambled everything away. Sadly, Dysart is not the man to restore the family fortunes as he has inherited his father's tendency to reckless spending. Tall and very good-looking with golden hair and an endearing smile, Dysart is an incorrigible rake, but he is also dangerously charming with laughter never far from his lips. Until he comes into his inheritance the only way to keep him out of trouble is to buy him an army commission and send him off to fight, but unfortunately his father won't hear of it. So with no other occupation to fill his time, he indulges in increasingly ridiculous wagers and hare-brained pranks with an old school chum.

E is for Earnshaw, Elliot, Eyre and more

Earnshaw, Catherine
From *Wuthering Heights* by Emily Bronte

The only daughter of Mr Earnshaw, a gentleman farmer who lives at Wuthering Heights on the Yorkshire Moors, Catherine is a beautiful girl with thick, dark hair and striking eyes. Spirited, passionate and headstrong, in her heart Catherine wants nothing more than to scramble across the moors with Heathcliff, her foster brother and soul mate, but these impulses are at war with her craving for prosperity and status. By choosing comfort and riches over a life with the man she

Top Withens, believed to have been the inspiration for *Wuthering Heights* photo by Dave Dunford.

really loves, she sets in train a chain of events that bring misery to herself and those that love her.

Although she is an iconic figure in English literature, Catherine Earnshaw is too arrogant and self-obsessed to be likeable. What she lacks in likeability, though, she makes up for by being completely original and entirely memorable. And she certainly deserves some sympathy for being in the unenviable position of having to choose between the conflicting desires of heart and head.

Earnshaw, Hareton
From *Wuthering Heights* by Emily Bronte

One of the few sympathetic characters in the book, Hareton is the only child of Hindley Earnshaw of Wuthering Heights and his wife Frances who dies shortly after Hareton's birth. Hindley survives her by about six years, after which care for the orphaned Hareton falls into the hands of Heathcliff. Having hated Hareton's father and schemed to bring about his downfall, he takes great satisfaction in raising the boy as an uncouth labourer instead of ensuring he is educated as a gentleman.

Although he is illiterate, uncultivated and quick-tempered, at heart Hareton is a decent man, honest, warm and intelligent. His rough upbringing conceals much of this, but a new arrival at Wuthering Heights is the catalyst that allows his true personality to shine through.

Earnshaw, Hindley
From *Wuthering Heights* by Emily Bronte

The heir of Mr Earnshaw of Wuthering Heights and about eight years older than his sister Catherine, Hindley is a boy with a jealous nature. He grows up harbouring a deep resentment towards Heathcliff, the orphan boy his father takes in and raises at Wuthering Heights. When Mr Earnshaw dies Hindley is able to exact his revenge by treating Heathcliff badly. A lighter side to his unpleasant character is shown in the strong affection he has for his wife, Frances. Unfortunately her early death sends him into a miserable spiral of drink and dissipation.

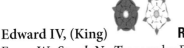

Edward IV, (King) **RP**
From *We Speak No Treason* by Rosemary Hawley Jarman

The oldest son of Richard, Duke of York, and his lovely wife Cicely, Edward has grown up during his father's turbulent struggle to establish his claim to the throne of England which is currently occupied by a Lancastrian rival, Henry VI. Edward was dealt a dreadful double blow when his father and brother Edmund were slain, leaving him head of the House of York aged just 18, with responsibility for continuing the fight and for the remaining members of his family. With help from the mighty Earl of Warwick he won a series of magnificent victories, ousted the hapless Henry and took the throne. Now, as the story begins, he is 21 and has been king for three years. The country is beginning to settle down after a prolonged period of civil war, so it seems a good time for Edward to think about looking for a wife, but while Warwick, his closest adviser, negotiates an important match with a foreign princess, Edward has ideas of his own.

Very tall, sturdily built, and crowned by bright gold hair, Edward is a dazzlingly handsome man. Healthy and virile, he is a brave, skilled fighter and a keen huntsman with an outsized appetite for good living and beautiful women. He has a genial, easy-going manner which can descend into indolence, yet his traumatic early experiences have left a mark on this pleasure-loving king and underestimating him is not advisable.

Elliot, Anne
From *Persuasion* by Jane Austen

Central protagonist of the last novel completed by Jane Austen, 27-year-old Anne is the middle daughter of Sir Walter Elliot, a conceited baronet whose ancestral home is Kellynch Hall in Somerset. She takes after her late mother in looks and nature, having inherited her sweet character and 'elegance of mind'. Eight years earlier, when Anne embarked on a romance with a young naval officer called Frederick Wentworth, she was very pretty, with delicate features and mild dark eyes, but in the intervening years her bloom has faded, leaving her looking thin and tired. The implication is that her lost

C.E. Brock illustration of Anne Elliot talking to Frederick Wentworth, 1909.

looks are due to her loneliness and unhappiness, for since pressuring Anne to break her engagement with Wentworth, an act that causes her great pain, her family have shown her little kindness. Her father and older sister virtually ignore her while her married younger sister regards her simply as a convenient person to have at her beck and call. Only her godmother, Lady Russell, recognises Anne's worth and is truly fond of her. Her friendship with Lady Russell, and her love for her ancestral home, are the only positive things in Anne's life, so she is dismayed when the family is forced to leave Kellynch Hall at the start of the book. This sets in motion a series of events that bring her face to face with her former fiancé, causing her further pain and anxiety before finally she is allowed to find happiness.

Less playful and vivacious than some Austen heroines, Anne is an attractive character all the same, exhibiting admirable restraint and fortitude in situations that would test the strongest character, and a genuine goodness that makes the reader really care about her welfare and resent the unjust treatment she receives from her family.

Elliot, Elizabeth
From *Persuasion* by Jane Austen

The oldest of Sir Walter Elliot's three daughters, at the start of *Persuasion* Elizabeth is a very handsome, unmarried woman of 29. Her father's favourite child by a considerable distance, Elizabeth is vain and self-important by nature and her high opinion of own worth has increased ever since she took over as mistress of Kellynch Hall, the family home, following the death of her mother thirteen years ago. Like most vain people she is very susceptible to flattery and this impairs her judgement, allowing her to become intimate with the scheming Mrs Clay, while treating her sister Anne with an indifference that borders on contempt.

Although she is confident in her looks and status, Elizabeth is conscious of the fact that she is no longer in the first flush of youth and has started to worry about finding a husband of suitable rank. Moreover, she is still smarting from the disappointment she experienced a few years ago when she failed to elicit a marriage proposal from Mr William Walter Elliot Esq., a distant cousin and the heir to Kellynch Hall.

Elliot, Sir Walter
From *Persuasion* by Jane Austen

Sir Walter Elliot of Kellynch Hall in Somerset is a deeply silly, conceited widower with three grown-up daughters, only the youngest of whom is married. Extremely handsome in his youth, at 54 he is still a fine-looking man but his good looks are not matched by good intellect. He is obsessed with rank and status and considers the 'blessing of beauty as inferior only to the blessing of a baronetcy'. Consequently, he foolishly values Elizabeth, his attractive but mean-spirited eldest daughter, far more highly than Anne, his sweet-natured middle child who has lost her former bloom, and Mary, the youngest daughter whose looks have never amounted to much. Although Anne is of little importance to him, nevertheless he intervened when she fell in love with a young naval officer since he felt the match was beneath the dignity of a baronet's daughter.

C.E. Brock Illustration of Sir Walter Elliot, 1909.

At the start of the book it is revealed that Sir Walter has run up huge debts and needs to make serious economies, but he is unable to contemplate living without the trappings he considers his due. Instead, he is persuaded by his agent to let Kellynch Hall while he and his single daughters move to Bath where they can live more cheaply, while retaining an outwardly high standard of living.

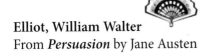

Elliot, William Walter
From *Persuasion* by Jane Austen

A distant cousin of Sir Walter Elliot and his heir in the event that Sir Walter does not produce a son, William Elliot is a good-looking and elegant young man with fashionable clothes and pleasing manners. In the past he has offended Sir Walter and his daughter Elizabeth Elliot, first by refusing their invitations to visit Kellynch Hall, and then by marrying a rich woman of inferior rank, in preference to Elizabeth. Some years later he reappears in their lives. Now a rich widower, he uses his considerable charm to make them forgive his former transgressions, and to rekindle in Elizabeth hopes that he might marry her. Although she finds him attractive, Elizabeth's sister Anne instinctively mistrusts him, inwardly questioning why he has suddenly decided to heal the breach between himself and his relatives.

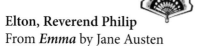

Elton, Reverend Philip
From *Emma* by Jane Austen

Recently arrived as the new vicar at Highbury, Philip Elton is an elegant young man with independent means and an inflated opinion of his merit and what he is due. Good looking and personable, he is charming in an oily way to those he wishes to impress, but is cold and indifferent to those he regards as his inferiors. It is his ambition to marry an heiress, but blissfully unaware of this, Emma Woodhouse has other plans for him.

Mr. Elton reads to Emma and Harriet. London: George Allen, 1898, illustration by Chris Hammond.

Elysande
From *We Speak No Treason* by Rosemary Hawley Jarman

A French gentlewoman in the retinue of Jacquetta of Bedford, Elysande befriends the Maiden - one of the novel's central characters - on her arrival at court. With smiles and affectionate words she wins the trust of the guileless Maiden, but all the while her green, catlike eyes are observing things which are then stored away for use in the future.

Eyre, Jane
From *Jane Eyre* by Charlotte Bronte

Eponymous narrator of Charlotte Bronte's most successful novel, Jane Eyre is first encountered as a 10-year-old orphan, living as a poor relation with Mrs Reed, her aunt-in-law who doesn't trouble to disguise how very much she resents being lumbered with the child. Bullied and abused by her cousins, in particular by the odious John, and treated with breath-taking unfairness by her aunt, Jane is a sad, scared, lonely and defiant child. Things scarcely improve when she is sent away to boarding school, for here she has to endure both physical and mental hardship. She is picked on and punished by those responsible for her well-being, yet Jane refuses to become a victim, surviving all the mistreatment and finding happiness of a sort in the kindness of a teacher and the friendship of a fellow pupil.

F.H. Townsend illustration of Jane Eyre.

In a different type of novel, Jane would grow up to be so staggeringly beautiful that all would fall at her feet, but Charlotte Bronte was more interested in her heroine's mind than in her outward appearance. As a result, the adult Jane is poor, petite and rather plain, with hazel hair, green eyes and elfin features. Although she is mousy and uninteresting at first glance, closer observation reveals that there is more to her than meets the eye. She is intelligent, caring, honest and resilient, refuses to be browbeaten and is determined to assert her independence. When she falls in love she discovers she has a deeply passionate nature, but this is tempered by a strong moral code. Echoing her experiences as a child, she undergoes physical and emotional trials that would crush a lesser spirit, but although she suffers greatly, Jane is strong and her instincts ultimately guide her to happiness.

F is for Falco, Ferrars, Fones and more

Fairfax, Jane
From *Emma* by Jane Austen

Tall, graceful and slender, Jane Fairfax is the poor, but gifted niece of Miss Bates. Brought up in London by a well-to-do couple called the Campbells, Jane is obliged to find a position as a governess following the marriage of the Campbell's daughter to whom she has been a companion. Before doing so, however, she returns to Highbury to spend time with her aunt and grandmother. With dark hair, deep grey eyes and a clear, pale complexion, Jane is a very handsome young woman who is quickly welcomed into Highbury society. Her many accomplishments are a source of great pride to her aunt, but her innate reserve does not endear her to Emma Woodhouse who never suspects that Jane is guarding a weighty secret.

Illustration by Chris Hammond of Jane Fairfax walking away from an admirer, George Allen, 1898.

Fairfax, Mrs (Alice)
From *Jane Eyre* by Charlotte Bronte

A clergyman's widow, the elderly Mrs Fairfax is distantly connected to Mr Rochester of Thornfield Manor through her late husband, and she is now employed as Rochester's housekeeper. A neat, comfortable person, she is kind and considerate to Jane Eyre. One of the few people aware of Mr Rochester's secret, she becomes decidedly uneasy when she realises that he has fallen in love with Jane.

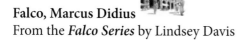

Falco, Marcus Didius
From the *Falco Series* by Lindsey Davis

The central character from a long-running series of novels set in Rome during the reign of Emperor Vespasian, Falco earns his living as a 'private informer' which is more or less what we know today as a private investigator. A committed republican, he comes from a working class (Plebeian) background and has a large, boisterous family which is headed by his tough, straight-talking mother, his father having absconded when Falco was a child. At the start of *The Silver Pigs*, the first book in the series, Falco and his family are still coming to terms with the death two years earlier of his older brother, Festus, who died fighting for Vespasian in Galilee. Falco himself has served in the army, joining at 19 and undergoing a miserable experience with the Second Augusta Legion in Britain during the Boudicca revolt.

When the reader first meets Falco he is 29 and living in a small apartment on the sixth floor of a seedy tenement block in the rough-and-ready Aventine district of Rome. He has an eye for pretty women, enjoys good wine, the occasional roister with his friend Petronius Longus, and frequently finds himself on the wrong end of a fist or boot through the course of his work. He narrates the books in a light-hearted, satirical style and talks to his family and clients in a nonchalant, jokey manner in an attempt to pass himself off as a bit of a rogue. From the start, however, there are clues that a sensitive, decent and ultimately soft-hearted individual, lurks beneath his deliberately blasé veneer. He voluntarily splits most of his earnings between his own mother and the mother of his dead brother's child, writes poetry in his spare time, becomes too attached to his clients and generally behaves with generosity and kindness to the weak and helpless, although he'd probably punch anyone tactless enough to mention these facts in front of him.

Favell, Jack
From *Rebecca* by Daphne du Maurier

The first cousin of Rebecca (deceased wife of Maxim de Winter), Favell is a heavyset man with florid good looks that promise to run to fat before too long.

He has reddish hair, sunburnt skin, a soft, pink mouth and blue eyes that reveal his fondness for a drink. Despite his close relationship to Rebecca - a woman who was said to be the epitome of elegant sophistication - Favell is slightly uncouth, with imperfect manners and an offensive laugh. Under the influence of alcohol he becomes even worse. Beatrice Lacy, the sister of Maxim de Winter, describes Favell as an 'awful bounder'. Short of money and aggrieved because Rebecca is dead, he is more than capable of stirring up trouble for de Winter.

Feake, Robert
From *The Winthrop Woman* by Anya Seton **RP**

A thin, weedy, young goldsmith with Puritan sympathies, Robert is nervous, highly strung and prone to memory loss. Believing himself guilty of a horrific crime (which he probably didn't commit, although there is some ambiguity on this point) he fleas London and begins a fresh life in the Massachusetts Bay Colony. There he plays a prominent part in the life of Bess and her Winthrop relations before completely losing his faculties.

Ferrars, Edward
From *Sense and Sensibility* by Jane Austen

The oldest brother of Fanny Dashwood and Robert Ferrars, Edward is heir to a sizable fortune, but he will only inherit if he remains in favour with his over-bearing widowed mother who expects him to marry well and pursue a glittering career. This is unfortunate as Edward desires a private life of domestic comfort and is keen to enter the Church. An unlikely hero, Edward is a quiet, unobtrusive young man with diffident manners. He is not handsome and his shyness makes it difficult for people to get to know him, but once they do they discover a good, honourable, intelligent and well-educated man hiding beneath the unpromising exterior. Elinor Dashwood recognises his true worth and develops strong feelings for him. She believes they are reciprocated, but Edward seems unable or unwilling to commit himself to her.

Oh Edward! How can you ?

Chris Hammond illustration of Edward Ferrars with Marianne Dashwood, George Allen, 1899.

Ferrars, Mrs
From *Sense and Sensibility* by Jane Austen

A ghastly, over-bearing woman, Mrs Ferrars has control of her late husband's fortune and is determined to use it to ensure her sons, Edward and Robert, make prestigious marriages. Ungenerous and narrow-minded, she has a bad temper and is vicious when thwarted, but can be won round by continuous, abject flattery.

Ferrars, Robert
From *Sense and Sensibility* by Jane Austen

The younger brother of Fanny Dashwood and Edward Ferrars, Robert is a vain, pompous, status-conscious young man - as unlike his pleasant, diffident older brother as it is possible to be. He is his mother's favourite son and takes full advantage of the fact.

Fitzgerald, Hugh Deveraux (Honourable)
From *Blanche* by Patricia Wendorf

Second son of an eminent surgeon and his aristocratic French wife, Hugh is raised by his aunt because his mother absconds with a lover when he is ten-days-old, and his despairing father commits suicide. Living in great comfort in a mansion in London's Russell Square, Hugh leads a pampered existence and is adored by his formidable aunt. Having inherited a fortune on his 21st birthday he is able to indulge his interest in the arts, ride to hounds with the Duke of Clarence, and even dine with the Prince of Wales. He is a very good-looking young man, with flaxen curls, brilliant blue eyes and a highly-flushed complexion. Although he has his faults, he is essentially a decent young man who admires great beauty and yearns for love and domestic happiness. He is also weak-willed with a tendency towards self-pity.

Flowerdew, Antony
From *The House at Old Vine* by Norah Lofts

The son of a tanyard owner, Flowerdew is a gentle, scholarly man who works as secretary for Sir Henry Saxham, a bluff Oxfordshire gentleman with Parliamentarian sympathies. When hostilities break out at the start of the Civil War, Flowerdew goes to war with Saxham even though he has no taste for soldiering. After his employer is killed he is recruited by a secretive intelligence organisation which exists to sniff out Royalist support. His life is changed when, at the age of 37 or so, he is sent on a mission to Baildon in Suffolk and opts to lodge at the Old Vine.

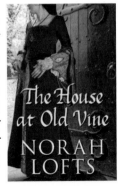

Follett, Hatton
From *The House at Sunset* by Norah Lofts

Follett and his twin sister Annabella have been brought up at the Old Vine in Baildon, Suffolk, by their Great Aunt Dorothea, their mother having died three weeks after their birth. As for their father, he was gone before they were born. Follett and Annabella are extremely close, their mutual devotion not affected by the differences in their personalities – he is steady and reliable while she is impulsive and not terribly bright. They are rich but their wealth is being gradually eroded. Follett's biggest headache, however, is his beloved sister who runs from one disaster to another, leaving him to pick up the pieces.

Fones, Bess (real name Elizabeth)   **RP**
From *The Winthrop Woman* by Anya Seton

Beautiful, passionate and lively, Bess is the oldest daughter of weak-natured London apothecary Thomas Fones. Her mother comes from the respected Winthrop family, God-fearing Suffolk landowners whose religious sympathies are not in line with the established Church. Bess finds that her genuine desire to be dutiful and conform to the expectations of her Puritan family is constantly at odds with her sensual nature and zest for life. Although she finds her stern, self-righteous uncle, John Winthrop, both

oppressive and frightening, she is unable to subdue her rebellious spirit, and as a result, frequently incurs his wrath. It is this spirit, however, that enables her to adapt and survive when the family leaves England to build a new life in the Massachusetts Bay Colony. Compassionate, affectionate and headstrong, Bess fights to win control of her own life and endures much hardship before finally achieving her aim.

Fones, Martha   **RP**
From *The Winthrop Woman* by Anya Seton

Bess Winthrop's younger sister, Martha is timid, sweet natured and far less robust in body and mind than her spirited sister. Unlike Bess, she generally has no problem accepting the authority of her controlling uncle, although she does find the courage to flout him when it comes to marrying. Leaving the familiarity of home for an uncertain future in New England hits her much harder than Bess.

Forrester, Mrs
From *Cranford* by Elizabeth Gaskell

The widow of an army officer, Mrs Forrester lives in the small town of Cranford in very reduced circumstances. Her income is just sufficient for her to keep a very small house with a young, inexperienced girl to look after her. Nevertheless, she remembers that she was born a member of the distinguished Tyrell family and always behaves with perfect decorum and gentility.

G is for Gaunt, Gloucester, Greypaull and more

Gardiner, Stephen   **RP**
From *Wolf Hall* by Hilary Mantel

A persuasive man, well-grounded in canon law, Gardiner is working as confidential secretary to Cardinal Wolsey when the main narrative begins. As a staunch upholder of the orthodox Catholic religion he seeks out heretics with fervour. He is rumoured to be the illegitimate offspring of a royal connection who had him brought up in secrecy by respectable wool-trade people. Conscious of the stories about his birth, Gardiner longs to be acknowledged as the King's cousin and resents the ordinariness of his stated origins. He detests Thomas Cromwell -

Cardinal Wolsey's man of business - because he is very lowborn and also because Wolsey holds him in high regard. There is also a suspicion that should it ever came to it, he knows Cromwell would beat him in a fight.

Garth, Caleb
From *Middlemarch* by George Eliot

Married to former schoolteacher Susan, Caleb is a decent man who earns an insubstantial living as a land agent and surveyor. An act of generosity to a young friend causes him hardship, but eventually his kindness and his faith in the young man are rewarded.

Garth, Mary
From *Middlemarch* by George Eliot

The daughter of Caleb Garth (see above) and his wife Susan, a former schoolteacher, Mary is a sensible, plain-featured girl who works as a nurse for a wealthy old man. She has strong feelings for Fred Vincy, son of the mayor of Middlemarch, but won't contemplate marrying him until he gives up on his parents' plans for him to become a clergyman, reforms his character and proves that he can hold down a steady job.

Gaunt, John of   **RP**
From *Katherine* by Anya Seton

With John of Gaunt, Anya Seton plucks an important, but largely overlooked, figure from the pages of medieval history, and creates a hero every bit as charismatic and unforgettable as Mr Darcy. Like Darcy, he is rich, handsome and arrogant, although there the similarities end because John of Gaunt is a royal prince, the third son of Edward III and his queen, Philippa of Hainault. He is 26 when the book begins, a manly, cultured prince who has increased his importance in the

John of Gaunt, second from left, from A Chronicle of England, BC 55 to AD 1485.

land by marrying a great heiress, Blanche of Lancaster. Thus, he has become Duke of Lancaster, and thanks to his wife's vast estates and fortune, has been transformed from a highborn, yet ultimately unimportant prince with little prospect of ever inheriting the throne, into one of the wealthiest and most powerful men in the country. Although he married Blanche principally for her great inheritance, as luck would have it he does actually love her and their marriage is successful. So far she has given him two little girls, Philippa and Elizabeth, and the longed for heir will surely arrive soon.

In looks John of Gaunt is every inch the hero. Tall, slender and strong, he is a magnificent specimen with bright blue eyes, thick, tawny-yellow hair, a close-cropped beard and shaven face which reveals his full, passionate mouth. Healthy and virile, he exudes vitality and pride. It would seem that he has everything going for him – good looks, youth, power, prestige, immense skill in knightly pursuits and a beautiful wife and family. Nevertheless, he is haunted by a dark dread, planted in childhood by a malicious tongue. Hard as he tries to suppress it, every so often this fear surfaces and gains control of his normally reasonable nature. Also, he finds he is not so entirely devoted to his lovely wife that he is incapable of being attracted to a beautiful newcomer at court, try as he might to dislike her.

Glenmire, Lady
From **Cranford** by Elizabeth Gaskell

Sister-in-law of one of the leaders of Cranford society, the Honourable Mrs Jamieson, Lady Glenmire is the widow of a poor Scottish peer. She comes to Cranford on an extended visit to Mrs Jamieson and soon becomes popular with the town's ladies because of her pleasant, relaxed manner and distinct lack of ostentation.

Gloucester, Richard, Duke of   **RP**
From *We Speak No Treason* by Rosemary Hawley Jarman

The youngest brother of King Edward IV, Richard is aged about 17 when he makes his first appearance in the narrative. Having been a sickly child and frail youth, through determination and hard training with weaponry he has grown up to be a strong, capable fighter whose battlefield skills are matched by his integrity and sound judgement. During his formative years his family was embroiled in a bitter power struggle against the House of Lancaster which saw England ravaged by civil war. He lost his father and a brother during the bloody conflict and at

Richard III

the age of 7 had to be taken out of the country for his own safety. But now the House of York has prevailed, his brother is on the throne and there has been peace for several years. However, discord is growing in unexpected quarters, and Richard is suffering as he watches resentment and hostility develop between three of the people he loves best in the world. Always true to his personal motto of *loyalte me lie* (loyalty binds me) he is distraught to discover that a similar level of faithfulness is not shared by two influential figures who mean a great deal to him. While Richard understands the reason for their discontent and sympathises to some extent, his first loyalty is always to the king. Thus he finds himself lonely and adrift as rival court factions vie for the upper hand.

An intense, slender man of below average height, Richard has deep-blue eyes, hair the colour of dark oak, and fine cheek bones. His expression is usually serious, and he has developed a nervous habit of twisting his rings around his fingers. A taste of early responsibility – he was mustering an army at the age of 12 – has given him a strong work ethic, while the several years he spent at Middeleham Castle in North Yorkshire have afforded him a genuine affection for that part of the country. Although he has not inherited the Plantagenet weakness for too much wine and too many women, he does have a passionate nature and a deep capacity for love. Hand in hand with this goes an almost limitless capacity for suffering.

Godolphin, Lord George
From *Frenchman's Creek* by Daphne du Maurier

A pompous, wig-wearing, heavy-set man with a florid face, protuberant eyes and an unfortunate growth on the side of his nose, Lord Godolphin is a Cornish neighbour and old friend of Sir Harry St. Columb. Conventional and exceedingly dull, he is anxiously awaiting the birth of his first child, and in the meantime fills his time making blustering plans to trap the French pirate who is outraging the Cornish gentlefolk with his audacious attacks on their property.

Graham, Helen
From *The Tenant of Wildfell Hall* by Anne Bronte

When she makes her first appearance in the book Helen is said to be a young widow of about 25 who has just moved into the badly neglected Wildfell Hall with just her 5-year-old son, Arthur and her maidservant, Rachel, for companionship. As a mysterious new arrival in Lindenhope – the small community to which Wildfell Hall

Title page from early edition of *The Tenant of Wildfell Hall.*

belongs - Helen is a figure of interest and soon becomes the subject of speculation and gossip. Her refusal to satisfy the curiosity of her neighbours simply serves to fuel the chatter which turns increasingly spiteful when two of the area's most eligible young men – gentleman farmer Gilbert Markham and Frederick Lawrence, local squire and owner of Wildfell Hall – are found to be paying her frequent visits. What only one of her acquaintances knows is that Helen has taken refuge at Wildfell Hall under an assumed name because she is in flight from her abusive and dissolute husband.

It is hardly surprising that she should attract so much attention since Helen is tall and beautiful, with raven-black hair worn in long, glossy ringlets, and a clear, pale complexion. With eyes a very dark grey colour and a perfect aquiline nose, her beauty is only slightly reduced by a hollowness about the cheeks and eyes, and lips that are pressed too firmly together, suggesting that there is severity in her character. In fact, Helen is sad rather than severe, although she is naturally disposed to be serious rather than frivolous. Intelligent, moral and unafraid to voice her own opinions, she has always been impatient with idle chit-chat, greatly preferring books, art and thoughtful conversation to light-hearted small talk, but her melancholy outlook has developed as a consequence of her disastrous marriage. What makes her seem even more peculiar in the eyes of her new neighbours is the extreme protectiveness she exhibits towards her young son. She cannot bear to have him out of her sight and has by her own admission done her best to make alcohol repugnant to him. That she has good reasons for her unusual behaviour never seems to occur to her detractors who want to believe the worst of her, either because she doesn't conform to their ideas of how a young mother should behave, or because they fear that she represents a threat to their personal schemes.

Greatorex, Hon. Reggie
From *My Last Duchess* by Daisy Goodwin

The younger son of Lord Hallam, Reggie is great friends with the Duke of Wareham with whom he was at Cambridge. In his late twenties, he is blond, polished, easy-going and charming. He is attached to Lady Sybil Lytchett, the Duke's stepsister, but their courtship is progressing at a very slow pace.

Greenwood, Joan
From *The House at Old Vine* by Norah Lofts

Joan is the only child of a miserly Suffolk farming couple who have never forgiven her for not being the son and heir they wanted, or for scuppering their plans to marry her to a neighbouring farmer by bearing a child out of wedlock. Once pretty, long years of hard work and cruel treatment have made her prematurely old. Having defied her parents once by stubbornly refusing to disclose the paternity of her daughter, she now obeys all their orders and endures her harsh life without complaint. In front of her parents she is careful to show her daughter no affection, but in private she is kind to her and tries to shield her from too much brutality.

Greenwood, Josiana
From *The House at Old Vine* by Norah Lofts

Growing up on her tight-fisted grandparents' farm in Suffolk in the late fifteenth century, Josiana leads a thoroughly miserable life. All the hardest and nastiest jobs are given to her and she is frequently beaten for imagined wrong-doings. She is treated thus because she is illegitimate, and her unexpected arrival put paid to a profitable match her grandparents planned to make between her mother and a neighbouring farmer. The only affection she receives is from her downtrodden mother, and then only when her grandparents are out of earshot. Not knowing any other life, Josiana puts up with her ill-treatment uncomplainingly until her grandparents arrange for her to marry a cruel, ugly old man. She is not quite 14 at the time, a small pretty girl with straight, smooth, black hair, unblemished pale skin and very blue eyes.

Grey, Elizabeth (née Woodville)   **RP**
From *We Speak No Treason* by Rosemary Hawley Jarman

The beautiful widow of a Lancastrian knight, Elizabeth is living with her mother and two young sons at Grafton Regis in Northamptonshire when the book begins. Although aged about 30 she looks much younger, and her beauty has the power to drive men to distraction. She is tall and slender, with long gilt-coloured hair, pale skin, broad brow, full lips and heavy, mysterious eyes.

Her husband died fighting for the Lancastrians so his estates have been confiscated by the Yorkist king, leaving Elizabeth perilously short of money. Now she and her mother plot to use her beauty to capture the heart of the most powerful man in the

Elizabeth Grey presenting a petition, from A Chronicle of England BC 55 to AD 1485.

country. To this end she presents herself to him as a lovely, chaste damsel in distress, encouraging him to fall in love with her but never yielding to his passion.

This is a tricky game to play since a false move could damage everything, but she plays her part with skill, maintaining calm piety in the face of his feverish desire. To help matters along she joins in with her mother's secretive and dangerous activities, albeit without a great deal of enthusiasm.

Elizabeth has a strong will and a swift temper which she has to keep hidden until she has won her prize. Her great beauty conceals a cold, haughty and aggressively acquisitive nature.

Greypaull, Annis
From *Larksleve and Blanche* by Patricia Wendorf

The fifth child and final daughter of Eliza and Philip Greypaull of Larksleve Farm, Buckland St. Mary, Somerset, Annisi is a sweetly pretty girl with blue eyes and fair, curly hair. She is brought up as much by her older sisters as by her overworked mother and, aged just 6, nearly dies from rheumatic fever because no one notices that she is ill until it is almost too late. When she is a little older Annis becomes very close to her mother and determines to be a good, dutiful child, one that never causes any anxiety, even if it means suppressing her own longing for excitement and finery.

Greypaull, Blanche
From *Larksleve* and *Blanche* by Patricia Wendorf

Conceived in anger, Blanche is the fourth child and third daughter born to Eliza and Philip Greypaull of Larksleve Farm. From the moment of her birth it is apparent that she is unlike her solemn-eyed, dark-haired siblings, and as she grows she develops into a real beauty with alabaster skin, violet eyes and copper-coloured hair. Nevertheless, she is disliked by her mother and unloved and resented by her siblings. Perhaps as a result, she becomes attention seeking and demanding, ungovernable and prone to violent fits of temper. Although clever, she refuses to learn to read and write, believing that her beauty is all she needs to get by. The only warmth in her life comes from Loveday Hayes, the strange woman who helps her mother in the dairy. Blanche adores her mother despite the coldness she receives from her, and detests her feckless father even though he is the only member of her family to truly love her. Proud, wilful and avaricious, she is absolutely convinced that a finer way of life is hers for the taking, and that wealth will make her happy. She is very certain that there is no place for romantic love in her drive towards financial attainment.

Greypaull, Candace
From *Larksleve and Blanche* by Patricia Wendorf

Candace is the first-born child of Eliza and Philip Greypaull of Larksleve Farm. Small, dark and thin, she is tough in body and spirit. She grows up to be capable, courageous and fiercely independent.

Greypaull, Eliza
From *Larksleve* and *Blanche* by Patricia Wendorf

Born into the nineteenth-century Somerset farming community of Buckland St. Mary, Eliza is small and angular, with opaque green eyes and fine white skin that freckles at the first sight of sun. Unfortunately for her, she also has red hair which is believed by her superstitious community to indicate a deceitful and jealous nature. As a result, dutiful, hardworking, tenacious Eliza remains unmarried at the age of 24, so her father, prosperous farmer John Greypaull, arranges for

Buckland St Mary, the setting for *Larksleve.* Image © Martin Bodman used under the Creative Commons Attribution-Share Alike 2.0 Generic license.

her to marry her cousin, Philip Greypaull, securing the match by promising to settle the coveted Larksleve Farm on the young couple. In doing so he is healing a longstanding family feud. Eliza is not in love with Philip - she dislikes his yellow curls and dimpled chin, and is at least partially aware of his failings - but she obeys her father's wishes out of a sense of duty and because she has no alternative. Given a choice, she would prefer to marry Philip's younger brother, Samuel, but nobody has thought to consult her feelings. A farmer's daughter through and through, without love in her life her only satisfaction comes from the orderly running of her farm and the rows of ripening cheeses in her dairy. Generally as cautious and conservative as her solid, taciturn family, Eliza's one act of rebellion is to be friends with a carefree gypsy girl called Meridiana Carew. It is a friendship that will have far-reaching consequences for both of them.

Greypaull, Madelina
From *Larksleve and Blanche* by Patricia Wendorf

Second child of Eliza and Philip Greypaull of Larksleve Farm, Madelina is a tiny girl, dark and neat like her older sister Candace, but much gentler and more caring. The only Greypaull child to have any sympathy for her weak-willed father, she grows up to be prim, respectable, and more than a little sanctimonious.

Greypaull, Philip
From *Larksleve* and *Blanche* by Patricia Wendorf

The apple of his mother's eye, tall, flaxen-haired Philip Greypaull shares just one thing in common with his red-headed cousin and bride, Eliza – neither of them resemble in the smallest degree their other Greypaull relatives, all of whom tend to be dark and compact. At 28, weak-willed Philip is a sorry disappointment to his thrifty father, Daniel Greypaull, as he greatly prefers gambling and carousing to toiling on the land. Good-natured and accommodating when left to his own devices, Philip craves warmth and affection, but finds neither with Eliza since she gives all her energy to running Larksleve, the Somerset farm they are given when they marry. He does not find Eliza attractive and resents being forced to marry her, but he does enjoy spending her handsome dowry. He also likes being master of Larksleve, even though he rarely knuckles down to the heavy work required.

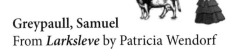

Greypaull, Samuel
From *Larksleve* by Patricia Wendorf

Younger brother of feckless Philip Greypaull, 25-year-old Samuel is a true Greypaull – short, stocky, dark-haired and conscientious. Hardworking and reliable, he is his father's favourite son and is too dutiful to complain when a match is arranged between his brother and his cousin Eliza for whom he has feelings.

Griet

From *Girl With A Pearl Earring* by Tracy Chevalier

Aged 16 at the start of the book, Griet is about to leave her parents' house in the Dutch town of Delft to take up a position as maid with the Vermeer family. She has a loving relationship with her parents and siblings, but since her tile-painter father was blinded in an accident he has been unable to work, and money has become very tight. Griet's 14-year-old brother Frans has already left to take up an apprenticeship at the tile factory and her sister Agnes is still young, so Griet has no choice but to go into service in order to help the family finances. Although her new employers live in the same town, they are Catholics, and live in the Catholic quarter which Griet, a Protestant, has never visited.

East German stamp, circa 1955, depicting Vermeer's 'Girl Reading a Letter by an Open Window'.

Small and wide-eyed with long, dark brown hair that is always carefully hidden by a cap, Griet is a tidy, efficient girl who works hard and conceals her feelings. Intelligent and acutely observant, she is very good at reading people and situations, and is not easily duped. Yet beneath her calm, submissive manner there exists another Griet, one who is sensitive to colour and light, who has an innate understanding of picture composition and who is capable of passionate feelings which she knows she must repress.

H is for Hamilton, Hampton, Heathcliff and more

Hallet, William 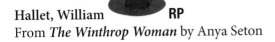 RP

From *The Winthrop Woman* by Anya Seton

Tall, muscular Will Hallet is a Dorset farmer's son, thrust into an aristocratic environment when he is raised by the Earl of Bristol in recompense for mistakenly killing Will's father. After six years with the Earl's family he is apprenticed to a joiner, but runs away when he is beaten too much. His humble origins combined with his fine education make him feel he belongs nowhere, so he takes ship to New England to start a new life there. On board ship he meets Bess, and a connection is formed between them even though, at not quite 16, he is several years her junior. A strong, intelligent and independently-minded man, Will leads a rootless, wandering life for several years until he re-encounters Bess, after which their destinies are permanently linked.

Hamilton, Charles
From *Gone With the Wind* by Margaret Mitchell

Brother of Melanie Hamilton (see below) Charles is an inexperienced young man – in fact little more than a boy – who lives with his sister and aunt in Atlanta. He has an understanding with his cousin Honey Wilkes, but on a visit to her home at Twelve Oaks in Clayton County, Georgia, he has his head turned by Scarlett O'Hara who is flirting indiscriminately with anyone in trousers in an attempt to make Charles's cousin Ashley notice her. When the afternoon culminates in the announcement of war with the Union, Charles loses his head in an excess of patriotic fervour and asks Scarlett to marry him.

Hamilton, Melanie
From *Gone With the Wind* by Margaret Mitchell

The cousin of the Wilkes's of Twelve Oaks, Melanie lives in Atlanta with her brother Charles at the home of her Aunt Pittypat Hamilton. A frequent visitor to the Wilkes plantation, Melanie has fallen in love with her cousin Ashley, and in his own way he loves her in return. As the book begins Ashley is preparing to propose to her at a sumptuous barbecue to which the entire neighbourhood has been invited.

A muted moth to Scarlett O'Hara's dazzling butterfly, Melanie Hamilton nevertheless has an inner radiance that transforms her into a beautiful woman when she is happy. A truly good person, Melanie is gentle, kind, tolerant and loving. Unlike some of her female companions, she is no simpering ninny, and her fragile and serene exterior hides a degree of courage and strength of character that surprise even those closest to her. She has a deep and abiding love for Ashley that never wavers, and an equally faithful love for the rampantly underserving Scarlett O'Hara. She also has a fondness for the dashing but disreputable Rhett Butler. Tranquil and soothing most of the time, she behaves like an angry lioness when those she loves are maligned. Since she is almost universally adored for her goodness, those under her protection who transgress the mores of society are by and large spared the hostility that would be their lot without it.

When the world she has known collapses Melanie's quiet certainty enables her to build a new life in the rubble of the old one. Deprivation and an altered way of life may take their toll on her physical strength, but they mean nothing to her as long as she has those she loves with her. Her strength inspires her friends and neighbours and many take their cue from her, rebuilding their lives as best they can. Yet Melanie's acceptance of the new order never means she has abandoned her loyalty to the Confederacy; in spirit she remains a true Southern lady even though she is forced to live under Yankee rule. It could be argued that in her own unobtrusive way, Melanie is as much the heroine of *Gone With the Wind* as the more colourful Scarlett O'Hara.

Hamilton, Pittypat (Aunt)
From *Gone With the Wind* by Margaret Mitchell

The real name of the dithering and perpetually flustered Aunt Pittypat is Sarah Jane, but she is referred to by everyone as 'Pittypat' because of the pattering sound made by her tiny feet. Fussy and prone to fainting fits, she lives in Peachtree Street, Atlanta, with Melanie and Charles Hamilton, her niece and nephew, whom she has raised following the death of their parents. Her financial affairs are looked after by her brother Henry from whom she is estranged, and her household is managed by a wonderfully capable and faithful slave called 'Uncle Peter'. Although she is a foolish, comedic figure she is an affectionate aunt and has done her best to care for Melanie and Charles.

Hampton, Cedric
From *Love in a Cold Climate* by Nancy Mitford

Born in Nova Scotia, Cedric is an unknown, distant relative of Lord Montdore. He is destined to inherit Hampton, his opulent home, because the Montdores' only child is a girl. Far from being the stereotypical uncouth colonial everyone imagines, Cedric turns out to be a fabulously exotic creature, fond of colourful clothing and much given to extravagant speech and gestures. A great lover of beauty, he talks intelligently about art and antiques to Lord Montdore, while transforming the dowdy Lady Montdore by means of a strict beauty and slimming regime. Blessed with the

Love in a Cold Climate, Folio Society edition.

Hampton goods looks, this tall, thin young man becomes a kind, thoughtful and affectionate friend to Fanny, the book's narrator. In case the reader is in any doubt, his homosexuality is made apparent by references to a German boy called Klugg and a handsome lorry driver called Archie. Nancy Mitford's portrait of Cedric Hampton is said to owe a great deal to her friend, the beautiful aesthete Stephen Tennant.

Hampton, Polly
From *Love in a Cold Climate* by Nancy Mitford

The beloved only child of Lord and Lady Montdore, Polly Hampton (real name Leopoldina) is exceedingly beautiful and this beauty is her one outstanding characteristic. Her parents had been married for twenty years before she was born and had quite given up hope of having children. As a little girl she is withdrawn and formal, with the poise of a Spanish Infanta, and she is reserved, single-minded and self-possessed as an adult. Having caused her parents no concern when younger, she now frustrates and dismays her overbearing mother by demonstrating a complete lack of interest in the potential suitors paraded before her. She confides to Fanny, her friend - and the book's narrator - that she finds the debutante obsession with falling love a tremendous bore, but as events reveal, she is already in love with a person her parents can only consider unsuitable in the extreme.

Hare, Barbara
From *East Lynne* by Mrs Henry Wood

The youngest daughter of Justice and Mrs Hare of The Grove, West Lynne, Barbara is a pretty girl of 19 when the story begins. She is fair-haired, blue-eyed and with a rosy complexion. At present she lives alone with her parents because her older sister Anne has married and left home, and her beloved brother Richard has fled the area as he is thought to be a murderer. Barbara, who refuses to believe in Richard's guilt, spends much of her time consoling her worried and ailing mother and keeping out of the way of her stern, authoritarian father who has vowed, given the chance, to turn his son over to the law. In her current gloomy situation the only thing that brings Barbara joy is seeing a long-term friend of the Hare family, Archibald Carlyle, with whom she is in love. Despite the fact that he has never treated

Back cover illustration of Barbara and Richard Hare from circa 1920s Readers Library edition of East Lynne.

her with anything more than brotherly affection, she harbours the hope that one day he will ask her to marry him.

The most striking aspect of Barbara's character is her steadfast determination to help her brother clear his name. Her attempts to do so demonstrate a fair degree of courage, not least because she risks incurring the wrath of her formidable father. Her resolve to help Richard continues long after her dream of marrying Carlyle has apparently been shattered. Putting aside her hurt pride and embarrassment she continues to work in secret with the lawyer as they attempt to unravel the truth about the murder.

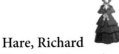

Hare, Richard
From *East Lynne* by Mrs Henry Wood

The only son of Justice and Mrs Hare of West Lynne, Richard is thought by almost everyone he knows to be the murderer of a man called Hallijohn. Although he is innocent of the crime, Richard has fled West Lynne to avoid being hanged. Even his own father believes in his guilt and has sworn to hand his son to the authorities if he ever discovers his whereabouts. With only his mother and sister Barbara prepared to fight for him, Richard is in a sorry state and is forced to find work as a stable lad. He keeps returning to West Lynne, however, to obtain money from his mother and during these visits he is able to throw light on the events of the night the murder took place.

Hargrave, Millicent
From *The Tenant of Wildfell Hall* by Anne Bronte

A cousin of the sophisticated heiress Annabella Wilmot, Milicent, 20, is gentle, timid and reserved. Plump and pretty with a pink and white face, she is a dutiful and loving daughter, and an affectionate sister to her brother Walter and sister Esther. She is also very fond of her friend Helen who is the niece of Mr and Mrs Maxwell, and is dismayed that Helen seems to have fallen in love with Arthur Huntingdon, a man she knows to be bold and reckless.

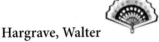

Hargrave, Walter
From *The Tenant of Wildfell Hall* by Anne Brontë

The owner of The Grove, a house in the same vicinity as Arthur Huntingdon's Grassdale, Walter Hargrave is a distinguished looking young man with habits and tastes that exceed his means. He neglects his estate in preference for a carefree existence in London, leaving his mother and sisters struggling to keep up an appearance of wealth. Although he is blessed with many gifts – he is a good conversationalist, has excellent taste and is always well-informed – there is something dislikeable about Hargrave. His selfish insistence on wearing expensive clothes and riding the best horses while his dependent females make do, shows a callous disregard for them, and the predatory circling of his friend's vulnerable wife reveals an unscrupulous streak.

Hatton, Felicity
From *The House at Sunset* by Norah Lofts

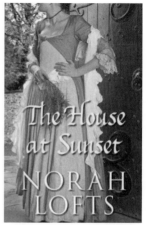

The daughter of a well-born wastrel and his respectable but penniless wife, Felicity grows up in London living a double life. When her father has done well at the gambling tables the family have elegant lodgings, eat well and wear silk and velvet, but when luck is against him they live in squalid rooms and pawn their finery to pay for bread. Thus, Felicity learns to be ladylike one month, and a pocket-picking guttersnipe the next. Finally, when her father's luck has run out once and for all, and her mother has died, she travels to Suffolk to throw herself on the mercy of the relatives she knows she has there.

Heathcliff (his only name)
From *Wuthering Heights* by Emily Bronte

Rescued as a young child by Mr Earnshaw who finds him ragged and starving on the streets of Liverpool, Heathcliff is taken to Wuthering Heights on the Yorkshire Moors where he is brought up with the children of the house, Hindley and Catherine Earnshaw. After a rocky start he and Catherine become intensely attached to one another, so he is devastated when he discovers that she plans to marry a richer, well-bred young man.

Athletic and handsome in a dark, gypsy-like way, Heathcliff has a personality driven by two things: his obsession for Catherine and his burning need for revenge. Although not without considerable talents, he

Heathcliff portrayed by André Huguenet in a South African production of Wuthering Heights, 1943.

is a man who bears grudges on an epic scale and enjoys grinding into the dust those he perceives to have done him wrong. Pitiless and tyrannical in pursuit of his vengeance, Heathcliff is a grim portrayal of obsessive love gone wrong. Today there is a tendency to view him as a desperately romantic figure, to be pitied for being tormented beyond endurance by his love for Catherine. That he is a tortured soul is undeniable, but considering the deliberate, unflinching cruelty of his actions, it is highly questionable whether he deserves any sympathy.

Heathcliff, Linton
From *Wuthering Heights* by Emily Bronte

Only offspring of a joyless marriage, Linton is a slight, sickly boy who inherits the pale good looks of his mother's family. Brought up in the south after his mother flees from her ill-conceived marriage, he is languid, peevish and prone to whining. When he is 13 his mother dies and he falls into the clutches of his father who loathes him on sight. Physically and temperamentally unsuited to the harrowing demands of life at Wuthering Heights, Linton's frail health deteriorates as he becomes a pawn in his father's quest for vengeance.

Henley, Lord Henry Hoste   **RP**
From *Remarkable Creatures* by Tracy Chevalier

The lord of Colway Manor and MP for Lyme Regis, Lord Henley is an important figure in his little corner of Dorset. Married with many children and a large extended family, he is at the centre of local society and knows everyone with any claim to gentility. As a collector of fossils he excites the interest of ardent fossil-hunter Elizabeth Philpot, but soon disappoints her when she discovers that he has no real knowledge or insight into the subject, collecting them only because they are fashionable and make him seem worldly and intelligent. Worse still, he harbours ignorant opinions, is patronising to intelligent women like Elizabeth, and is entirely dismissive of the contribution made by the working-class Mary Anning in finding a magnificent and mysterious skeleton. With a piggish face, limited intelligence and an impatient nature he is not an appealing character.

Henry VIII (King) **RP**
From *The Other Boleyn Girl* by Philippa Gregory

Aged about 30 when the story begins, Henry has been King of England for thirteen years and married to Katherine of Aragon, his brother Arthur's widow, for the same period. Tall, well-built and handsome with a ruddy complexion and golden hair, Henry is a strong, athletic man who excels at hunting, jousting and hawking. However, he is also devout, and enjoys the company of learned men including scholars such as Sir Thomas More. For the time being he is happy to allow his closest adviser, Cardinal Wolsey, to run the country on his behalf while he enjoys himself in tournaments and masques, but that is soon to change.

The one shadow hanging over Henry's life is his lack of a legitimate male heir. A former mistress has provided him with a healthy boy, but with one exception all the children borne by Katherine, his legal wife, have been stillborn or have died within a few weeks. Now that Katherine is approaching the change of life he is becoming increasingly anxious that he does not have a son to inherit his throne. However, he still loves his wife and although he is unfaithful to her he has not yet thought of divorcing her. Soon, though, his desperation to have a son will make him harden his heart against Katherine, altering the balance of power at court and causing a seismic shift in his religious observances. The catalyst for these changes will be a beautiful, terrifyingly determined young lady-in-waiting who is propelled by her ambitious family into the forefront of court politics.

Henry is a classic example of a promising young king corrupted by over-indulgence and too much power. With no steady hand to rein him in, all his good characteristics such as his intelligence, piety, and geniality are tarnished by the atmosphere of frenetic sycophancy that prevails at his court. Encouraged to believe that he is more handsome, clever and courageous than any of his contemporaries, and with courtiers falling over themselves to flatter and delight him, his vanity and sense of entitlement become monstrously over-inflated. Like a sulky child, he descends into dark moods when he can't have his way, but unlike a child, he has the authority to impose his will on everyone in his kingdom, from the highest to the lowest, however unpopular his decisions might be. With such a man, nobody – friend, counsellor, wife, mistress or daughter - can ever be entirely safe.

Hethersett, Felix
From *April Lady* by Georgette Heyer

The cousin of wealthy Lord Cardross, Felix Hethersett is a gentleman of comfortable fortune who makes himself useful escorting his cousin's pretty young wife and half-sister to balls, masques and so on. Neither handsome nor especially articulate, he is well-regarded by Society even so, on account of his impeccable lineage and faultless dress sense. A graceful dancer and a stickler for etiquette, he can be relied upon to instinctively know the right shade of ribbon to trim a particular gown, or the correct angle at which to fix a feather in a fashionable bonnet. The author describes him as 'not much of a lady's man' which is perhaps a gentle hint that his interest in women is entirely non-sexual.

Hoggins, Mr
From **Cranford** by Elizabeth Gaskell

Cranford surgeon Mr Hoggins was born the son of a well-to-do farmer who lived close to the town. Now he looks after the health of the local citizens. He is generally liked and considered an able healer, but his inelegant name and lack of refinement are viewed as regrettable by the genteel ladies of the town.

Holbrook, Thomas
From **Cranford** by Elizabeth Gaskell

A cousin of Miss Pole, one of the spinster ladies that make up much of Cranford society, Mr Holbrook is an elderly bachelor living on a small estate about five miles from the town. Although educated and gentlemanly, he is content to remain nothing more than a yeoman farmer and stubbornly refuses to call himself 'esquire'. He reads aloud beautifully and takes a great delight in the natural world.

Hugh Thomson illustration of Mr Holbrook, 1891.

Holly, Annie
From *South Riding* by Winifred Holtby

Married to Barnabas Holly, a feckless labourer to whom she has born seven children, Annie is a competent woman of 43 whose spirit has been worn down by hard work and incessant pregnancies. She now believes that her child-bearing days are behind her, which is just as well since the doctor has said another baby will kill her. Raising her family in two compartments of a railway coach situated in a run-down cliff top area known as The Shacks, she struggles to feed, clothe, and keep clean her many offspring. In her own way she is very proud of Lydia, her oldest daughter, who has won a scholarship to Kiplington High School, and is desperate for her clever daughter to escape the poverty trap.

Holly, Barnabas
From *South Riding* by Winifred Holtby

An easy-going, irresponsible man with a large family to provide for, Barnabas Holly earns his living as a labourer when the work is available, and when it isn't he draws unemployment benefit. Keen on beer and congenial company, he believes himself to be a soft-hearted man and a fond father, but when there is trouble he makes himself scarce. His inability to leave his tired wife alone has resulted in them having more children than they are able to manage.

Holly, Lydia
From *South Riding* by Winifred Holtby

The oldest daughter of Annie and Barnabas Holly, Lydia is a fat, agile, untidy girl of 14 who helps her mother look after the large brood of Holly children. When she's not washing the little ones or putting them to bed, Lydia has her nose in a book because she is exceptionally bright and has a passion for learning. At 11 she won a scholarship to Kiplington High School, but was unable to take her place as she was needed at home to help with the children. Now she is filled with excitement because her sister Daisy is old enough to take over from her and so she can start at Kiplington after all. She adores her mother and greatly admires her bravery and resilience.

Howard, Katherine   RP
From *The Lady Elizabeth* by Alison Weir

A member of the noble Howard clan and first cousin to Anne
Boleyn, Henry VIII's second wife, Katherine is a very young
woman when she catches the eye of the lecherous king, and
becomes his fifth wife. Small, plump and pretty with chestnut
hair and a generous pouting mouth, Katherine adores jewels,
gowns and gaiety. She is too young to have much interest in
her stepchildren – indeed, she is younger than Mary, Henry's
daughter by Katherine of Aragon – preferring to dance and
play with puppies. Sadly, however, she is not too young to
have had a past which can come back to blight her present.

Catherine Howard

Huggins, Alfred
From *South Riding* by Winifred Holtby

Large and lusty, Councillor Alfred Ezekiel Huggins is a Methodist lay preacher
who runs a not-very-successful haulage business in the comically-named Pidsea
Buttock area in Yorkshire's (fictitious) South Riding. Better at preaching rousing
sermons than running his two-lorry business, he entertains hopeless dreams of
entering Parliament as a Liberal MP. Instead, he serves on the County Council
where his genuine compassion for those living in poverty, which stems from his
own childhood in a Kingsport slum, is at variance with his appetite for bodily
comforts. Beset by debts and saddled with a hypochondriac wife, he has been
known to seek solace with Bessie Warbuckle, a young woman of regrettably easy
virtue.

Huntingdon, Arthur
From *The Tenant of Wildfell Hall* by Anne Bronte

A good-looking young man in possession of Grassdale Manor, a considerable
country estate, Huntingdon appears at first glance to be precisely the sort of catch
Regency mothers desire for their unmarried daughters. Personable and gifted with
easy charm, he is well-bred, courteous and totally at ease in Society. Beneath this
veneer of respectability, however, there lurks a far less attractive character, one
which is not so well concealed that a discerning chaperone cannot detect it. A

dissipated lifestyle has already made inroads into his inheritance, and although he is not yet beyond redemption, Huntingdon seems set fair to continue a downward spiral into debt, drunkenness and debauchery. Keeping company with similarly circumstanced young men, he is encouraged to behave badly, and without an inner morality to whisper to him that his excesses are getting out of hand, he roisters without constraint.

Yet while an experienced woman can see the degeneracy behind his façade of charming respectability, it is a different story for a naïve young girl fresh from the schoolroom. Attracted by her beauty, innocence and goodness, Huntingdon sets out to woo her, even though he has no intention of changing his ways once he has caught her.

I, J and *K* are for Ingram, Jenkyns, Knightley and more

Ingram, Blanche
From *Jane Eyre* by Charlotte Brontë

Blanche is a beautiful, well-connected young woman with designs on Mr Rochester, the owner of Thornfield Manor. Shallow, mercenary and snobbish, she is unpleasant to Jane Eyre whom she regards as her social inferior.

Illustration of Blanche Ingram by F.H. Townsend.

Jamieson, the Honourable Mrs
From *Cranford* by Elizabeth Gaskell

A large widow of comfortable means, Mrs Jamieson lives in a sizeable house just outside Cranford. Her household is managed by a manservant called Mr Mulliner who performs his duties in a lazy, sullen manner. Mrs Jamieson herself is 'dull and inert and pompous and tiresome' but nevertheless she is pre-eminent in Cranford society because of her aristocratic connections. She is much attached to her little dog, Carlo.

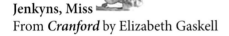

Jenkyns, Miss
From *Cranford* by Elizabeth Gaskell

In a society populated almost exclusively by widows and spinsters, Miss Jenkyns is acknowledged as the arbiter of gentility and good manners. Known only to her sister by her first name, Deborah Jenkyns is the oldest child of the former rector of the small northern town of Cranford. Her status as a clergyman's daughter is enhanced not only by her family's kinship with a titled gentleman by the name of Sir Peter Arley, but also by her serious demeanour and innate sense of decorum. In Cranford Miss Jenkyns sets the tone.

   Notwithstanding the deep love and respect she bore for her late father, Miss Jenkyns believes that women are superior to men and she in no way regrets the town's dearth of gentlemen. Having left the large rectory – where they were served by three maids and a manservant – following the death of their father, she and her sister now live in a much smaller house with only a servant-of-all-work to see to their needs. Nevertheless, their financial circumstances are never alluded to since to do so would be vulgar and vulgarity is a cardinal sin in the eyes of Miss Jenkyns. Her forceful personality ensures that her opinions always hold sway at home and are usually deferred to by friends and acquaintances. Clever, stately and grand, her somewhat domineering personality is lightened by a sympathetic sensibility which moves her to little acts of kindness, albeit within the strict boundaries of Cranford decorum.

Jenkyns, Miss Matilda (Matty)
From *Cranford* by Elizabeth Gaskell

Miss Matty

Illustration of Miss Matty by Hugh Thomson, 1918.

The younger sister of Miss Jenkyns (see above), Miss Matty is very much in the habit of following her sibling's lead in everything. Although only in her fifties throughout the narrative, her appearance and mannerisms suggest an older woman. She is nervous, timid, and perpetually anxious to be seen to conform to the peculiar notions of gentility that pervade Cranford society. Unlike her clever, severe sister, Miss Matty is sweet-natured and kind, and generally sees the good in everyone. She is very fond of children and would have made a loving mother had she ever married. That she never did appears to be the fault of her overbearing father and sister, although it would never occur to Miss Matty to harbour feelings of resentment. Despite her timidity she is such a good, gentle, soul that she is universally loved by her friends and neighbours.

Jenkyns, Peter
From *Cranford* by Elizabeth Gaskell

The younger brother of Deborah and Matty Jenkyns, Peter was a serial prankster who ran away from home after one joke too many earned him a severe beating from his domineering father. His disappearance broke his fond mother's heart and she died within a year of his leaving. Shortly afterwards, news reached Cranford of his arrival in India, but when the book begins he has not been heard of for many years and is never spoken of by the Jenkyns sisters.

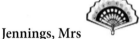

Jennings, Mrs
From *Sense and Sensibility* by Jane Austen

Fat, jolly Mrs Jennings is a well-meaning chatterbox who delights in the company of young people. Good-humoured and full of jokes, she is less refined than the Dashwood family, but her genuinely kind heart does much to compensate for her vulgarity. A widow who has successfully married off her two daughters – one of them to Sir John Middleton, the bluff country squire who offers the Dashwood women a home in Devon – Mrs Jennings is now intent on helping her young friends make good matches and remains oblivious to the embarrassment she often causes them.

Mrs Jennings with Sir John Middleton, Chris Hammond 1899.

Jukes, Anne
From *Rebels and Traitors* by Lindsey Davis

The pretty wife of Lambert Jukes, son of a London grocer, at first glance Anne is a sensible young woman with a light hand for pastry and the happy knack of getting on with her mother-in-law. In time, however, she is revealed to be an independent thinker, and as the society she lives in becomes increasingly radicalised, she develops some unusual ideas of her own.

Jukes, Gideon

From *Rebels and Traitors* by Lindsey Davis

MITCHELL'S CIGARETTES.

1643.
Time of Battle of Naseby.

A tall, reasonably well-built young man with square features, pale skin, blue eyes and tow-coloured hair that suggests a Viking ancestry, Gideon is the youngest son of John and Parthenope Jukes, two decent and hard-working London grocers. At the age of 13 he is apprenticed to a printer because he needs to learn a trade, as the family business is destined to pass to his brother Lambert, fifteen years his senior. Over seven years he serves his time, learning enough to become a competent, but not exceptional, printer. During that time he changes from a surly, rebellious boy into a calm, good-natured young man, gifted with intelligence and a thoughtful, steady character. When his apprenticeship is complete he goes into business with his former master and his future seems set, except that the world he knows is about to collapse as civil war grips the country. When King Charles falls out with Parliament and flees London, Gideon becomes a musketeer in one of the regiments formed to protect the city from his anticipated return. He is destined to participate in some

English Civil War musketeer from Mitchell's Cigarette Card series Arms & Armour, 1916.

of the most memorable events of the Civil War, experience deprivation and injury, and along the way encounter the love of his life in a most unexpected quarter.

Jukes, Lambert

From *Rebels and Traitors* by Lindsey Davis

The oldest son of John and Parthenope Jukes and brother of Gideon (see above), Lambert is a big, blond, thickset man who has served an apprenticeship with another London grocer and is now helping with his parents' business. He is married to Anne, a pretty, dark-eyed, sensible girl from Bishopsgate who helps his mother in the kitchen. Popular, strong, level-headed and reasonable, Lambert is an enthusiastic regular with the London Trained Bands' Blue Regiment - he likes the uniform and the camaraderie. When tension erupts between King and Parliament he has no hesitation in turning out to defend the city as a pikeman. Like his brother, his life is destined to be disrupted in unimaginable ways by the Civil War.

English Civil War pikeman.

Julius, Master
From *Niccolò Rising* by Dorothy Dunnett

A highly-trained notary educated at the University of Bologna, Julius is an ambitious young man of 28 who is working for the Charetty company in Bruges when the story begins. Having been employed by Cornelis de Charetty, he now finds himself answering to Cornelis's widow and isn't happy to be working for a woman. Sensible and reliable most of the time, he is still young enough to succumb to occasional outbursts of laxity, particularly when in the company of Felix, his employer's son, and Claes, Felix's servant-companion. This is slightly unfortunate since one of Julius's duties is to keep the younger men out of trouble. Despite the fact that they cause him trouble he is fond of them and does his best to look after their interests, although he is rarely able to spare Claes a beating.

A pleasant-looking man with slanting eyes and a blunt, heavy-boned face, Julius is keen to build himself a career, and he cuts a confident figure in the collared black gown of his profession. He is loyal and intelligent, but is not sharp enough at first to detect an unexpected spark of brilliance in someone he knows very well.

Justa, Julia
From the *Falco Series* by Lindsey Davis

Wife of Senator Decimus Camillus Verus, Julia Justa is a staid Roman matron who lacks the warmth and humour of her husband. She behaves conventionally and regrets that her daughter, Helena Justina (see below) does not always do likewise. Usually reserved and cool, she does unbend just a little as the *Falco Series* progresses.

Justina, Helena
From the *Falco Series* by Lindsey Davis

Helena is first encountered in *The Silver Pigs*, the debut novel in the *Falco Series*, and thereafter she appears in all the ensuing books. She is 23 when the reader first meets her, recently divorced and spending time with relatives in Britain. Her father, the Senator Camillus Verus, has a high opinion of her intellect and allows her rather more independence than is normal for a respectably brought up Patrician girl.

Spirited, intelligent, sensible and resourceful, Helena is also passionate, witty and kind, although these attributes are not immediately made evident. When necessary she can be acerbic and formidable. She is not afraid to flout convention, especially in matters of the heart. Physically, she is tall, good looking and graceful with a 'bonny figure' that is more voluptuous than slender, although it is made clear that she is not overweight. She has soft brown eyes and long dark hair which is usually worn twisted up and secured with ivory hairpins.

Kate
From *The Town House* by Norah Lofts

Aged 17, Kate lives on the manor of Rede in Norfolk where she helps her shepherd father look after his sheep. Her life, that of her father, and all the other Rede villeins, is determined by the will of Lord Bowdegrave, the great nobleman who owns the manor. She is a tiny, delicate girl with eyes of speedwell blue and hair 'the colour of new run honey'. When she first appears in the story she is being severely beaten by her new stepmother who wants her out of the way. She is rescued by Martin, the blacksmith's son, who is entranced by her smallness and immediately resolves to marry her. Thereafter, her life follows a path she could never have predicted.

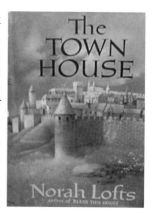

Katherine, (of Aragon), Queen   **RP**
From *The Other Boleyn Girl* by Philippa Gregory

The daughter of Isabella of Castile and Ferdinand of Aragon, Katherine is aged about 37 at the start of the book and for thirteen years has been married to Henry VIII, seven years her junior. She has born him six children including several boys, but only a daughter called Mary has survived. Now it is feared that she is getting too old for further pregnancies and Henry is becoming increasingly desperate for a legitimate male heir. Although she adores her daughter, Katherine is well aware of the need for a boy to succeed his father, but as a devoutly Catholic woman she accepts that it is God's will that they do not have a son. She does not for a moment believe that it has anything to do with her previous marriage to Henry's older brother, Arthur, who died just four months after their wedding. Although a man is forbidden under canon law to marry his brother's widow, Katherine is confident that the special dispensation granted by the Pope at the time of her marriage to Henry has made their union legal.

Once a beautiful woman, Katherine is now starting to age; her lustrous auburn hair is streaked with grey, her face is puffy and her appearance is not improved by the unflattering Spanish fashions she wears. Nevertheless, she still has flashes of her former beauty and her blue eyes remain clear and bright. As the daughter of two powerful Spanish monarchs she has a naturally regal bearing which is tempered by a sweet and gracious disposition. Katherine is also extremely well-educated, pious and acutely intelligent. She has learned to ignore her husband's infidelities, behaving with calm dignity where lesser woman would lose control. Deep down she believes that although he may stray, the bond between them is too strong to be broken. So far her policy of turning a blind eye has stood her in good stead with the king who dislikes being made to feel guilty, but she is soon to face her toughest challenge and will need all her religious conviction to get through it.

Keevil, Lacy
From *Rebels and Traitors* by Lindsey Davis

Lacy is an unmarried girl of 16 who comes to London from her country home to help her aunt Elizabeth Bevan manage her large brood of children. She isn't especially pretty, but she has a womanly figure and exotic, almond-shaped eyes that get her noticed by men. Her uncle-in-law, Bevan Bevan, introduces her to his nephew Gideon Jukes in a deliberate attempt at match-making.

Kennedy, Frank
From *Gone With the Wind* by Margaret Mitchell

An unattractive, well-meaning, but fatally dull middle-aged man, Frank Kennedy is engaged to Suellen O'Hara, middle daughter of Gerald and Ellen O'Hara of Clayton County, Georgia. He isn't a very exciting 'beau' for Suellen, but he is the best she has been able to attract and she is genuinely fond of him. Sadly for both of them, Frank is weak-willed and as susceptible to deceit and flattery as any man. He would do well to remember the old adage, 'marry in haste, repent at leisure'.

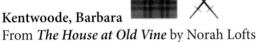

Kentwoode, Barbara
From *The House at Old Vine* by Norah Lofts

The youngest daughter of Mr and Mrs Hatton of Mortiboys in Suffolk, Barbara is married at 18 to John Kentwoode, the 30-year-old heir to a prosperous silk business based at Old Vine in Baildon. Although she barely knows John when they marry, their life together gets off to a promising start until a malicious relative drops a few words deliberately chosen to sour their joy. Her happiness ruined, Barbara discovers unusual strength of character that sees her through the difficult years ahead.

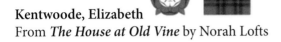

Kentwoode, Elizabeth
From *The House at Old Vine* by Norah Lofts

A pretty little girl of 8 with wide blue eyes, a sweet smile and coppery hair, Elizabeth lives at the Old Vine in Baildon, Suffolk, with her parents, baby brothers and grandfather. Much of her time is spent with her grandfather who spoils her and speaks in her defence when she is being scolded by her mother. This happens frequently because Mrs Kentwoode knows that behind Elizabeth's pretty smiles there is a sly, manipulative little minx. Even she, however, is unaware of the full extent of her daughter's calculating nature.

Kerkyon
From *The King Must Die* by Mary Renault

Kerkyon is the name given to all the young men who marry the Queen of Eleusis for one year, and then fight to the death when their allotted twelve months are over.

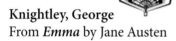

Knightley, George
From *Emma* by Jane Austen

In his late thirties, George Knightley is the major
landowner in the village of Highbury and nearby
Donwell. His large estate, Donwell Abbey, is very close
to the Woodhouse's home and he is a good friend of
both Emma and her father. He is also related to them
by marriage, his brother John having married Emma's
older sister, Isabella, and he is now a devoted uncle to
the couple's children. Tall, strong and upright, Mr
Knightley is a very sensible man with a cheerful
manner. He is honest, kind and perceptive, and even
though he is very fond of Emma he is not afraid of
criticising her when he thinks she is at fault, even going
so far as to deliver a crushing reprimand when she
allows her sharp wit to humiliate well-meaning Miss
Bates. Although more solid and less romantically

Illustration by Chris
Hammond of George
Knightley with Emma
Woodhouse, 1898.

appealing than aloof Mr Darcy, Jane Austen's best known hero, George Knightley
is generally more amiable, and one suspects he will turn out to be a very
considerate husband.

Kroesig, Tony
From *The Pursuit of Love* by Nancy Mitford

Son of the Governor of the Bank of England, Tony Kroesig is brought as a stopgap
guest to the shared coming out ball of Fanny Logan and her cousin, Linda Radlett
(one of the daughters of Lord and Lady Alconleigh). Tall, blond and heavily built,
he initially appears to be good humoured and part of the cultured and witty set
that Linda admires. Unfortunately, he is in fact a pompous bore, drearily
unimaginative and entirely dedicated to furthering his career as a banker and
Conservative MP. He loathes the working classes, admires Hitler and is utterly
committed to capitalism. All this makes him a desperately unsuitable match for
any member of the charmingly dotty, aristocratic Alconleigh family.

L is for Ladislaw, Logan, Loveridge and more

Lacy, Beatrice
From *Rebecca* by Daphne du Maurier

The sister of Maxim de Winter, Beatrice is a forthright , no-nonsense woman who lives for horses and dogs. Tall, broad-shouldered and very handsome, she dresses in tweeds as befits an English lady whose life is rooted in country pursuits. Married with one son, Roger, who is about to go to Oxford, she lives in Devon, approximately fifty miles from Manderley, her brother's house in Cornwall where she spent her childhood. A kind and sincere woman despite an unfortunate tendency towards tactlessness, Beatrice is very fond of her brother although she bickers with him incessantly. When she meets his new, very young and very inexperienced wife, she makes a point of being friendly to her.

Lacy, Major Giles
From *Rebecca* by Daphne du Maurier

The brother-in-law of Maxim de Winter, Major Lacy lives in Devon with his wife Beatrice and his son, Roger, who is about to go to Oxford. Large, bluff and hearty, he has a big moon face and genial smiling eyes that look out from behind horn-rimmed glasses. He shares his wife's fondness for country pursuits and is something of a trencher man. When he has had a bit to drink he enjoys putting on mock theatricals.

Ladislaw, Will
From *Middlemarch* by George Eliot

Will Ladislaw comes from a family with a habit of producing problematic females. His maternal grandmother was disinherited by her well-to-do kin for marrying a Polish musician with no money, and in due course his mother ran away from home and lost touch with her family. Related through his grandmother to Reverend Edward Casaubon of Lowick, Ladislaw is an idealistic and gifted young man who lives a fairly bohemian life without a great deal of focus in it. Things change when he meets and falls in love with a remarkable young woman with whom he has much in

Will Ladislaw from The Works of George Eliot, Vol 11, Middlemarch part 3 published by The Jenson Society, NY, 1910.

common. Unfortunately, she is already married and his obvious affection for her leads to problems with her husband. Unlike many characters in the book, Ladislaw sets little store by money and sticks to his principles even when doing so proves disadvantageous.

Lee, Bessie
From *Jane Eyre* by Charlotte Bronte

A nursemaid at Gateshead Hall (the home of Jane Eyre's aunt, Mrs Reed), Bessie is the closest thing the orphaned Jane has to a friend. A pretty, slim young woman with black hair, dark eyes and a clear complexion, she is basically good at heart, although she is often careless, abrupt and quick-tempered. All the same, she is the only resident at Gateshead Hall to show Jane any kindness, on occasion singing to her, holding her hand for comfort and bringing her tasty treats from the kitchen. It might not sound like much but for a child starved of any affection, anything is better than nothing.

Lestrange, Archie
From *The Cazalet Chronicle* (the second, third and fourth novels only: *Marking Time, Confusion* and *Casting Off*) by Elizabeth Jane Howard

A new character introduced for the first time well into the second half of the second volume of the *Cazalet Chronicle*, Archie immediately becomes a key player in the story. A close friend of Rupert Cazalet with whom he was at Art School many years previously, Archie arrives at Home Place in the summer of 1941, on sick leave from the Army following a leg injury. In need of rest and recuperation, he is made welcome by the Cazalets on the basis of his long friendship with Rupert, and the particular fondness the Duchy has for him. He soon discerns the true nature of the friendship between Rachel and Sid and is relieved because it soothes his injured pride. Seventeen or eighteen years previously, Archie had fallen in love with Rachel and asked her to marry him. When she rejected him with barely concealed revulsion, Archie had been deeply hurt and he went away for a long time to lick his wounds. Now, seeing Rachel and Sid together, he is able to understand, and the lingering remnants of an old hurt are healed once and for all. During this, and subsequent visits to Home Place, Archie becomes a trusted confidant and adviser to many of the Cazalet family, especially Clary for whom he feels a special bond because she is Rupert's daughter. As Clary is going through a terribly difficult time, the presence of Archie is a tremendous boon.

Archie's appearance is described more vividly than some of the other major characters in the book. He is immensely tall, with a domed forehead and fine, black receding hair. His eyes are heavily lidded and there is often an expression of secret amusement in them. His war injury has left him with a pronounced limp in one leg.

Levison, Captain Francis
From *East Lynne* by Mrs Henry Wood

The heir-presumptive to rich old Sir Peter Levison, Captain Levison is a young, elegant Guardsman with clear cut features, white teeth and raven hair. In short, he is extremely attractive, but astute observers notice that there is something shifty in his appearance. A 'graceless spendthrift', he has a terrible reputation as a seducer, but is received all the same in good company where he continues to prey on innocent young girls. Using honeyed words and meaningful glances, he manages to insinuate himself into the affections of the impressionable Lady Isabel Vane. This is most unfortunate since Levison is a thoroughly dangerous individual without any redeeming characteristics whatsoever.

Linton, Cathy (baptismal name Catherine)
From *Wuthering Heights* by Emily Bronte

Perhaps the closest thing to a heroine to be found in this unconventional novel, Cathy is brought up in comfort at Thrushcross Grange by her father and nursemaid, her mother having died soon after giving birth to her. She is very pretty, slim and healthy with her father's fair hair and skin, and her mother's dark eyes. In character, she has her mother's high spirits and is clever, affectionate and occasionally mischievous. Unlike her mother, however, she has a gentle, considerate side to her personality.

> **WUTHERING HEIGHTS**
>
> **EMILY BRONTË**

Unfortunately, a dramatic change in her personal circumstances has an adverse effect on her character and she becomes reserved and rather hostile. Beneath the unfriendly exterior, however, the old Cathy remains, ready to resurface when her icy facade is thawed by love.

Linton, Edgar
From *Wuthering Heights* by Emily Bronte

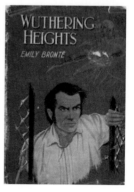

Brought up with his younger sister at comfortable Thrushcross Grange, Edgar is a pleasant, civilised young man who has benefitted from receiving every material advantage. His fair-haired, blue-eyed good looks contrast with the brooding, Byronic appearance of his neighbour and romantic rival, Heathcliff.

Affectionate, emotional and highly sensitive, Edgar's tragedy is that his timid, irresolute character is no match for the volatile woman he falls in love with, and even less so for the violent obsessive who wants to destroy him.

Linton, Isabella
From *Wuthering Heights* by Emily Bronte

With blonde hair, blue eyes and a pale complexion, Isabella Linton is a pretty young woman, although sadly for her, these good looks are not what it takes to inspire admiration in the man with whom she recklessly falls in love. About a year younger than her neighbour Catherine Earnshaw, in every respect the two are as dissimilar as chalk and cheese. Isabella is refined, sensitive and perilously naïve when it comes to affairs of the heart. Indulged by doting parents and a fond brother, she is immature and has little understanding of the world beyond the safe confines of Thrushcross Grange. Foolish and susceptible, she proves easy prey for an unscrupulous suitor and stubbornly refuses to listen when she is warned to stay away from him.

Lock, William
From *Remarkable Creatures* by Tracy Chevalier

An ancient ostler working at the Queen's Arms in Charmouth, Lock – nicknamed Captain Cury by the Anning family – scours the beaches with a spade searching for fossils to sell to coach passengers breaking their journey between London and Exeter. An unpleasant old man, he steals the finds of other fossil hunters and spies on them to see what they have uncovered.

Lockwood, Mr
From *Wuthering Heights* by Emily Bronte

A gentleman of means from the south of England, Mr Lockwood comes to the Yorkshire Moors in order to recuperate from an illness. Having rented Thrushcross Grange, he pays a visit to his landlord at Wuthering Heights, and becomes intrigued by the bizarre mix of people who live there. With plenty of time at his disposal, he asks his housekeeper, Ellen Dean, to tell him their stories.

   Mr Lockwood's main purpose in the book is to stand in for the reader, eliciting information about the highly-charged events at Wuthering Heights and Thrushcross Grange. As an outsider, he is also useful in underlining how impenetrable the strong local dialect can be, and how alien the landscape and some of its inhabitants can seem to those not used to them.

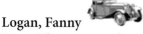

Logan, Fanny
From *The Pursuit of Love* and *Love in a Cold Climate* by Nancy Mitford

Daughter of divorced, dysfunctional parents, Fanny Logan is brought up in Kent by her Aunt Emily and spends most of her holidays with her Aunt Sadie (Lady Alconleigh) and her family at Alconleigh. As narrator of *The Pursuit of Love* and *Love in a Cold Climate*, Fanny features prominently in both books, although hers is not a starring role. Instead, she acts as friend and confidante to the central characters. Unlike her eccentric cousins Fanny has been educated at school, a fact that perhaps explains why she is sensible and well-behaved, while they are rather too high spirited and unruly. Fanny is, however, lively enough to appeal to her cousin Linda and become her closest friend. Not very tall and with round pink cheeks and rough curly black hair, she is not a beauty like Linda or her friend Polly Hampton, and her manner is rather diffident. Aunt Sadie likens her to a little pony which might at any moment toss its shaggy mane and gallop off. It's a rather endearing image, but it does not suggest elegance or poise.

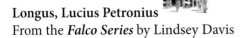

Longus, Lucius Petronius
From the *Falco Series* by Lindsey Davis

The closest male friend of Marcus Didius Falco, Petro (as he is known to his friend) is the Patrol Captain of the Aventine Watch, a job that makes him responsible for fighting fires and maintaining law and order in his district. He joined the army on the same day as Falco and the two quickly became friends. The normal bonds of friendship were strengthened by their experiences in Britain where they served in the Second Augusta Legion, disgraced during the Boudicca uprising.

A big, placid, sleepy-looking man with an impassive face, Petro is married and has three little girls to whom he is devoted. He is good at his job and often lends Falco a helping hand when he is investigating something.

Sculpture of a Roman legionary by Johann Baptist Moroder-Lusenberg.

Lovell, Orlando
From *Rebels and Traitors* by Lindsey Davis

An unscrupulous young adventurer whose background is shrouded in mystery, Lovell allies himself to the King's cause in the Civil War because he thinks the rebellion is doomed to failure. Sturdy and tanned, he cuts a dashing figure with his light brown eyes and uptwirled moustache. His manner is persuasive and he is capable of great charm, but he is also untrustworthy and inherently callous. He enjoys warfare and has a cruel streak which surfaces from time to time.

Charles I, for whom Orlando Lovell is fighting.

Loveridge, Meridiana (Meri)
From *Larksleve and Blanche* by Patricia Wendorf

A tall, straight-backed gypsy girl aged 17 at the start of the Larksleve books, Meridiana has a compelling gaze and a head swathed in thick black braids. She is fully aware of the impact she has on men and is steelily determined to snare Luke Carew, the handsome stone mason on whom she has set her heart. For Meri, to want is to have, and in her headlong pursuit of Luke she doesn't stop to consider the consequences of marrying a man not born to the gypsy way of life. Regarded as the jewel of her family, Meri has been raised on the 'drom' – the Romany word for road – and cannot contemplate any other way of life. Although in general she doesn't care for non-gypsy people, she has formed a friendship of sorts with Eliza Greypaull, the red-headed daughter of a farmer in Buckland St. Mary.

Lowborough, Lord
From *The Tenant of Wildfell Hall* by Anne Bronte

A tall, thin, gloomy-looking man aged somewhere between thirty and forty, Lord Lowborough has had the misfortune to be friends with Arthur Huntingdon and his gang of dissipated cronies. Through his notorious gambling he has lost his fiancée, a girl he really loved, as well as his entire fortune. All that now remains to him is his title and family seat. Having found the willpower to stop gambling for good, he immediately finds solace in the bottle and when he attempts to stop drinking he is thwarted by his malicious friends. Eventually he distances himself from their toxic influence and manages to stop his descent into alcoholism. When the novel begins Lowborough is a reformed character, although his reputation remains poor amongst society mammas. He has become acquainted with Annabella Wilmot, the niece and putative heiress of a very rich old man, and is well on his way to falling in love with her. Since she already has a fortune and expects to inherit even more, it is a match that will make his financial embarrassment a thing of the past. Thus the future is looking rosy for Lowborough but will his luck hold out?

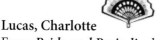

Lucas, Charlotte
From *Pride and Prejudice* by Jane Austen

Charlotte, 27, is the oldest daughter of Sir William and Lady Lucas who live at Lucas Lodge, a short distance from Longbourn, the home of the Bennet family. Plain, sensible and intelligent, Charlotte is great friends with Elizabeth Bennet, yet she is far more pragmatic and accepting than her friend. She understands that it is the responsibility of single young women to find suitable husbands so that they do not become a burden to their families, and she believes that romantic attachment is a luxury few can afford. With little fortune and less physical beauty, she knows that her chances of matrimony are slim, but should a respectable offer come her way, she will not hesitate to accept it.

Hugh Thomson illustration of Charlotte Lucas and Mr Collins, George Allen, 1894.

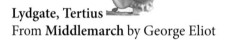

Lydgate, Tertius
From **Middlemarch** by George Eliot

An idealistic young doctor, Lydgate was born into a prosperous family from which he has become alienated by entering the medical profession against their wishes. He is now short of money but finds it hard to live within his means, partly because he is used to a certain standard of living, and partly because he has grand ideas about not charging for some of his work. Although he is a good doctor with advanced ideas about medicine, he is naïve and inexperienced in his relationships with patients and colleagues. Furthermore, he fails to adapt to Middlemarch ways because of an arrogant belief in the superiority of his own methods. This inability to get on with people leaves him vulnerable when circumstances turn against him.

If Lydgate has a difficult time professionally his private affairs are little better. He makes the mistake of falling for a pretty, shallow, young woman who values money and status above all. An unhappy character, Tertius Lydgate is a warning of the damage that can be wrought by too much self-belief and too little self-knowledge.

Lytchett, Lady Sybil
From *My Last Duchess* by Daisy Goodwin

Daughter of the Duke of Buckingham, Lady Sybil occupies much of her time serving as a kind of unofficial lady-in-waiting to her stepmother, Duchess Fanny. A pleasant, unassuming young woman who seems content to remain in her glamorous stepmother's shadow, she is quite good-looking despite her dowdy clothes and red hair that clashes with her frequent blushes. A longstanding romantic attachment to Reggie Greatorex appears to be going nowhere.

M is for McGrath, Merlyn, Mortmain and more

McGrath, Hal
From *Tilly Trotter* by Catherine Cookson

Big, brutish Hal McGrath is a young miner who lives with his parents and brothers in a village on the Sopwith estate in County Durham. The McGraths are known troublemakers, vicious, violent and untrustworthy, and Hal is no exception. He has taken a shine to young Tilly Trotter and means to make her his wife, regardless of whether or not she wants him. His obsession with Tilly stems partly from straightforward lust, but also from the suspicion that she is the key to helping his family recover something important that they lost many years ago.

McGrath, Steve
From *Tilly Trotter* and *Tilly Trotter Wed* and *Tilly Trotter Widowed* by Catherine Cookson

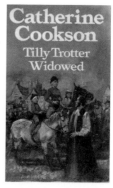

Aged 14 at the start of the trilogy, Steve is violent Hal McGrath's youngest brother. Completely unlike his family in both looks and appearance, Steve has a long face, sandy hair and skinny legs. Where his brothers and parents are surly and rough, Steve is pleasant and funny. He is very fond of Tilly Trotter and goes out of his way to help her, even when he puts himself at risk by doing so.

Magda
From *The Town House* by Norah Lofts

Magda is a thin, sinewy girl of Romany extraction who lives only to dance. Food, comfortable surroundings and human company mean nothing compared to the euphoria she feels when she picks up her tambourine and dances. As a foreign traveller she is viewed with suspicion by most people, but when she dances their hostility is forgotten until she stops.

Early postcard showing dancing girl with tambourine.

Maiden, The
From *We Speak No Treason* by Rosemary Hawley Jarman

When the story opens the Maiden is a 12-year-old orphan living at Grafton Regis in Northamptonshire, in the service of the widowed Dame Elizabeth Grey. Brought up in a nunnery in Leicestershire, she came to Grafton having been willed into Dame Grey's care by her father just before he died of wounds sustained in the service of Dame Grey's father, Sir Richard Woodville. At Grafton the Maiden earns her keep by sewing, running errands and generally helping her beautiful, but cash-strapped mistress look her best in clothes that have seen better days. She admires Dame Grey's beauty and calm piety, but fears her temper since it can lead to beatings, and is made extremely uneasy by certain covert activities she accidentally observes.

The Maiden is tiny and lovely with large dark brown eyes, but her best feature is her hair which is thick, falls to her knees and features all the colours of an autumn forest. She has a sweet, gentle disposition and is distressed by bear baiting and cock fights as she cannot abide cruelty to animals. An eager, innocent young girl on the brink of womanhood, she is greedy for knowledge about the wider world, and dreams at night of a faceless lover. Truthful and straightforward most of the time, her longing to experience life outside Grafton is such that she is prepared to flatter and ingratiate in order to achieve her aim. She has a happy nature and laughs often, but underlying her gaiety is an intensity that suggests a deep capacity for love and suffering.

Although the Maiden is the central female character in this wonderful book her real name is never mentioned. Nevertheless, given that at one point St Catherine's blessing is invoked for her, it seems likely that this is her name. (There is further evidence to support the idea that she is called Catherine but stating it would constitute a spoiler). In any case, the absence of a name for the Maiden underlines the fact that although she narrates a significant part of the story, her place in it for the most part is on the sidelines.

Martha
From *Cranford* by Elizabeth Gaskell

A 'rough, honest-looking country girl', Martha comes to work as a servant-of-all-work for Miss Matty Jenkyns. She is blunt and plain-spoken to a fault, but she is also trustworthy and utterly loyal to her employer.

Hugh Thomson illustration of Martha with Mary Smith, 1918.

Mammy
From *Gone With the Wind* by Margaret Mitchell

A slave owned by the O'Hara family of Clayton County, Georgia, Mammy has the coveted position of children's nurse which gives her great status in the slaves' pecking order. Having previously helped raise Ellen O'Hara (nee Robillard), she is now doing the same for Ellen's daughters. Since all three are on the brink of womanhood her duties now involve helping them dress, making sure they eat properly,

Early book mark promoting film version of Gone With the Wind.

and at every opportunity reminding them to behave with suitable decorum. Mammy has very cogent ideas about what constitutes ladylike behaviour and although a slave, she is on familiar terms with her charges and is not in the least afraid to give them a piece of her mind. In fact, she is forever scolding Scarlett, the oldest O'Hara daughter, who is more wilful and prone to acts of disobedience than her sisters. Despite, or perhaps because of this, Mammy adores Scarlett and watches her with a motherly gaze that is both affectionate and critical. She stays with Scarlett through thick and thin, long after she has been given her freedom, and becomes a rock on which her turbulent mistress can always rely.

Man of Keen Sight, The
From *We Speak No Treason* by Rosemary Hawley Jarman

The name of 'the man of keen sight' is never revealed, although the author discloses that he is a young knight who, following the death of his father and his mother's subsequent entry into a convent, has been raised by a guardian in a castle in Kent. When he first appears in the story, he is a tall, eager lad of 17 with a gift for archery and an ability to see further into the distance than is usual. Long-sightedness is normally something of a drawback for an archer, but he has worked hard to overcome any disadvantage. With money to inherit when he comes of age and a mooted betrothal to a suitable girl, he has every reason to remain comfortably at home when a new episode in the violent struggle between the Houses of York and Lancaster threatens the peace of the nation. Yet following a chance encounter with Richard of Gloucester, the youngest brother of Edward IV, he joins the young Duke's entourage and heads off with him to war. In so doing he follows a course that will bring him friendship, doubt and a great test to his loyalty, but above all will teach him to understand the true nature of Richard of Gloucester.

Markham, Gilbert
From *The Tenant of Wildfell Hall* by Anne Bronte

The hero and sometime narrator of this novel, Gilbert Markham is a young gentleman farmer who lives at Linden Grange in the rural community of Lindenhope with his widowed mother and younger brother and sister. Although farming is not the occupation he would have chosen for himself, Markham has shouldered the burden of managing the family farm with reasonably good grace and is going about his work in a diligent manner. He is an amiable, intelligent young man whose personality

Gilbert Markham and lady from an early edition of The Tenant of Wildfell Hall.

has perhaps been injured a little by the unapologetic favouritism constantly shown him by his mother on account of his being her oldest male child. He has an affectionate, if teasing, relationship with his sister Rose and manages to be moderately forbearing to his mischievous brother, Fergus. While he wants to be good and generally manages to listen to his conscious, he has a tendency to be sulky, and occasionally allows his fierce temper to gain control of his better self.

At the start of the book he is conducting a half-hearted courtship of Eliza Millward, the pretty daughter of the vicar of Lindenhope. He is mildly infatuated with her, but is prevented from becoming too serious by the disapproval of his mother who thinks Eliza is not good enough for her son, and moreover, deplores the fact that she will bring very little money when she marries. Markham is not so enamoured of Eliza as to remain disinterested when the mysterious widow Helen Graham arrives in the neighbourhood. At first he is merely intrigued by her and cultivates a friendship with her young son in order to get to know her better. Having achieved his aim, against his will he finds himself gradually falling in love, but just as he begins to believe that his feelings are reciprocated, he allows suspicion and jealousy to cloud his judgement about his beloved.

Marnesse, Sophie de la
From *Milady Charlotte* by Jean Plaidy

The teenage daughter of the Comte and Comtesse de la Marnesse, Sophie has been engaged since she was a child to her cousin, Jean Pierre de la Vaugon. Small and blonde, she has led a privileged, sheltered life but with revolution in the air she is about to be plunged into terror and uncertainty.

Martin, Robert
From *Emma* by Jane Austen

Twenty-four year old Robert Martin is a respectable, neatly-dressed tenant farmer on the Donwell Abbey estate owned by George Knightley. He shares his comfortable home with his mother and two sisters who went to school with Emma Woodhouse's friend, Harriet Smith. Intelligent, sincere and good-humoured, Robert is well thought of by Mr Knightley who has no hesitation in describing him as a gentleman farmer. Emma, however, finds his appearance very plain, and although she accepts he is a worthy young man, she believes he is socially inferior to her friend and therefore not a suitable marriage prospect.

Hugh Thomson illustration of Robert Martin conversing with Harriet Smith, 1915.

Mason, Bertha
From *Jane Eyre* by Charlott Brontë

Daughter of Mr Mason, a prosperous Jamaican planter and merchant, Bertha is a beautiful, unattached woman aged 31. Tall, dark and majestic, she is admired by many young men, but makes a point of flattering and dazzling the young, inexperienced Mr Rochester who has been sent by his father to Jamaica in order to marry her. Sadly, Bertha is not all she seems; in reality she is violent, foul-mouthed and promiscuous, but with her family's connivance she manages to conceal this from Rochester because they want the marriage to proceed. Their deception has dire consequences not only for Rochester, but ultimately also for Jane Eyre and Bertha herself.

Maudelyn, Hawise   **RP**
From *Katherine by* Anya Seton

The daughter of a prosperous London fishmonger, Hawise is a stout, big-boned young lass with freckles, sandy hair and a missing front tooth. Her less than beautiful appearance is offset by other virtues – she is wholesome, healthy and happy – and these qualities have helped her secure the affections of a young weaver's apprentice, Jack Maudelyn. However, as Jack still has to serve time before he can become a master weaver, Hawise's father refuses to give the match his blessing. Unperturbed, Hawise reasons that if Jack gets her pregnant her father will have to give in.

Hawise meets Katherine de Roet shortly before the latter's wedding day and instantly likes her. Loyal and full of common sense, she is destined to become Katherine's most trusted servant and friend.

Maxwell, Mrs (Peggy)
From *The Tenant of Wildfell Hall* by Anne Bronte

Mrs Maxwell is a grave, elderly woman who promised her dying sister she would take care of her daughter, Helen, and has thus raised the girl since she was a very small child. At times she can seem stern and disapproving, but she loves her niece and has her best interests at heart. Although Helen's father is still alive, he has abdicated responsibility for his daughter to her competent aunt and is happy to let her live permanently at Staningley Hall, the home of Mr and Mrs Maxwell.

A sensible, cautious woman, Mrs Maxwell has done her best to make her beautiful niece aware of the perils of marrying unwisely prior to introducing her to London society. Her warnings contain a hint, which Helen observes, that her own marriage has not been entirely without difficulty. In London she endeavours in vain to steer her niece towards steady, wealthy and ultimately, dull older men, in the belief that they will make better husbands than the handsome young rake who is making a play for Helen.

Medea
From *The King Must Die* by Mary Renault

A Priestess who is also an enchantress, Medea is close to King Aigeus of Athens and people believe she will soon become his wife. She has a dark past which she keeps concealed.

Fresco of Medea, Herculaneum.

Merion, Lady Letitia (Letty)
From *April Lady* by Georgette Heyer

The 17-year-old half-sister and ward of Lord Cardross, Letty has been brought up by her maternal aunt, a good-natured but unduly lax woman who has allowed her young charge to become flighty and difficult. Since her brother's marriage to Lady Helen Irvine, Letty has been living at his house in Grosvenor Square, but although she is now under the supervision of a more responsible guardian, her character has yet to show an improvement. Flirtatious, conceited, pleasure-seeking and far too knowing for her years, dark-haired Letty is a very attractive girl, and as she is also an heiress, she is a tempting prospect for fortune hunters. However, she has formed a serious attachment with Jeremy Allandale, an honourable young man of good family who loves her but is not rich enough to win the approval of Letty's brother. While the reckless Letty is capable of flouting Cardross's wishes and eloping with Allandale, he is far too upright and conventional to contemplate such a desperate move.

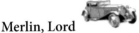

Merlin, Lord
From *The Pursuit of Love* by Nancy Mitford

Although a relatively minor character, the beauty and culture-loving Lord Merlin is important for several reasons, not least of which is the fact that he inadvertently introduces Linda Radlett to the pompous Tony Kroesig. In many ways the absolute antithesis of his neighbour Lord Alconleigh - pictures by Watteau hang in his hall rather than the dead animal heads that are to be found at Alconleigh – he is just as eccentric in his own way. Having taken a shine to Linda at her older sister's wedding, he makes it his business to supervise her cultural education and becomes exceptionally fond of her.

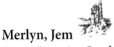

Merlyn, Jem
From *Jamaica Inn* by Daphne du Maurier

The youngest brother of Josh Merlyn (see below), Jem is a horse thief who lives alone in his old family home near Kilmar Tor on Bodmin Moor. His family has a dismal history – his father was hanged for killing a man, his grandfather transported as a convict and his middle brother drowned in a marsh. Josh, many years Jem's senior, disappeared for a time to America and came back with a bad reputation. Jem left home to go to sea but disliked the life and came back to discover his mother was ailing. Since her death he has lived on and off at the cottage, making money from selling stolen horses and ponies.

Kilmar Tor, home of Jem Merlyn. Image © Neil Hanson used under the Creative Commons Attribution-ShareAlike 2.0 license.

   Good-looking with a firm mouth and fine eyes, Jem resembles his older brother, although he is less tall, and his appearance has not been raddled by alcohol. He is a bold character with a callous and amoral outlook on life, yet he is not without charm and possesses considerably more humanity than his brutish brother.

Merlyn, Josh
From *Jamaica Inn* by Daphne du Maurier

The landlord of Jamaica Inn, a hostelry with a terrible reputation situated on the desolate road that runs between Bodmin and Launceston, Merlyn is a drunken brute of a man with thick dark hair that falls into his eyes, and strong white teeth. Unnaturally tall and broad, he has powerful shoulders, long gorilla-like arms and fists like hams. His face is now ravaged by the effects of alcohol, but enough of his former looks remain to show that he was once a handsome man. He routinely bullies and beats his pitiful wife, and engages in activities that have already driven her half-mad with horror.

Merlyn, Patience
From *Jamaica Inn* by Daphne du Maurier

The wife of Josh Merlyn, landlord of Jamaica Inn, Patience has been terrified out of her wits by the cruel behaviour of her vicious husband. Once a pretty, particular woman, she is now a dismal, grey-haired slattern who creeps about like a whipped dog. Most of the time she is scared witless, yet in spite of all she has suffered she retains a cringing devotion to her husband.

Miller, Fanny
From *Remarkable Creatures* by Tracy Chevalier

Fanny Miller is the one-time friend of Mary Anning, the fossil hunter from Lyme Regis. Where Mary is tall and plain, Fanny is small and pretty with delicate features, fair hair and blue eyes. Her father is a wood cutter who sells wood to Richard Anning for his cabinet making business, and her mother works at a local factory. When she is young Fanny attends the same chapel as Mary and the two amuse themselves playing finger games during dull services. Outside they romp

Blue Lias cliffs at Lyme Regis. Image ©Michael Maggs under the Creative Commons Attribution-Share Alike 2.5 Generic license.

together along the banks of the river and occasionally play on the beach although Fanny is nervous near the sea and scared of the fossils that Mary loves to find. She has a superstitious nature and is fearful of things that cannot be easily explained. This inherent timidity and narrow-mindedness is in sharp contrast with Mary's enquiring mind and is the reason they stop being friends.

Milliment, Miss

From *The Cazalet Chronicle* (comprising 4 novels: *The Light Years, Marking Time, Confusion and Casting Off*) by Elizabeth Jane Howard

The governess of Louise Cazalet and her cousin Polly (and Clary and others later on), Eleanor Milliment is a quietly tragic character. She is an impoverished, aged spinster when the story starts, and the narrative reveals that life has not been kind to her. Unattractive to an unusual degree, she nevertheless found love with a young curate but he perished in the Transvaal during the Boer War. Thereafter, she was doomed to take care of her tyrannical old father, a retired clergyman, until his death, whereupon she was left free but virtually penniless. In order to supplement her minuscule inheritance, Miss Milliment found work as a governess. As *The Cazalet Chronicle* commences she is teaching two of the young Cazalet girls, one of whom is the daughter of a former pupil, Villy Cazalet (nee Rydal).

Miss Milliment is a wonderful portrait of a woman whose beauty is entirely on the inside. Large and shapeless, she is extremely ugly with a face like 'a huge old toad', and she dresses in cheap, hideous clothes which are seldom clean because she cannot afford to have them laundered. This, combined with the fact that she bathes just once a week, means that she has a noticeably musty smell. These shortcomings are outweighed by the fact that she is kind, exceedingly intelligent and devoted to Villy and the Cazalet girls. She is passionate about art and books and passes her erudition on to her pupils. Overwhelmingly grateful to Villy for rescuing her from penury, she nevertheless lives in silent dread of the day when the family will no longer require her services. Fortunately for her, the cloud of approaching war has a silver lining as far as her personal circumstances are concerned.

Millward, Eliza

From *The Tenant of Wildfell Hall* by Anne Bronte

The youngest daughter of Reverend Millward, the vicar of Lindenhope, Eliza is a small, pretty young woman with a charming, flirtatious manner which she utilises in an attempt to ensnare Gilbert Markham, a local gentleman farmer. Since she has virtually no money of her own, she must utilise all her wiles to make him love her enough to propose marriage. For a time she seems to be succeeding, although Gilbert is never fully committed to her and soon ceases to admire her at all when his affections are captured by a more deserving subject. Eliza is not the kind of girl to take rejection in good spirit; playful as a kitten when she is contented, she becomes a spiteful cat when she realises her plan to marry Gilbert is not going to succeed. The malicious delight she exhibits when bringing him bad news about the woman he loves demonstrates her venomous character and underlines how fortunate Gilbert is to have escaped her clutches.

Millward, Mary
From *The Tenant of Wildfell Hall* by Anne Bronte

Older and taller than her sister, Mary is a plain, quiet, sensible girl with none of Eliza's kittenish charm. Since the death of her mother she has taken on the role of housekeeper and general dogsbody, and is valued by no one except her father and those to whom her kindness is very welcome such as the local poor, small children and animals.

Millward, Rev. Michael
From *The Tenant of Wildfell Hall* by Anne Bronte

The elderly vicar of Lindenhope, the parish in which Wildfell Hall stands, Reverend Millward is a self-opinionated man who believes his views are the only ones that matter, and that it is incumbent upon him to indoctrinate his flock with them at any given opportunity. That these opinions extend way beyond his theological remit concerns him not at all, and thus he holds forth to his neighbours ceaselessly about his peculiar dietary ideas that involve the consumption of plenty of meat and strong liquor. When he gets hold of a belief, nothing will persuade him that it is wrong and nothing will prevent him from delivering his judgement as if it were set in stone. A tall, powerfully-built man who habitually wears a large shovel hat, he has a square face with massive features.

Minos (King)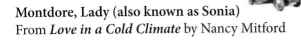
From *The King Must Die* by Mary Renault

The powerful King of Crete, Minos is seldom seen by his people. When he makes a rare appearance to officiate at a sacred ceremony, he wears a fearsome bull-mask made from gold and set with crystal eyes.

Bull head with gilded horns found at Knossos, now in Heraklion Archeological Museum. In Crete © Edisonblus, used under the Creative Commons Attribution-Share Alike 3.0 Unported license.

Montdore, Lady (also known as Sonia)
From *Love in a Cold Climate* by Nancy Mitford

Lady Montdore is a brilliant evocation of a magnificently monstrous old battle axe, or 'hell-hag', to use Lord Alconleigh's epithet. Born Miss Perrotte, the handsome daughter of an undistinguished country squire, she hit the jackpot when she married the rich and universally respected Lord Montdore. Now aged about 60 (assuming she married at 20 and gave birth to her only child, Polly, at the age of 40), she is greedy, snobbish, selfish, rampantly vulgar, and has a slavish devotion for impoverished European royalty. Although she is as heartily disliked as her husband is adored, her invitations are accepted because she is an excellent hostess and is occasionally capable of immense charm. Having successfully managed her husband's career in public life, her main object in life now is to arrange a glittering match for Polly.

Montdore, Lord
From *Love in a Cold Climate* by Nancy Mitford

Very grand and very rich, Lord Montdore is blessed with godlike good looks, a noble and ancient lineage, and a formidable wife whose ambition has propelled him to greatness. A scholarly gentleman, a pillar of the Conservatives and the best-looking Viceroy ever sent to India, he is universally considered a wonderful old man. Or almost universally, because the young Radletts and their cousin Fanny think he is an old fraud.

More, Thomas   **RP**
From *Wolf Hall* by Hilary Mantel

A scholar admired throughout Europe, More holds the post of Chancellor of the Duchy of Lancaster at the start of the narrative. He is something of a religious zealot, wearing a jerkyn of horsehair under his clothes and beating himself with a scourge. As a staunch upholder of the faith, he has a keen interest in sniffing out heretics and doesn't shy away from using torture to extract confessions. A misogynist at heart, he treats his womenfolk with contempt apart from his daughter Meg whom he adores - perhaps a little too much for comfort. His appearance is usually dishevelled, his clothes untidy and his face not properly shaven. He has known Thomas Cromwell since the latter was a small ragged boy and he sneers at him for growing prosperous through money-lending activities.

Statue of Sir Thomas More Cheyne Walk. Image © Alexander K Papp, used under the Creative Commons Attribution-Share Alike 2.0 Generic license.

Morland, Catherine
From *Northanger Abbey* by Jane Austen

The protagonist of Northanger Abbey, Catherine Morland is brought up in the pleasant rural community of Fullerton, said to be about nine miles from Salisbury. One of ten children born to a comfortably off clergyman and his good-natured wife, Catherine grows up something of a tomboy, romping with her older brothers while her mother is busy with the younger offspring. As she enters her teens she becomes more feminine and her looks, unpromising to begin with, greatly improve so that at seventeen she is pretty in an unremarkable way.

Catherine Morland reading, from 1833 Bentley edition of Jane Austen's novels .

An affectionate and cheerful girl, Catherine is unlike some other Austen heroines in that she is not especially witty, clever or beautiful; she is, in fact, a relatively ordinary girl. Having led a sheltered existence until now, she is inexperienced, naïve and gullible, and her glimpses into the wider world have come mostly from the pages of the overblown gothic novels she loves to read. As a result, she has poor judgement and makes serious errors when she makes her first entry into society, accompanying wealthy friends called Mr and Mrs Allen to Bath. She is easily taken in by people unworthy of her trust and allows her vivid imagination to run riot with embarrassing consequences, but she learns from her mistakes and suffers her setbacks with dignity. As the story progresses Catherine matures and her intelligence develops. At heart she is a decent, caring girl who only needs some experience of life to make her as sensible as she is likeable.

Morland, James
From *Northanger Abbey* by Jane Austen

Catherine Morland's affectionate older brother, James is easy going and good-natured. Normally he is a sensible lad but having met and fallen for Isabella, the beautiful sister of John Thorpe, a fellow student at Oxford, he has formed a better opinion of the morally dubious Thorpe family than they truly deserve. Unfortunately, his opinion influences his naïve sister Catherine, who understandably defers to her more experienced brother.

Mortmain, Cassandra
From *I Capture the Castle* by Dodie Smith

Heroine and narrator – through her journal - of this much-loved book set in the 1930s, Cassandra Mortmain, 17, lives with her eccentric, cash-strapped family in a crumbling medieval castle in the English countryside. Less pretty than her sister Rose, Cassandra is bright and witty and she harbours literary ambitions. Quirkily charming and thoroughly original – a character in the book describes her as 'Jane Eyre with a touch of Becky Sharp'

Manorbier Castle, used as the Mortmain's home in the 2003 film version of the book. Image © Mr M Levison used under the Creative Commons Attribution-ShareAlike 2.0 license.

- Cassandra is a convincing portrait of a girl on the verge of adulthood, learning about life and ready to experience the joy and pain of her first romance.

Mortmain, James
From I *Capture the Castle* by Dodie Smith

The father of Cassandra, Rose and Thomas Mortmain, James is a once-successful experimental novelist who is now struggling with severe writer's block. A fine-looking man in his youth, his face is just starting to run to fat and his bright colouring is fading. His inability to write anything for more than a decade has depleted the family's finances and they now live a hand-to-mouth existence in the castle he leased at the height of his success. Over the years he has become eccentric and unsociable, spending all his time in the castle's freezing gatehouse where he does nothing but read detective novels. His children have stopped believing that he will ever write again, but his genius is simply lying dormant, waiting for something to spark it back into being. In the meantime, he seems unconcerned that his wife and children are living in poverty.

Mortmain, Rose
From *I Capture the Castle* by Dodie Smith

Oldest child of acclaimed writer James Mortmain, Rose is a very beautiful 20-year-old who deeply resents the poverty and monotony of her life. She longs for beautiful clothes, a comfortable home and the little luxuries that only money can buy, and believes a loveless marriage is a fair price to pay for acquiring them.

Mortmain, Topaz
From *I Capture the Castle* by Dodie Smith

James Mortmain's second wife – his first having died when his children were 12, 9 and 7 – Topaz is a free spirit with what would today be recognised as New Age sensibilities. An artist's model before her unexpected marriage to James Mortmain, she is stunningly beautiful with very pale skin and an abundance of white-blonde hair. Although she likes to wander around wearing little or nothing, she is a kind soul who does her best to hold things together for her step-children as the family descends deeper and deeper into poverty.

Mortmain, Thomas
From *I Capture the Castle* by Dodie Smith

The youngest Mortmain child, 15-year-old Thomas is a cumbersome school boy with mousey hair that stands up in tufts. A scholarship boy, his daily commute to school involves a five-mile bicycle ride followed by a slow, ten-mile train journey. Bright like his sister Cassandra, he is a perceptive boy who notices things that other members of the family are too wrapped up in their own concerns to see.

Moulin, Jeanette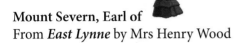
From **Milady Charlotte** by Jean Plaidy

A working-class woman employed as a cook in Paris, Jeanette has endured great hardship. Her daily struggle for survival has bred within her a deep hatred of the French ruling class, and she longs for revolution so that the aristocracy can be made to pay for doing nothing to improve conditions for the starving masses. Yet for all her hatred and revolutionary zeal, Jeanette is not a bad woman and she is capable of responding with gratitude to acts of kindness.

Mount Severn, Earl of
From *East Lynne* by Mrs Henry Wood

Aged 49 when the novel begins, William, Lord Mount Severn, looks much older; he is grey haired, gout-ridden and wrinkled. His premature aging has been brought about by a life of dissipation, and he now faces a dismal future since all his money is gone and his creditors are catching up with him. Yet until the age of 25 he was nothing more than a poor law student, managing to live within his meagre means. Then he unexpectedly inherited an earldom together with £60,000 a year, and at once found himself surrounded by flattering new friends. Allowing his newfound wealth and popularity to go to his head, he became a reckless spendthrift, squandering his fortune in extravagant living. His marriage to Mary, daughter of a respectable General, didn't help his financial situation since the General disapproved of Mount Severn's lifestyle and refused to give his consent to the match until the Earl reformed. Instead, the couple eloped to Gretna Green, thereby foregoing the financial settlement the General would have given his daughter had they waited for his blessing.

Mary bore him just one child, Isabel, and died when her daughter was 13-years-old. Since then the Earl's financial situation has been worsening and now, as the book begins, he is faced with the prospect of selling his only remaining asset, a country estate called East Lynne that he purchased some eighteen years previously. He insists, however, that the new owner must agree to keep the sale a secret for as long as possible or else his creditors will demand that he gives them the proceeds to settle his debts.

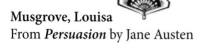

Musgrove, Charles
From *Persuasion* by Jane Austen

Heir to the Uppercross estate, Charles Musgrove is the husband of Mary, Anne Elliot's discontented youngest sister. He is also the brother of Louisa and Henrietta Musgrove. He is a decent, uncomplicated young man who would have liked to marry Anne Elliot but has settled for her sister, and seems happy enough with his tiresome wife. A keen sportsman, he has little interest in anything else and has a tendency to be idle.

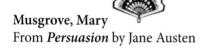

Musgrove, Louisa
From *Persuasion* by Jane Austen

Lively, high-spirited 20-year-old Louisa is the eldest daughter of Mr and Mrs Musgrove of Uppercross in Somerset. At the start of the book she and her sister Henrietta have just returned from school in Exeter and are now looking forward to a life dedicated to being fashionable and merry. When she meets Captain Wentworth, a very handsome and eligible naval officer who is staying with his sister at nearby Kellynch Hall, she pays him a great deal of attention which he finds flattering. He is also impressed by this pretty, pleasant girl's eager and impulsive nature which is in sharp contrast to the more cautious and reserved character of Anne Elliot, Louisa's sister-in-law and his own former fiancée.

C.E. Brock illustration of Louisa Musgrove and others, 1909.

Musgrove, Mary
From *Persuasion* by Jane Austen

The youngest and least attractive of Sir Walter Elliot's daughters, Mary is married to Charles Musgrove, heir to the Uppercross estate which neighbours the Elliot's ancestral home of Kellynch Hall in Somerset. (She was not Charles's first choice – he had originally wanted to marry Mary's sister Anne but she refused as she was still in love with Frederick Wentworth). Although better

C.E. Brock illustration of Mary Musgrove with Anne Elliot, 1909.

natured than Elizabeth, her oldest sister, Mary is weak-willed and selfish, and she is overly proud of her status as a baronet's daughter. When she is bored or discontented – which is often – she imagines herself ill and requires others to dance attendance on her.

Myton, Lady (Agnes)
From *Tilly Trotter* by Catherine Cookson

In her late twenties, Agnes Myton is the new wife of a wealthy man many years her senior who has a country seat in County Durham. A fine horsewoman with an excellent figure, she is a bold, sexually voracious woman who is unfaithful to her husband and doesn't trouble to cover her tracks.

N and *O* are for Neville, O'Hara and more

Neville, Anne **RP**
From *We Speak No Treason* by Rosemary Hawley Jarman

Second and youngest daughter of the powerful Earl of Warwick, Anne is a gentle, shy girl in her mid-to-late teens who has spent happy years at Middleham Castle in Yorkshire, growing up surrounded by well-born youths including her cousin, Richard of Gloucester, for whom she has tender feelings. Her contentment is shattered when her father uses her to secure an important alliance with an enemy of the crown and she is drawn, against her will, into a treasonous plot.

Anne Neville, on the left of this Fifteenth century illustration from the Rous Roll.

Thereafter her fate depends on whoever comes out on top in the forthcoming struggle for control of the country.

Although she is delicate and frail, Anne has quiet courage and a steadfast nature. She is slender and pretty, with golden hair, smoky grey eyes, a small mouth and a rounded chin.

Neville, Isabel  **RP**
From *We Speak No Treason* by Rosemary Hawley Jarman

The oldest daughter of the Earl of Warwick and joint heiress, with her sister Anne, to his vast fortune, Isabel is a lovely-looking young woman whose health is not robust. Like her sister, she is destined to be used as a pawn in her father's machinations.

Norfolk, Thomas (Duke of)   **RP**
From *The Other Boleyn Girl* by Philippa Gregory

Referred to throughout the book as 'Uncle Howard', Thomas Howard is in fact Earl of Surrey at the commencement of the novel and within three years he inherits the Dukedom of Norfolk from his father, although these titles are never mentioned in the text. One of the country's premier noblemen, he is a key figure at Henry VIII's court. Even though he already has great power and influence, he is hungry for even more. When he sees that his Boleyn nieces – Mary and Anne, daughters of his sister Elizabeth – are extremely beautiful, he doesn't hesitate to use them to attract the favour of the king. His nephew George is also pressed into service, promoting the girls to the king and helping them win and keep his attention. Uncle Howard expects them all to follow his commands unhesitatingly and to do all they can for the advancement of the Howard clan, however much it may conflict with their personal wishes. At the same time he makes it clear that as individuals they are of little importance. A skilled courtier with spies everywhere, he reads the king's mood, and should he ever suspect that the Boleyns are falling out favour, he will not hesitate to abandon them to their fate.

Norris, Sir Henry   **RP**
From *Wolf Hall* by Hilary Mantel

One of Henry VIII's closest friends, 'Harry' Norris holds the post of Groom to the Stool which means he sees the king in some of his most intimate moments. He is a polished courtier with graceful manners, always ready with a smile or laugh to smooth over awkward moments.

Norris, Mrs
From *Mansfield Park by* Jane Austen

The sister of both Lady Bertram and Fanny Price's mother, Mrs Norris is quite possibly the nastiest character to be found in any of Jane Austen's novels. The widow of the Mansfield Park parson, she revels in her close connection with the Bertram family and does all she can to ingratiate herself with them. She flatters and indulges the Bertram girls to such an extent that their personalities are ruined, at the same time losing no opportunity to bully her poorer niece, Fanny Price, and rub her nose in her charity status.

C.E. Brock illustration of Mrs Norris with Fanny Price, 1908.

Interfering, miserly and malicious, Mrs Norris manipulates and meddles her way throughout the book without ever revealing the smallest sign of kindness or generosity. Due to the indolence of Lady Bertram and the cold detachment of Sir Thomas, this odious woman is allowed to exert her malign influence over the inhabitants of Mansfield Park for far too long.

O'Hara, Carreen
From *Gone With the Wind* by Margaret Mitchell

The youngest daughter of Gerald and Ellen O'Hara, Carreen – really name Caroline Irene – is a sweet, dreamy girl with none of her sister Scarlett's vivacity or wilfulness. She is a dutiful daughter and when her circumstances change she adapts to them with a better grace than her other sister, Suellen. When the privations and losses of the Civil War take their toll on her gentle nature she finds comfort and peace in her religious faith.

O'Hara, Ellen
From *Gone With the Wind* by Margaret Mitchell

A gracious, elegant and refined woman twenty-eight years younger than her husband, Ellen O'Hara runs Tara, her plantation home, with an effective mixture of compassion and discipline. Always lady-like, she achieves her end with soft words and reproachful glances. She is revered by her husband, whom she married after the cousin she loved was killed in a fight, and adored by her three daughters, particularly the oldest, Katie Scarlett, who knows she can never live up to her mother's example of gentle goodness however hard she tries. Ellen is the mainstay of the O'Haras, the deceptively soft cog around which the rest of the family turns.

O'Hara, Gerald
From *Gone With the Wind* by Margaret Mitchell

The owner of Tara, a rich cotton-growing plantation in Clayton County, Georgia, Gerald O'Hara is a self-made man who came to America from Ireland with next–to-nothing and used his wits to make his way in life. By persuading the refined, well-bred Ellen Robillard to be his wife, Gerald has become socially acceptable, and his three children – Katie Scarlett, Suellen and Carreen – can expect to make good matches with sons from neighbouring plantations. Yet despite his veneer of respectability, Gerald remains rough around the edges; he drinks too much, rides recklessly and generally exerts his strong will. Having made his own way in life he knows the value of stability and is passionate about his adopted country and his land. Tara, his wife and family mean everything to him and without them he would be a broken man.

O'Hara, Scarlett
From *Gone With the Wind* by Margaret Mitchell

The oldest child of first-generation Irish immigrant Gerald O'Hara and Ellen, his genteel wife, Scarlett (real name Katie Scarlett) grows up at Tara, a slave-owning plantation in Clayton County, Georgia. Her story begins in 1861, just as the South is poised to secede from the United States of America and form a Confederacy, an action that results in civil war. A strikingly pretty and vivacious 16-year-old with dark hair, green eyes and a tiny waist, Scarlett knows how to make

Cropped screenshot of Vivien Leigh as Scarlett O'Hara from the trailer for the film version of *Gone with the Wind*, retouched by Wilfredor.

young men think she is the most fascinating and ravishing female they have ever met. At first glance her personality is not impressive as she is spoilt, wilful, superficial and vain. She flirts outrageously with the local boys, trampling heedlessly over the feelings of their outraged sweethearts. However, her heart belongs to Ashley Wilkes, the son of a neighbouring plantation owner and she has long since made up her mind to marry him. As she is used to getting her way she is not prepared for disappointment and when things don't go to plan, her impulsive and irrational reaction has long-lasting repercussions.

The reality is that beneath Scarlett's self-centred and shallow exterior, a much more complex character exists. Although unable to empathise with others, and far too easily governed by her temper and selfish desires, she does have a conscience; admittedly it doesn't surface very often but when it does Scarlett can be relied upon to do the right thing, albeit grudgingly. One of the main problems with her personality is that she possesses more drive, vitality and chutzpah than is considered fitting for a genteel Southern belle. She is frustrated by the restrictions society places on her and, lacking tact and guile, she follows her own path come what may. This wins her many enemies, but since she cares for the opinion of very few people, their dislike doesn't bother her. In times of need Scarlett is courageous, resourceful and tenacious and when it comes to business she is very astute, but in affairs of the heart she is infuriatingly slow on the uptake. Her dogged devotion to Ashley blinds her to the real love of her life, and for a long time she fails to recognise the strong bond of friendship that has formed between herself and someone she has always preferred to regard as an enemy. Ultimately, Scarlett is a survivor and as long as she has the security that her beloved Tara represents, she will always rise from the ashes of her latest disaster to make the best of whatever life throws at her.

O'Hara, Suellen
From *Gone With the Wind* by Margaret Mitchell

Middle daughter of Gerald and Ellen O'Hara, Suellen (real name Susan Elinor) is less pretty than her older sister Scarlett and less tractable than her younger sister, Carreen. Selfish and small-minded, she constantly feels slighted and hard done by, especially where Scarlett is concerned. As events turn out, Suellen is right to distrust and resent her older sister because when the O'Hara family is at its lowest ebb, Scarlett deals her a cruel blow, not out of spite, but in order to save her beloved Tara. Not surprisingly, this further embitters Suellen who is faced with the terrible prospect of dying an old maid. Luckily for her, fate has different plans.

Old Agnes
From *The Town House* by Norah Lofts

In her youth Agnes married a game warden and lived with him in a cottage that came with his job. She kept the cottage tidy and snug, fully enjoying all the cooking and cleaning. Then after just two years of married life and with a baby on the way, her husband died of a fever and Agnes was turned out of her home. Mad with grief and worry, she took to drink, lost her baby and spent many years thereafter existing in poverty and squalor, using any spare penny she could obtain to get drunk. When she first appears in the book she is still living a desperate, hand-to-mouth existence, but a casual act of kindness to a grieving man is about to change her life forever.

P is for Parker, Parr, Philpot and more

Parker, Jane   RP
From **The Other Boleyn Girl** by Philippa Gregory

A rabbit-faced lady-in-waiting to Queen Katherine, Jane Parker is chosen by the ambitious Boleyn/Howard families as a suitable wife for George, brother of Mary and Anne Boleyn. Her bridegroom is extremely reluctant and he avoids Jane as much as he can, greatly preferring the company of his beautiful sisters and his roistering male companions to that of his fiancée. This obvious aversion cannot be anything but hurtful to Jane, yet she makes no attempt to endear herself to him. Instead, she continues as she has always done, listening at keyholes, spying on fellow ladies-in-waiting – particularly Mary and Anne Boleyn – and passing on sleazy titbits of information to anyone willing to listen to them. This insatiable, unsavoury appetite for gossip ultimately combines with her resentment of the Boleyns to devastating effect.

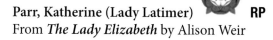

Parr, Katherine (Lady Latimer) RP
From *The Lady Elizabeth* by Alison Weir

Already twice-widowed when she comes to the attention of Henry VIII, Katherine Parr is an intelligent and good-looking woman of 31 with auburn hair, hazel eyes and a gentle and dignified manner. Now that her second husband is dead she hopes to be able to marry Thomas Seymour, the man she loves, but her plans are scuppered when the king decides he wants her for himself. Although she is reluctant, Katherine dutifully accepts his proposal and becomes his sixth and final wife.

Finally it seems that Henry has made a good choice. Katherine has a loving relationship with all three of his children, and interests herself in the education of Elizabeth and Edward. She persuades Henry to allow Elizabeth to live at court, and uses her nursing skills to tend his stinking leg wound when it troubles him. Such is Henry's regard for her that when he goes to war in France he leaves her in charge of the country. However, her secret sympathy with religious reformists leaves her dangerously open to attack from enemies such as the staunchly Catholic Bishop Gardiner. Furthermore, her cleverness does not make her immune to the charms of a handsome rogue, nor does it help her notice when that same rogue is shamelessly attempting to seduce her stepdaughter under her very nose.

Patch RP
From *We Speak No Treason* by Rosemary Hawley Jarman

An entertainer working at the court of Edward IV, Patch (real name Piers) is a professional fool who jokes, capers and performs tricks for the amusement of the king and his courtiers. Although the jesting business is in his blood - his father and grandfather were also fools and an ancestor was a jongleur during the reign of Richard the Lionheart - he honed his craft travelling with a group of itinerant minstrels, playing at the great houses they visited. Now his father is dead and his mother owns a comfortable cook shop business in London where Patch visits her whenever he remembers.

Jester illustration extracted from an opera poster. Image © Chalumeau used under the Creative Commons Attribution-Share Alike 3.0 Unported license.

A short, lithe, acrobatic man, Patch has tight, buttery curls and grey eyes which take in more than his light-hearted buffoonery suggests. Although he is aged about 18 when he makes his first appearance in the book, the lines on his comical face belie his youth. He is bold and unafraid to take risks, and as a result, the king values him even though his immediate superior, the Master of Revels, disapproves of his brazen antics. Patch has a quick temper, and his time at court has taught him to be cynical, but underneath all the tomfoolery he hides a good heart and a profound capacity for devoted, lasting love.

Percy, Henry   **RP**
From *The Other Boleyn Girl* by Philippa Gregory

The heir to the Duke of Northumberland, Henry is young, handsome and inexperienced at the start of the book when he is serving in the household of Cardinal Wolsey, the most powerful man in the country apart from the king. Susceptible to beauty and charm, he falls headlong in love with a young woman at court and allows her to rush him into a betrothal even though he knows the Cardinal and his family will disapprove of the match.

When Wolsey finds out about the betrothal he orders Henry to break it even though it has been consummated, but Henry holds firm until he is tricked into believing his beloved has abandoned him. Thereafter, he makes a loveless marriage with the noblewoman his family has chosen for him but still harbours romantic feelings for the girl he loved and lost.

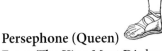

Persephone (Queen)
From *The King Must Die* by Mary Renault

The Queen of Eleusis, a city about two hours' ride from Athens, Persephone rules a matriarchal society in which women make the laws and men are used only for mating and fighting. Every year she presides over a sacred ritual in which her current husband is obliged to wrestle a challenger; they wrestle to the death and if the challenger wins he becomes king in turn. His reward is to sleep with the queen and enjoy a life of luxury but only until his allotted year is up, whereupon he will be expected to wrestle to the death.

A stately woman of about 27, Persephone has copper-red hair, a broad face and a fine figure. She is a strong,

Persephone shown in fragment of Great Eleusinian Relief, image © Marie-Lan Nguyen used under the Creative Commons Attribution 2.5 Generic license.

sensual woman whose life is ruled by her devotion to the Mother Goddess. Her name, Persephone, is sacred and men are forbidden to speak it so she is also called by her other name, Core.

Pert Tom
From *The Town House* by Norah Lofts

An itinerant of indeterminate age who travels from town to town with his dancing bear, Tom is a black-hearted rogue who pursues his own selfish ends regardless of the consequences. His affable manner disguises a cunning character devoid of conscience.

Philpot, Elizabeth   **RP**
From *Remarkable Creatures* by Tracy Chevalier

A respectable solicitor's daughter with three sisters, only one of whom is married, and one brother, Elizabeth grows up in London where she is able to enjoy the conversation of learned men discussing the latest scientific ideas. Following the death of her parents, however, her brother decides to marry and makes it clear that he expects his unmarried sisters to move out of the family home in order to make way for his bride. Thus, Elizabeth finds herself at the age of 25 swapping life in a large, comfortable house in London for a small cottage in Lyme Regis with her sisters Louise and Margaret for company, and a faithful servant, Bessie, to look after them all. With an income of just £150 per annum for the three sisters to exist on, their lifestyle is of necessity fairly frugal but Elizabeth soon adapts to her new circumstances, enjoying the novelty of not having to share her home with a man for the first time in her life.

Although she is still young when the book begins, Elizabeth has already resigned herself to perpetual spinsterhood. Her appearance is not conducive to attracting a husband as she is small, bony and has a prominent jaw of which she is painfully aware, and her manner when speaking to men is scarcely better as she is unable to flirt. Instead, she talks to them about serious matters which they find off-putting in a woman. Yet the realisation that she is unlikely to find a husband does not make Elizabeth immune to the attraction of a good-looking man, particularly one who shares her interest in geology. As newcomers to Lyme Regis, the Philpots are introduced to local society and made moderately welcome, but Elizabeth finds assemblies, card parties and so on tiresome. Instead, rather oddly as far as society is concerned, she prefers to study the area's natural history and takes long walks on the beach. There she discovers an ammonite which sparks a lifelong passion for fossils. Her attempts to discuss this interest with the local gentry prove frustrating, but when she meets Mary Anning, a working class girl with a natural gift for fossil hunting, she finally finds someone who understands the fascination of these relics from another era.

Philpot, Louise (real name Mary) **RP**
From *Remarkable Creatures* by Tracy Chevalier

The oldest of the Philpot siblings, Louise is very tall with large hands and feet. Although she is a sensible woman, in public she is very quiet and retiring, a quality which, when she was young and in the company of potential suitors, had a tendency to make them think she was judging them. Having long since given up any thoughts of marriage, Louise contents herself with her love of botany and gardening. At the Philpot sisters' new home in Lyme Regis she takes charge of the garden, devoting to it all the time and energy Elizabeth spends on fossil hunting.

Philpot, Margaret **RP**
From *Remarkable Creatures* by Tracy Chevalier

The youngest Philpot sister, Margaret is 18 when she moves from London to Lyme Regis with her sisters Elizabeth and Louise. While her sisters are resigned to spinsterhood, Margaret is still young enough to entertain hopes of finding a husband, and when she first enters Lyme society these hopes are encouraged as her youth and novelty value make a favourable impression on the community. Although not precisely pretty – her face is too long and her mouth too thin for that – Margaret is fresh and lively, and her lovely dark ringlets and long, graceful arms make her attractive enough to have no shortage of dancing partners. At first she is very happy flitting from ball to ball, making friends, playing cards and generally being sociable, but disappointment sets in when a nascent romance fails to develop. Insufficiently rich to attract a fortune-hunting husband and insufficiently pretty to make men overlook her lack of money, Margaret seems destined to lose her bloom and become another Philpot spinster.

Pieter
From *Girl With A Pearl Earring* by Tracy Chevalier

Son of a prosperous butcher (also called Pieter), Pieter is a tall, handsome youth with thick curly blond hair and bright blue eyes. A decent young man, he will make someone a good husband – and not just because a butcher's wife and family need never go hungry. Once he meets the girl he wants to marry, he pursues her with patience and dogged determination.

Pittheus (King)
From *The King Must Die* by Mary Renault

King of Troizen, a small city in Greece, Pittheus is a big man who has ruled his land wisely for twenty years. In that time he has fathered many children, legitimate and otherwise, but all the sons born in wedlock have died, leaving his daughter Aithra his sole legitimate child. Now her son, Theseus, is being raised as Pittheus's heir.

Pole, Miss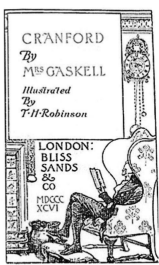
From **Cranford** by Elizabeth Gaskell

Another of the unmarried elderly ladies who populate the small northern town of Cranford, Miss Pole is an assiduous gossip, expert at insinuating herself into any situation in order to glean interesting snippets of information. As obsessed as any of her friends with appearing respectable and genteel, she is excitable and prone to exaggeration and rumour-mongering. She may once have pursued the unmarried rector with a view to matrimony, but now pretends to regard the institution of marriage with abhorrence.

Title page of Cranford with illustration by T. H. Robinson, 1896.

Poole, Grace
From *Jane Eyre* by Charlotte Brontë

A mysterious servant working at Thornfield Manor, Grace Poole is a plain, solid, red-haired woman in her mid-thirties. Apparently employed to sew and generally assist the housemaid, she is said to be responsible for the eerie noises and strange occurrences that sometimes disturb the household. In fact, she has a secret, very specific role in the house, but her effectiveness is sometimes compromised by her fondness for alcohol.

Price, Fanny
From *Mansfield Park* by Jane Austen

Probably Jane Austen's least engaging heroine as far as modern sensibilities are concerned, Fanny Price is a shy young woman of 18 when the main action of the story begins (although she is first encountered as an equally shy 10-year-old). Passive, timid and lacking in spirit, she is the absolute antithesis of lovely, vivacious Elizabeth Bennet. Yet Fanny is not without admirable qualities: she is loyal and loving, and has good instincts and an unexpectedly resolute character which enables her to reject an unwelcome suitor, even though by doing so, she incurs the disapproval of those she habitually seeks to please.

C.E. Brock illustration of Fanny Price, 1908.

Taken as a child from a seedy, overcrowded home to live as a charity case with her much grander relations at Mansfield Park, Fanny initially suffers agonies as she gets to know her uncle, aunts and cousins. Sir Thomas terrifies her, Lady Bertram is vague and careless, Mrs Norris bullies and verbally abuses her, and as for her four cousins, the oldest scarcely notices her existence, while the two girls make her an object of scorn and spite. Only one, Edmund, is kind and concerned for her well-being so it is hardly surprising that she falls deeply in love with him. Fanny knows, however, that her chances of marrying him are virtually nil, partly because of her humble status but also because much as Edmund genuinely loves her, he does not think of her in a romantic light.

R is for Radlett, Reed, Rochester and more

Radlett, Linda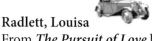
From *The Pursuit of Love* by Nancy Mitford

The second oldest daughter of Lord and Lady Alconleigh, Linda is the central character in *The Pursuit of Love*. Her father's favourite child, she is vibrant, wildly funny, impulsive, highly strung and extreme in her emotions. She is also beautiful, with regular features, straight brown hair, large blue eyes and a furious intensity that is evident even when she is laughing, which is often. Her various attempts to find the romantic love she craves form the bedrock of the story. Believed to be a distillation of the personalities of the author's famous sisters, Linda is an eccentric, fascinating and occasionally infuriating, force of nature, adored by many – including her cousin Fanny who narrates the book - and despised by a few.

Radlett, Louisa
From *The Pursuit of Love* by Nancy Mitford

The oldest daughter of Lord and Lady Alconleigh, Louisa has the good looks common to all her siblings and some of their spirit. She teases her sensitive sister Linda remorselessly and generally joins in with the family banter. However, she is frightened of her ferocious father who despises her because he thinks she is a fool. Consequently, at the earliest opportunity she swaps her nervous

existence at Alconleigh for a happy if unexciting life as wife and mother.

Rancon, Lady
From *The House at Old Vine* by Norah Lofts

The widow of a great knight, Maude Rancon is intent on restarting her family's once successful wool business at Old Vine, her house near Baildon in Suffolk. She is now an old lady but her wits are still sharp and she commands the respect of most people with her quietly courteous manners. Her only son is dead but she has a young grandson, Walter, who helps her run the business.

Rancon, Walter
From *The House at Old Vine* by Norah Lofts

A serious young man, Walter lives at Old Vine in Baildon with his grandmother, Lady Maude Rancon. He has strong principles which, whilst admirable, may one day prove to be his undoing.

Reed, Eliza
From *Jane Eyre* by Charlotte Bronte

The youngest daughter of Jane Eyre's aunt and uncle, Mr and Mrs Reed of Gateshead Hall, Eliza is a hard and selfish creature, jealous because she is less beautiful than her older sister. Ultimately she chooses a religious way of life but her vocation is driven by self-righteousness rather than genuine Christian goodness.

Reed, Georgiana
From *Jane Eyre* by Charlotte Bronte

The oldest daughter of Jane Eyre's aunt and uncle, Georgiana is a very pretty girl who grows into a beautiful woman. Complacently aware of her good looks, and spoiled and petted by her mother, she is self-obsessed and can be spiteful, but she is not as thoroughly rotten as her brother, nor as vindictive as her sister.

Reed, John
From *Jane Eyre* by Charlotte Bronte

At the start of the book John Reed is a fat, greedy, pasty-faced boy of 14. He is a sadistic and arrogant bully who mercilessly torments his young cousin, Jane Eyre. In the eyes of his doting mother, however, he can do no wrong. Not surprisingly, he grows up wild and undisciplined, drinking to excess and running up vast gambling debts.

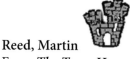

Reed, Martin
From *The Town House* by Norah Lofts

Born in 1381, the year of the failed Peasants' Revolt, Martin is the son of a blacksmith who works on the Norfolk manor of a great nobleman called Lord Bowdegrave. As villeins, neither he nor his father may leave the manor, marry or change their occupation without their Lord's consent. A strong, capable lad, Martin grows up around his father's forge, initially working the bellows and going on to more skilled work as he develops. Although it is hard work, food is plentiful and the family hut provides adequate shelter. Martin's first setback occurs when the parish priest recognises his intelligence and asks permission

Reconstruction of a medieval blacksmith's shop. Image © Marc Werner used under the Creative Commons Attribution-Share Alike 3.0 Unported license

from Lord Bowdegrave to send him to the monks' school in Norwich. Permission is refused because Martin is an only son and cannot be spared from the forge. Unused to determining their own fates, father and son accept this ruling without rancour and Martin continues his training as a blacksmith. Only when he is a grown man of 20 does he again seek permission from Lord Bowdegrave, and this time it is to marry. The reply he is given sets in motion a sequence of events that are to transform Martin's life in ways he never imagined possible.

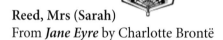

Reed, Mrs (Sarah)
From *Jane Eyre* by Charlotte Brontë

Widow of Jane Eyre's maternal uncle, Mrs Reed lives in comfortable circumstances at Gateshead Hall with her own children - John, Eliza and Georgiana – and Jane, the niece-in-law she reluctantly agreed to care for when her husband died. She is a doting mother, especially to her son whom she indulges to a ridiculous degree, but to the orphan in her care she is cold and deliberately cruel, punishing her childish misdemeanours with excessive harshness.

F.H. Townsend illustration of Mrs Reed with the young Jane Eyre.

Rivers, Diana
From *Jane Eyre* by Charlotte Brontë

A slender, graceful young woman with pale skin and darkish brown curls, Diana has two siblings, Mary and St. John. Well-bred and intelligent, she is obliged to work as a governess because her family lacks money. Vital and spirited, she has a kind, generous personality and is not afraid to state her opinions. When she encounters Jane Eyre in dramatic circumstances she becomes a very supportive friend.

Rivers, Mary
From *Jane Eyre* by Charlotte Brontë

F.H. Townsend illustration of St. John Rivers with one of his sisters and a lady visitor.

Sister of Diana and St. John Rivers, Mary is employed as a governess a long way from home. Physically she resembles her sister except that her hair is a lighter shade of brown. In temperament, she is also rather like Diana, although she is more reserved and her manner is less engaging.

Rivers, St. John
From *Jane Eyre* by Charlotte Brontë

A devout young clergyman in his late twenties, St. John Rivers lives in genteel poverty, usually with just Hannah, an old family retainer, to look after him although when he is first encountered his unmarried sisters, Mary and Diana are visiting. The reason for their visit is the recent death of their father. Very handsome with regular features, large blue eyes and fair hair, he is cold, reserved and utterly dedicated to doing God's work as a missionary. He lives a life of self-denial, refusing to give in to his love for a very eligible young woman because he is convinced she would not make him a good wife. Stern and austere, Rivers is proof positive that good looks and strong faith are not enough on their own to make a man a good marriage prospect.

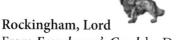

Rochester, Mr Edward Fairfax
From *Jane Eyre* by Charlotte Bronte

The wealthy, well-travelled master of Thornfield Manor, Mr Rochester is a man with a past he is keen to keep hidden. Having sowed his wild oats as a young man – and paid a heavy price for doing so – he is now in need of peace and serenity. Unconventional, obstinate and moody, he is also on occasion capable of immense charm. Living alone at Thornfield with just his housekeeper and young ward for company, he broods on the past and the unhappy situation in which he finds himself. To his surprise, however, he discovers there is comfort and contentment to be found in a most unexpected quarter.

   Although not conventionally handsome, Rochester's dark, Byronic appearance has a compelling quality that many women find attractive. He is also intelligent and passionate, but his morality is dubious, and the dark secret he conceals has the power to destroy him should it ever become known.

Rockingham, Lord
From *Frenchman's Creek* by Daphne du Maurier

A close friend of Sir Harry St. Columb and a keen admirer of Dona, Sir Harry's beautiful wife, Lord Rockingham is a dissolute rake who rackets about London, proceeding from theatre to tavern to gaming table, behaving badly and attempting to seduce his friend's wife at every opportunity. His narrow, cat-like eyes and knowing smile are sure signs that he is not to be trusted, but although Dona St. Columb is shrewd enough to pick up the clues, her dim-witted husband is not. Unluckily for Dona, the sinister Rockingham is obsessed with her, scrutinising her every word, action and expression with unhealthy avidity.

de Roet, Katherine   **RP**
From *Katherine* by Anya Seton

Aged fifteen-and-a-half at the start of the book which is set in fourteenth century England, Katherine is the orphaned daughter of an obscure royal herald from Hainault and his wife, a girl from Picardy who died giving birth to Katherine. Following the death of her father, fighting in France for Edward III shortly after he had been knighted by the same monarch, 10-year-old Katherine and her 13-year-old sister Philippa were sent to England where they were given into the care of Edward III's consort, Queen Philippa. The older girl was immediately given a minor post in the queen's household, but as Katherine was as yet too young to be useful, she was packed off to be raised in a convent. Now, five years later, at the urging of Philippa de Roet the Queen has remembered Katherine and has summoned her to court.

It is clear from the outset that Katherine is possessed of a remarkable beauty. She is tall, with large grey eyes fringed by dark lashes, long, burnished bronze hair and a full, sensuous mouth. Her unblemished complexion is milky white with a rose flush on her cheekbones, and her teeth are small and white. Her smile is both radiant and wistful. Yet lovely as she is, Katherine is a convent-bred innocent and though intelligent and educated, she emerges from the nuns' care devout, demure and quite unaware of the potential power of her beauty. Furthermore, while she craves excitement much like any girl her age she is as yet unconscious of her passionate nature that, once woken, will have far-reaching consequences not just for herself and her family, but also the English monarchy. Soon after her arrival at the Windsor court she encounters two men who are to play pivotal roles in her life; one she marries against her will at the urging of her friends and royal patrons, the other she falls helplessly in love with even though he is even further above her station than the man she is being forced to marry. Anya Seton relates Katherine's story with vivid brilliance, creating an unforgettable portrait of a woman whose life careers backwards and forwards from triumph to tragedy, and for whom the reader can feel genuine empathy.

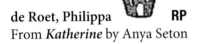

de Roet, Philippa **RP**
From *Katherine* by Anya Seton

A brisk, no-nonsense young woman of about 19 when the book begins, Philippa has been living at court in the household of Queen Philippa for over five years. Through her honesty and efficiency she has found favour with her namesake and now holds the post of Queen's panterer which involves keeping the pantry maids on their toes. Through the queen's good offices she has just become engaged to a young man called Geoffrey Chaucer. It is not a love match but she likes him well enough and feels his prospects are good if only he can be persuaded to put aside his incessant scribbling.

Unlike her sister, Philippa does not have a romantic disposition and her appearance is in marked contrast to Katherine's, as she is small, dark and 'plump as a woodcock'. Bustling and busy, she loves her sister and wants the best for her, but in Philippa's practical mind this translates to nothing more than early marriage to a sensible, experienced man of modest rank.

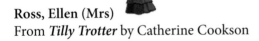

Ross, Ellen (Mrs)
From *Tilly Trotter* by Catherine Cookson

Married to the parson of Tilly Trotter's County Durham village, Ellen Ross is a petite 26-year-old with light brown hair and eyes that are a startlingly clear blue. Animated and impulsive, she is not particularly suited to the life of a country parson's wife because she has no truck with stuffy conventions and is inclined to behaviour that shocks the deeply conservative villagers. However, she has a good heart and cares passionately for the welfare of others, hence her interest in educating miners. When faced with a crisis, she reacts promptly and decisively even though she puts herself at risk by doing so.

Rushworth, Mr
From *Mansfield Park by* Jane Austen

Dim, dull Mr Rushworth is a young man with one important thing in his favour – he is the wealthy owner of a large estate not too far from Mansfield Park. This makes him interesting to Maria Bertram who is in a

C.E. Brock illustration of Mr Rushworth, 1908.

hurry to marry and get away from the stultifying atmosphere of home. Although he is generally slow on the uptake, he is made uneasy by Maria's flirtation with Henry Crawford but isn't perceptive enough to realise that if she misbehaves before her marriage, she's unlikely to be any better once she has become Mrs Rushworth.

Russell, Lady
From *Persuasion* by Jane Austen

Anne Elliot's godmother and a close family friend, Lady Russell is a sensible, middle-aged widow who loves Anne and is one of the few people in her intimate circle with the wit to appreciate her fine qualities. However, eight years ago she did Anne a grave disservice when she was instrumental – together with Sir Walter Elliot – in persuading her to break off her engagement to Captain Wentworth, a naval officer who at the time had no fortune and no eminent connections. Her genuine affection for Anne and desire for her well-being is always tempered slightly by the undue respect she feels for people of rank and fortune. Nevertheless, she tries to look out for what she perceives to be Anne's best interests.

S is for Seymour, Sidney, St. Columb and more

St. Pol, Jordan de
From *Niccolò Rising* by Dorothy Dunnett

Introduced initially as the Vicomte de Ribérac, the true identity of this imposing middle-aged nobleman is soon revealed as Jordan de St. Pol, younger brother of a Scottish lord called Alan de St. Pol. With no land and little fortune, the younger St. Pol went to France in his youth where he found favour with the king and was rewarded with the estate of Ribérac. Having invested his newfound fortune in trade and shipping, he is now a wealthy and important man who advises the French king. He has been estranged from his adult son, Simon de St. Pol, for some time, but nonetheless keeps informed of what is happening in Simon's life.

Tall and extremely fat, St. Pol dresses sumptuously in fur-trimmed velvet and ornate jewels. He is clean-shaven and has many chins, but more noticeable than anything else are his eyes which are chillingly cold even when his mouth is smiling. Despite his sonorous voice and exaggeratedly polite manners, there is something unnatural and deeply unpleasant about the man.

St. Pol, Simon de
From *Niccolò Rising* by Dorothy Dunnett

A Scottish nobleman aged around 34 at the start of the *House of Niccolò* series, Simon de St. Pol expects one day to inherit the Scottish and French estates of his uncle, Alan de St. Pol. As a very young man he lived in France where he earned a reputation for wildness and, disgraced, was sent to live with his uncle in Scotland. Handed over for taming to Alan de St. Pol's steward, he resisted for five years before calming down sufficiently to take over the steward's work when he died. Now, when he arrives in Bruges on business, he is already reasonably rich and will become richer when he inherits his uncle's money, land and title. This makes him, at first glance at least, an attractive proposition for a well-bred girl in search of a husband.

His attractiveness is not solely linked to his circumstances since St. Pol is an extremely handsome man with broad shoulders, a muscular physique, golden hair and a strikingly beautiful face. He dresses elegantly and carries himself with the casual confidence of one born to privilege. When it suits him he he can be amusing and charming, but the smooth, handsome Scot is also arrogant, impatient, and a dangerous enemy when crossed, and he is something of a bully when it comes to dealing with his inferiors. In the opinion of another major character in the book he acts like an oaf and has the talents of a girl. He is also a renowned rake, famous for never being refused by a woman because the rich ones think he'll marry them and the poor ones don't care.

Sadler, Rafe   RP
From *Wolf Hall* by Hilary Mantel

A slight young man of 21, with pale blue eyes and sandy-brown hair, Rafe has lived as part of Thomas Cromwell's household since the age of 7. His father, a respectable man who holds the post of steward with a well-connected knight, put him into Cromwell's care so he can learn about business. Rafe has done well and is now Cromwell's chief clerk. Quick-witted, dogged and sardonic, he has the absolute trust of his master.

A Tudor boy with his father.

Salter, Rhoda
From *Larksleve and Blanche* by Patricia Wendorf

Appearing in the books only through her correspondence with Eliza Greypaull, her friend and cousin, Rhoda is a young woman who has travelled from her close knit community of Buckland St. Mary in Somerset to New York in order to marry George Salter, a butcher recently widowed by the death of Rhoda's sister. With two motherless youngsters to care for, George needed a new wife, and so Rhoda set off to fill the vacancy left by her sister's death. Full of fascinating detail about life in nineteenth century America, her letters to Eliza make an interesting counterpoint to the main story, while Eliza's replies allow certain key events in her life to unfold in her own words.

Sauveterre, Fabrice, Duke of
From *The Pursuit of Love* and *Love in a Cold Climate* by Nancy Mitford

A rich, charming and urbane French aristocrat, Fabrice has spent fifteen years flitting from one mistress to another following the death of his beloved fiancée. Deeply attractive to women despite being short, stocky and very dark, he is renowned throughout French and English society for his love affairs. There is, though, a more serious side to Fabrice. He knows that war is coming and is determined to do his bit to

1930s Paris, home of Sauveterre.

defend France when the Nazis arrive. He features prominently in *The Pursuit of Love* but makes just a cameo appearance in *Love in a Cold Climate*.

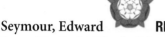

Seymour, Edward   **RP**
From *The Lady Elizabeth* by Alison Weir
Originally a relatively unimportant gentleman at the court of Henry VIII, Edward's star rises when his sister Jane secures the affections of the king and becomes his wife. He is then made Earl of Hertford and assumes the very grand mannerisms of the newly ennobled. Fiercely ambitious, but also cautious and intelligent, Seymour is a sober-looking man with a thin face and a thick russet

Prince Edward, nephew of Edward Seymour.

beard. A secret Protestant, he grasps the chance to remove the last vestiges of Catholicism from England when his nephew, Henry's son Edward, inherits the throne. Seizing control of the Regency Council set up to rule in Edward's minority, he has himself made Duke of Somerset and proclaimed Lord Protector.

Seymour, Jane  **RP**
From *The Lady Elizabeth* by Alison Weir

The daughter of a relatively unimportant knight, Jane is a rather plump girl with long blonde hair and a very pale, almost marble-like complexion. With blue eyes, a long nose and small mouth, she is not especially attractive until she smiles and then her face becomes beautiful. She is wooed by Henry VIII and marries him very soon after his second wife, Anne Boleyn is beheaded. Naturally modest, compassionate and kind to Henry's daughters, Jane is a promising queen and she seems to be genuinely loved by Henry who only wants a son from her to be perfectly content. Obedient as ever, Jane duly delivers an heir, but at a terrible personal cost.

Jane Seymour

Seymour, Thomas **RP**
From *The Lady Elizabeth* by Alison Weir

The brother of Edward and Jane Seymour, Thomas is a bold, daring adventurer, handsome and dashing with a flamboyant personality. He is every bit as ambitious as his brother Edward, but without the careful intelligence that allows Edward to prosper in his bid for influence and high office. What Thomas lacks in intelligence, however, he makes up for in good looks. Blessed with a broad, muscular chest, finely boned features, dark, wicked eyes, a straight nose and a dark, bushy beard, he is a fine physical specimen and women find him hard to resist. When Henry VIII marries Katherine Parr, a woman thought to have been romantically linked to Thomas, he is given a diplomatic mission and then created Lord High Admiral in order to keep him away from court. He returns and is made Lord Seymour of Sudeley when his nephew Prince Edward becomes king. Throwing caution to the wind, he then proceeds to cause trouble for his brother and entangle himself in the lives of the widowed queen and her stepdaughter, Elizabeth.

Sidney, Margot (always known as Sid)
From *The Cazalet Chronicle* (comprising 4 novels: *The Light Years, Marking Time, Confusion* and *Casting Off*) by Elizabeth Jane Howard

Sid is the daughter of a Portuguese Jewess and a classical musician who abandoned his wife and two children for a new life in Australia. She had a hard, impoverished childhood which involved caring for her ailing mother who eventually died of TB, and coping with Evie, her difficult and demanding sister. She makes just enough to live on working as a violin teacher, sharing her home and sometimes her wages with Evie. The great passion of her life is Rachel Cazalet who returns her affections while insisting on keeping the relationship asexual. This torments Sid, as does Rachel's selfless devotion to her family which frequently results in the ruination of plans she and Sid have made. As a result, much as Sid adores Rachel, a slightly bitter edge has crept into their relationship which, in any case, is usually conducted long distance by letter and the occasional telephone call. Believed by the Cazalets to be no more than Rachel's great friend, Sid is always made welcome at Home Place – her musicality makes her a particular favourite with the Duchy – but because of her job and the dependence of her sister she is unable to visit very often.

Sid is described as having cropped hair, a nut-brown face and 'eloquent, wide-apart eyes' in a face that usually looks tired. She wears tweed suits and carefully tied cravats. Given her appearance, her adoption of a male name and her forthright, 'What ho!' manner of speaking, it is perhaps surprising that none of the Cazalets realise the true nature of her relationship with Rachel (although, engrossed as they all are in their own concerns, they scarcely have time to consider Rachel as anything more than a very dear, conveniently obliging daughter, sister or aunt who, due to her unmarried state, has no real life of her own and is, therefore, more than happy to dedicate herself to their needs). Although she is generally fond of the Cazalets, this attitude towards Rachel hurts Sid, as does their occasional and accidental anti-Semitism.

Smeaton, Mark   **RP**
From *Wolf Hall* by Hilary Mantel

A young musician of Flemish origin, Smeaton is working for Cardinal Wolsey when he first appears in the narrative. He is an arrogant young man who feels no loyalty or compassion for his employer.

Smith, Harriet
From *Emma* by Jane Austen

The illegitimate daughter of an unknown father, Harriet is brought up at a school for young ladies run by Mrs Goddard in Highbury. Having completed her education, Harriet now lives with Mrs Goddard as a paying guest, the arrangement paid for by her mysterious benefactor. The rich and socially influential Emma Woodhouse is impressed by Harriet's pretty looks - a plump figure, blue eyes, fair hair and a sweet face – and although she realises she is not terribly bright, she is flattered by the girl's gentle manners and deferential air. Convinced that Harriet must be the daughter of a nobleman, Emma takes her under her wing and decides to arrange an advantageous marriage for her. For her part, Harriet is very grateful for the attention and is beguiled by her new friend's ambitions for her, even though she is already more than half in love with someone else.

C.E. Brock illustration of Harriet Smith, Robert Martin and Mrs Martin, 1909.

Smith, Mary
From *Cranford* by Elizabeth Gaskell

The book's narrator, Mary Smith gives little away about her personal circumstances. The young daughter of a brusquely capable businessman, she lives in Drumble, a large town some twenty miles distant from Cranford, but pays long, frequent visits to the quiet little town where she stays with Deborah and Matty Jenkyns who are old family friends, and possibly even distant relatives. Knowing the town's residents very well, she has a lively interest in everything that occurs in Cranford society and takes every possible step to help Miss Matty when the occasion arises.

Smith, Mrs
From *Persuasion* by Jane Austen

A former school friend of Anne Elliot, Mrs Smith is a semi-invalid who has fallen on hard times. Widowed and with very little money, she lives in rented rooms in

Title page for 1909 J.M. Dent & Co edition of *Persuasion*.

a seedy part of Bath, relying on her well-informed nurse for news of the outside world. She is delighted when her kind friend Anne comes to the city and makes the time to visit her regularly. Her personal circumstances could be much better than they are if only a man she once thought of as a friend would bestir himself on her behalf.

Snaith, Alderman
From *South Riding* by Winifred Holtby

A confirmed bachelor, Anthony Snaith is a very wealthy man living in a comfortable modern house situated on a hill between the large industrial town of Kingsport and the seaside resort of Kiplington. Psychologically scarred by an encounter with paedophiles when he was a young boy living with his maiden aunt in Kingsport, he now eschews intimate relationships with other humans, preferring the warmth and companionship of cats. A clever, fastidious man with a quiet voice, he amuses himself with Council schemes, cultivating allies and advancing his plans without ever clearly revealing his hand. He is small, neat and precise, with horn-rimmed spectacles, long, pale eyelashes, and a taste for wearing innocuous grey suits.

Sopwith, Eileen
From *Tilly Trotter* by Catherine Cookson

Having produced four children for her husband Mark Sopwith, 37-year old Eileen has decided to put an end to the physical side of her relationship with her husband by becoming a semi-invalid. Four years earlier, she took to her couch with vague female complaints and now refuses to stir from her bedroom for anything. As a result, her household is in chaos – the children run wild, the servants steal and swindle, and her frustrated husband is nearing the end of his tether. None of this makes any impression on selfish Eileen who sees her children for five minutes once a day, and at all other  times, relies on her creepy maid, Mabel Price, for companionship.

Sopwith, Mark
From *Tilly Trotter* by Catherine Cookson

A member of the landed gentry with an estate and coal mine in County Durham, 40-something Mark Sopwith is a man beset with problems. His mine is failing, his children are unruly, his servants are cheating him and his wife has decided to become an invalid in order to avoid her marital duties. He is an inherently decent man who takes an interest in the welfare of his workers, ensuring their cottages are habitable and permitting them to educate themselves, unlike his neighbour Mr Rosier who immediately sacks any miner daring to learn to read and write. But even though Sopwith is a considerate employer by the standards of the time, there are young children working twelve-hour shifts in his mine, crawling on their hands and knees as they haul coal-filled carts to the surface. This is not because he is heartless, but because it is accepted practice, and he hasn't ever stopped to consider what it really means. Lonely, weary and sexually frustrated, Sopwith is an unhappy man desperately in need of some affectionate female companionship.

Sopwith, Matthew
From *Tilly Trotter* and *Tilly Trotter Wed* by Catherine Cookson

Aged 10 at the start of the *Tilly Trotter* trilogy, Matthew is the oldest of Mark and Eileen Sopwith's four children. He has fair curly hair and an angelic appearance, but there's nothing angelic about his personality for he is a disobedient, wilful little boy who delights in tormenting his nursery maids and inciting his siblings to do likewise. It remains to be seen whether his delinquency is caused by his mother's apathetic attitude to her children's upbringing or by some deep-rooted flaw in his character.

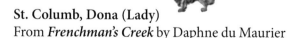

St. Columb, Dona (Lady)
From *Frenchman's Creek* by Daphne du Maurier

A beautiful woman just short of her thirtieth birthday, Dona St. Columb has dark hair worn in ringlets and large, lovely eyes. She is married to Sir Harry St. Columb, a wealthy landowner, and has two small children by him, Henrietta and James. At her luxurious home in a fashionable

Looking into Frenchman's Creek from the Helford River. ©David Stowell, used under the Creative Commons Attribution-ShareAlike 2.0 license.

part of London she lives a life of idleness and plenty, wanting for nothing and outwardly enjoying the risqué, devil-may-care reputation she has acquired by participating in outrageous antics with her husband and his roistering cronies. Yet beneath the surface Dona feels jaded by the incessant round of pointless pranks and over-indulgence, and is suffocated by her adoring husband who irritates her almost to breaking point with his indolence and stupidity. She especially dislikes and distrusts his closest friend, Lord Rockingham, who is attempting to seduce her and once managed to steal a kiss from her when her guard was down.

The book starts with Dona making an impulsive escape from London with just her children and their nurse for company. The discontent she feels for her London life has become unbearable, and in her need to get away she finds herself instinctively drawn to Navron, her husband's estate on the Helford River in a remote corner of Cornwall. There she finds the peace and serenity she craves and a great deal more besides. Dona is not the most sympathetic heroine, but what she lacks in likeability she makes up for in strength of personality. What's more, her dubious morality makes her an interesting and believable character in a book that often requires considerable suspension of disbelief.

St. Columb, Harry (Sir)
From *Frenchman's Creek* by Daphne du Maurier

A prosperous member of Society with estates in Hampshire and Cornwall, and a smart London house, Sir Harry is a good-looking, amiable man with an abundance of good nature and precious little intellect. Fond of his two children and devoted to his lovely, capricious wife, he is happy to spend his life carousing with like-minded companions, his two spaniels forever yapping at his heels. The only blight on his contentment is the persistent remoteness of his wife who treats him with affectionate disdain. Harry longs to get closer to her but he is hopelessly adrift when it comes to understanding the complex Dona, and his clumsy efforts simply drive her further away. His naïvety about the intentions of his friend Lord Rockingham towards Dona is part and parcel of his general dim-wittedness.

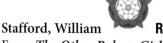

Stafford, William   **RP**
From *The Other Boleyn Girl* by Philippa Gregory

A minor gentleman in the service of the Duke of Norfolk, William Stafford dreams of one day having a small farm of his own with a wife and children to keep him company. For now, however, he serves the Duke and looks with longing at a beautiful young lady-in-waiting who is very much out of his league. Stafford is a decent, handsome young man who wants to make his own way in life away from the toxic Court circle.

Starling, Jem
From *Rebels and Traitors* by Lindsey Davis

A highway robber of some notoriety, Jem Starling is a fit, good-looking rogue aged about 30. In his youth he was apprenticed to a Shoreditch weaver but ran away because his master was cruel, and thereafter took to a life of crime. He thinks he is clever but in reality is no match for the cunning, streetwise slip of a girl who comes into his life.

Steele, Lucy
From *Sense and Sensibility* by Jane Austen

C.E. Brock illustration of Lucy Steele with Elinor Dashwood, 1908.

Lucy Steele and her older, dim-witted sister Anne enter the story when they pay a visit to their distant relative, Mrs Jennings, at Sir John Middleton's house in Devon. In her early twenties, Lucy is pretty, lively and smart, with a civil manner and a sharp wit. She is also sly, scheming, unscrupulous and absolutely committed to marrying well, come what may. This is not necessarily an easy task since she has no fortune, her background is undistinguished and her education has been sketchy at best. Nevertheless, Lucy possesses all the determination and cunning necessary to achieve her end, using an arsenal of flattery, fake humility and false friendship. Unlikeable as she is, given the hand fate has dealt her she can hardly be blamed for wanting to better herself, and since matrimony is the sole career option open to her, she does what she must to achieve her end. In this she is not unlike Thackeray's anti-heroine, Becky Sharp.

Suffolk, Duke of **RP**
From *Wolf Hall* by Hilary Mantel

Henry VIII's great friend, Charles Brandon, Duke of Suffolk is a fair, florid man. Although not overly bright, he is a good, reliable soldier and knows a great deal about hunting. He is currently married to Henry's youngest sister, Mary,

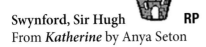

Swynford, Sir Hugh   **RP**
From *Katherine* by Anya Seton

A landed knight in the service of John of Gaunt, Duke of
Lancaster, Hugh Swynford is the antithesis of the chivalrous
knights that grace the court of Edward III. Of Saxon descent,
he despises elegant Norman manners and the rituals of
courtly love. Although he does attend church it is only in
order to keep up appearances because at heart Hugh is an
unreconstructed pagan. Awkward, morose and uncouth, he
is a figure of fun to his fellow knights but they are careful not
to mock him openly because Hugh is a shrewd and terrifying
fighter. In fact he is a devastating force to be reckoned with,
tolerated by his feudal lord for his courage and brute
strength. Living only for battlefield glories, Hugh is
impatient of lesser matters and thus neglects the running of his remote
Lincolnshire estates. This is unwise since his sole income derives from these estates
and if they are badly run his pocket suffers. What he really needs is a sensible wife
with a comfortable dowry who can supervise the estates while he is away fighting.
Unfortunately, before such a wife can be found he becomes wholly fixated on a
very beautiful but penniless new arrival at court.

Hugh's rough-and-ready personality is matched by an equally unenticing
appearance. Chunkily built and with bandy legs, he has a florid face disfigured by
a jagged purple scar that puckers his right cheek. (The scar is said to have come
from a wolf which he strangled with his bare hands). His hair and beard are the
colour and texture of rough ram's wool and his eyes are small and usually scowling.
All in all, he's about as far removed from the stuff of girlish dreams as it is possible
to be whilst remaining human.

T is for Tilney, Trotter, Tudor and more

Tacita, Junila
From the *Falco Series* by Lindsey Davis

Matriarch of the working-class Didius family, Junila
Tacita has been toughened by what today would be
termed the school of hard knocks. Deserted by her
dodgy auctioneer husband when their children were
still small, the ensuing struggle to bring them up

respectably has turned her into an indomitable matron with a sharp tongue and a critical eye. The death of her oldest son, Festus, has been a bitter blow and her anger and resentment is usually directed at Falco, her one surviving son, who consistently fails to live up to her expectations. Despite, or perhaps because of this, she never ceases to interfere in his life, taking it upon herself to clean his apartment, offer unwanted advice and nag him whenever the opportunity presents itself.

Talbot, Christian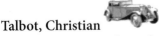
From *The Pursuit of Love* by Nancy Mitford

An extremely attractive and charismatic young journalist with strong Communist sympathies, Talbot is the son of a professor who lives in the same village as Tony Kroesig's parents. With his careless dress sense and intense political views, he makes an immediate impact on the impressionable Linda Radlett. Sadly for her, he turns out to care more for the welfare of the masses than for any individual person.

Tanneke
From *Girl With A Pearl Earring* by Tracy Chevalier

Tanneke is a large, grumbling maid who works at the household of Johannes Vermeer, the painter. In fact the house belongs to Vermeer's mother-in-law, Maria Thins, for whom Tanneke has worked since she was 14. She is now 28 years old, but looks older, and her appearance is not enhanced by her pockmarked face, bulbous nose and thick lips. Petty, jealous and bad-tempered, she is often sloppy in her work yet she retains a fierce loyalty to her employer.

Telaka
From *The Winthrop Woman* by Anya Seton

A scarred, one-eyed 'Indian' woman from the Long Island Siwanoy tribe, Telaka is taken captive by the New England settlers and becomes a maidservant to Bess, central character of *The Winthrop Woman*. She and Bess forge an unusual friendship which endures even after Telaka regains her freedom and rejoins her tribe. A woman with strong mystical qualities, she ultimately helps Bess discover the spiritual peace for which she has always hankered.

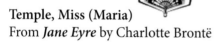

Temple, Miss (Maria)
From *Jane Eyre* by Charlotte Brontë

Tall, fair and shapely, 29-year-old Miss Temple is the Superintendent of Lowood Institute. A kind, compassionate woman, she does what little she can to improve the appalling conditions her pupils have to endure, and she stands up for Jane when she falls foul of the odious Mr Brocklehurst. As Jane grows up she becomes her friend.

THE SCHOOLMISTRESS.

Tew, Kinchin
From *Rebels and Traitors* by Lindsey Davis

A 14-year-old vagrant when she first appears in the novel, Kinchin is 'a starved, scab-encrusted runt' who roams the streets of her native Birmingham searching for food or money to scrounge or steal. Her feckless parents care little for her, regarding her merely as a body to sell to the highest bidder when the time comes. The Tew family have been living on the edges of society since a local landowner enclosed the common land on which they once scratched a meagre living. Now they are unscrupulous scavengers, beholden to no one, and disinterested in the looming power struggle between King and Parliament.

Kinchin is a pitiful scrap, all skin and bone, hollow eyes and tangled, greasy hair. She can't read or write, but her hard life has taught her the value of everything. Looking out for herself without parental support has made her shrewd and streetwise, attributes she is going to need to survive the cataclysm that is about to rip the land asunder.

Theseus
From *The King Must Die* by Mary Renault

The grandson of King Pittheus of Troizen (a small Greek city southwest of Athens), Theseus grows up not knowing the truth about his paternity. His mother tells him he was fathered by Poseidon and, this being Ancient Greece where it's not unusual for gods to bed human girls and produce semi-divine offspring, Theseus initially accepts her story. His doubts begin when he fails to develop the physique he feels appropriate to a demi-god. To compensate for his lack of stature he pushes himself to become a fine athlete and unbeatable wrestler, using his agility and sharp wits to defeat bigger opponents. Finally, when Theseus is about 17 his mother reveals the identity of his father and he sets off to meet him, experiencing a series of fantastic adventures along the way.

Thins, Maria 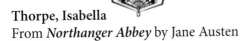 **RP**
From *Girl With A Pearl Earring* by Tracy Chevalier

The mother-in-law of Johannes Vermeer, grey-haired, pipe-smoking Maria Thins shares her home with the painter, her daughter Catharina, and their large, ever-growing family. She is a shrewd old woman who observes everything and hides a benevolent heart beneath her gruff exterior. The true mistress of the household despite her ineffectual daughter's pretence at being in charge, she has the manner of someone accustomed to looking after the less able.

Thorpe, Isabella
From *Northanger Abbey* by Jane Austen

Oldest daughter of an acquaintance of Mrs Allen, Catherine Morland's chaperone in Bath, Isabella is a very attractive, worldly young woman with a coquettish air. Seemingly good-natured and pleasant, she is in truth shallow, superficial and flighty. She befriends and then manipulates the naïve Catherine for her own purposes, but ultimately falls victim to her own unbridled flirtatiousness.

C.E. Brock illustration of Isabella Thorpe walking with Catherine Morland, 1907.

Thorpe, John
From *Northanger Abbey* by Jane Austen

Brother of Isabella Thorpe, the friend Catherine Morland makes in Bath, and a university chum of Catherine's beloved brother James, John is a stout, plain young man who is extremely full of himself for no good reason. Fonder of talking than listening, he has scarcely a sensible thought in his head so his conversation is trivial and tiresome in the extreme. Vain, arrogant and manipulative, his boastful stupidity creates a misunderstanding that is central to the plot.

Tilney, Eleanor
From *Northanger Abbey* by Jane Austen

The youngest of General Tilney's three children and his only daughter, warm-hearted, sweet-natured Eleanor has led a lonely life since her mother died when she was 13. Now aged about 22, she is an attractive young woman with a good figure, pretty face and pleasing manners. Although her solitary life has made her rather quiet and reserved, she has an intelligent, lively mind and engages in bantering conversation with her adored brother Henry. She bears the dictatorial behaviour of her father with quiet composure but is made uncomfortable by his scheming.

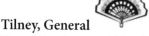

Tilney, Captain Frederick
From *Northanger Abbey* by Jane Austen

Oldest son of General Tilney of Northanger Abbey, Captain Tilney is closer in personality to his father than his younger siblings, Henry and Eleanor. His callous feelings are made evident by his habit of pursuing attractive young ladies without serious intent, heedless of the damage he does to their prospects of making a good marriage.

Tilney, General
From *Northanger Abbey* by Jane Austen

The owner of Northanger Abbey in Gloucestershire, stern, oppressive General Tilney has been a widower for nine years. He is a prestige-obsessed, controlling man who seeks to impose his will on his three children, Frederick, Henry and Eleanor. His domineering personality makes life particularly hard for Eleanor who, as a single woman, is obliged to stay at home while Frederick and Henry can escape into their professions. Although selfish, materialistic and calculating, he is capable of appearing pleasant and attentive when it suits his purpose. When he think his grandiose plans have been thwarted he gives full vent to his anger, but an unforeseen, advantageous event placates his essentially avaricious nature. His worst crime is in valuing material advantage more highly than emotional happiness.

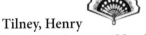

Tilney, Henry
From *Northanger Abbey* by Jane Austen

The second son of General Tilney (see above), Henry Tilney is a clergyman in his mid-twenties. Quite tall and almost handsome, he is intelligent, lively and agreeable with a wry sense of humour and a rather cynical view of life. Literate and something of a people-watcher, he has little in common with his older brother, Frederick, but is very fond of his sister Eleanor, and is a dutiful son to his father even though he does not always agree with him. When he meets Catherine Morland on her first trip to Bath he is amused by her innocence, and gently tries to open her eyes to the realities of human nature. Essentially kind and fair, he can on occasion be roused to anger.

C.E. Brock illustration of Henry Tilney and Catherine Morland.

Trent, Homer
From *Milady Charlotte* by Jean Plaidy

The narrator of the story, Homer is a young girl of 16 living in a remote Cornish parsonage when the novel begins. Her odd name is accounted for by her clergyman father's fixation on having a son called Homer to continue a long line of Homer Trents. His first wife bore two daughters before dying and his second wife, a mysterious travelling fortune teller, stayed with him just long enough to produce yet another girl. Before leaving her husband she mockingly decreed that the child should be called Homer.

Homer has grown up feeling like an outsider in her own home, ignored by her father and ill at ease with her very genteel half-sisters. The only people she feels comfortable with are the servants. Hemmed in by convention and aware that the only feelings she arouses in her family are those of disappointment and disapproval, she longs to escape the oppressive atmosphere of the parsonage. From the moment she hears about her cousin Charlotte who has left home to become an actress, she feels uncannily certain that her fate is bound up with Charlotte's.

Homer is a striking-looking girl with thick, virtually unmanageable nut-brown hair, and eyes that change from tawny to topaz to green depending on her mood.

While not conventionally beautiful she is very attractive but is singularly unaware of the fact. She has a passion for living and an innate ability to sense atmosphere and impending events which she believes she must have inherited from her mother. Although she is young and innocent, she is nobody's fool and quickly learns to stand up for herself. Unlike many of her class, she recognises, and is concerned by, the conditions of miserable poverty in which many people are forced to live. Loyal to her friends and sympathetic to those less well off than she, Homer is also strong-willed, courageous and clear-headed, though when it comes to affairs of the heart she can be frustratingly obtuse.

Treves, Edmund
From *Rebels and Traitors* by Lindsey Davis

A tall, chunkily built lad of 18 with red hair and the pale skin that usually goes with it, Treves is an Oxford scholar when he first appears in the novel. He is at Oxford because he doesn't really know what else to do with his life. His family are minor gentry with little money or influence and with younger children to care for, his widowed mother is struggling to provide for him. Loyal to the king, when help is needed to fortify Oxford against attack from Parliamentarian forces he pitches in willingly. This is how Treves meets an unreliable adventurer called Orlando Lovell who persuades him to join the King's army and hatches a plan for him to marry a rich heiress.

Trotter, Tilly
From *Tilly Trotter, Tilly Trotter Wed* and *Tilly Trotter Widowed* by Catherine Cookson

Arguably the best loved of all Catherine Cookson's heroines, Tilly is a 16-year-old orphan at the start of this trilogy which begins in the north east of England. Since the age of 5 she has been brought up by her kind grandparents who live rent-free in a comfortable cottage on the Sopwith estate, courtesy of the local landowner, Mark Sopwith. Now Tilly looks after her ageing grandparents, chopping wood, fetching water and generally making sure they have everything they need. Her hard work on their behalf has made her very strong although she doesn't look it with her spare, rangy figure. Although Tilly is unusually tall for a woman and completely devoid of womanly curves, she is possessed

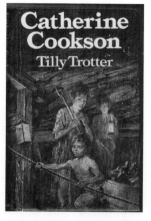

Catherine Cookson
Tilly Trotter

of a beauty most men find irresistible, with rich, shining brown hair and disturbingly clear brown eyes that bewitch the unwary. Tilly herself is unconscious of her beguiling appearance and is disconcerted whenever, as frequently happens, women take an immediate and unaccountable dislike to her, unaware that their hostility is prompted by envy.

As far as personality goes, Tilly is a cheerful, hardworking girl who wishes no harm to anyone. She adores her grandparents, and harbours an innocent love for Simon Bentwood, a neighbouring farmer who shares a secret with Tilly's grandfather. Brighter than average, she has a thirst for knowledge and has learned to read and write with the help of Mrs Ross, wife of the local parson. The same lady has also taught her to dance. What Tilly is to discover in the course of the trilogy is that she is courageous, resourceful and passionate, and has the fortitude to withstand all the injustices and calamities that come her way.

Tudor, Elizabeth   **RP**
From *The Lady Elizabeth* by Alison Weir

Aged not quite 3 when the novel begins, Elizabeth is the daughter of Henry VIII and his second wife, Anne Boleyn. Born a royal princess and declared heir to the throne in the event of her father dying without a male heir, Elizabeth's circumstances change dramatically following her mother's fall from favour. The story begins as the young Elizabeth is given the news of her mother's execution and her own demotion from princess to illegitimate daughter of the king.

Elizabeth is a pretty child with red hair, black eyes, fair skin and freckles. She has a quick wit and is an eager pupil, studying hard and excelling in all subjects, especially languages. Her mercurial temperament keeps her attendants on their toes, while her vanity and love of fine gowns are flaws that give her rather startlingly precocious personality a reassuring touch of imperfection. She adores her magnificent father and revels in being the daughter of such a powerful, almost god-like figure, but she also knows that she sometimes angers him with her forwardness. As for her dead mother, when she learns of her execution she is distraught and the manner of her death – beheading by sword – imprints a shadow of fear on her young mind. After the first shock has waned she never speaks of her mother, but throughout her life Elizabeth cherishes memories of the beautiful woman who brought her gifts, walked with her and played to her on the lute.

Elizabeth is toughened by the experiences of her childhood – in favour one moment, out of it the next – and through the fate of her mother and various stepmothers she learns that for a woman, marriage is a hazardous occupation.

This thought is always uppermost in her mind and so, apart from one dangerous wobble when she is a teenager, an ingrained fear of marriage enables her to resist the temptations of love and romance. The shadow of the block is never far from Elizabeth's consciousness and in her attempts to avoid her mother's fate she learns to rely on her quick wits. She also learns a lot from the religious conflicts of the age as exemplified by the extreme, opposing views of her half-brother Edward and half-sister Mary. Their dogmatism teaches her to develop a tolerant and pragmatic approach to faith. Thus, with a character forged by the traumatic experiences of her youth, when the time comes for Elizabeth to inherit the throne, England will at last have a truly worthy Tudor monarch.

Tudor, Mary   **RP**
From *The Lady Elizabeth* by Alison Weir

A young woman of 20 when the novel begins, Mary is the daughter of Henry VIII and his first wife, Katherine of Aragon. Although she is only a girl and therefore of little importance according to the attitudes of the era, Mary has for many years been Henry's sole legitimate heir because her mother's many pregnancies failed to produce a boy. Her status changes when Henry puts Katherine aside in order to marry Anne Boleyn. Declaring his first marriage to be invalid on the grounds that Katherine was previously married to his dead brother Arthur, Henry makes Mary illegitimate and debars her from the succession. Witnessing her beloved mother being driven from Court has been a bitter experience for the young princess who bravely defies her terrifying father by remaining resolutely faithful to Katherine. Denied permission to visit her mother in a cruel attempt to bring them both to heel, Mary suffers the misery of knowing that Katherine has been neglected and ill.

Only after Katherine's death – which according to some rumours was not caused by natural circumstances – has Mary been able to bring herself to acknowledge, albeit unwillingly, that her parents' marriage was unlawful and that her father is the Supreme Head of the Church of England. Having finally forced her to do what he wanted, Mary has been restored to Henry's favour although she remains illegitimate and has to endure being usurped from her former title of royal princess and heir to the throne by her new half-sister, Elizabeth.

All that she has suffered has had a very detrimental effect on the development of Mary's character. Although naturally inclined to be kind and compassionate, she is too full of resentment and bitterness to forget the injuries of the past. Moreover, heavy reliance on religion during her darkest days has turned her into a devout Catholic unable to tolerate any kind of heresy. While Elizabeth, the daughter of her own mother's nemesis, is still small, Mary is able to put aside her resentment and love her, but this changes as Elizabeth leaves the innocence of childhood behind. Seeing her half-sister turn into an attractive and charming young woman, Mary is forcibly reminded of the scheming Anne Boleyn and all the damage she caused. She also has a recurring doubt about Elizabeth's paternity based on rumours at the time of Anne Boleyn's death that a musician called Mark Smeaton was the father.

Mary's burgeoning dislike of Elizabeth is not helped by the contrast between their appearances. While Elizabeth is young, fresh and pretty, Mary is plain and skinny with a melancholy face and sparse, frizzy red hair. Her hopes of marriage have been repeatedly dashed and now she is rapidly turning into a sour old maid. Ultimately, she is a sad woman whose character has been defined by the ugly struggle between her parents.

V is for Van der Poele, Vane, Vermeer and more

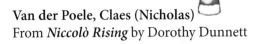

Van Der Leyden, Teddy
From *My Last Duchess* by Daisy Goodwin

The good-looking son of an American society family that has more pedigree than money, Teddy is set on trying to make it as a painter in Paris when the book begins. The only thing that could stand in his way is his liking for Cora Cash, an attractive young heiress for whom he has tender feelings. But Teddy knows that Cora's future husband is meant to have a title, and in any case, he realises that a romantic entanglement will get in the way of his painting.

Van der Poele, Claes (Nicholas)
From *Niccolò Rising* by Dorothy Dunnett

Aged 18 at the start of the novel (the first in a series of eight), Claes is an apprentice dyer with the Charetty company in Bruges which is currently run by the widowed Marian de Charetty. He has been with the Charettys since the age of 10, having been taken in by them because he is the illegitimate son of a distant relative by marriage. Now, as well as serving his apprenticeship in the dye shop, he has become a servant-companion to Felix, the Charetty heir. Built like an oak tree, with dun-coloured hair and dimpled cheeks, Claes is frequently involved with Felix in

mischievous exploits, and just as frequently receives beatings which he accepts uncomplainingly. In fact, Claes seems never to mind about anything, smiling his wide happy smile at the most inappropriate moments. His perpetual good nature makes him popular with most people, especially young women, and it is said that no female under the age of 20 is safe from him.

Claes frustrates those that care for him as he never protects himself and comes across as a little slow-witted. In reality there is nothing slow about Claes who is actually a polymath; brilliant at languages, figures and complex puzzles, he soaks up knowledge and information and has an innate understanding for business, strategy and warcraft. The reader soon learns that nothing is ever as it seems with this fascinatingly complex, multi-layered character.

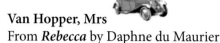

Van Hopper, Mrs
From *Rebecca* by Daphne du Maurier

A rich American woman with more money than delicacy, Mrs Van Hopper travels from one glamorous location to another in search of amusement and gossip. While staying at a hotel in Monte Carlo she accosts Maxim de Winter, a distinguished Englishman who has recently lost his wife, in the hope of obtaining an invitation to visit Manderley, de Winter's beautiful Cornish estate.

Stupid, snobbish, greedy and crass, Mrs Van Hopper has a vast bosom, small piggy eyes and a sharp, staccato voice. Avid for titbits of personal information about anyone remotely well known, she uses a lorgnette to spy on her fellow hotel guests and pounces on the unwary. Devoid of tact and self-awareness, she is insensitive and patronising to the young woman unfortunate enough to work as her paid companion.

van Ruijven   **RP**
From *Girl With A Pearl Earring* by Tracy Chevalier

The rich patron of the painter Johannes Vermeer, van Ruijven has a plump body and face, a moustache and an oily smile. He has an unfortunate reputation for pursuing attractive maids and getting them into trouble.

Vane, Lady Isabel
From *East Lynne* by Mrs Henry Wood

Young, innocent and very beautiful, Isabel is the only child of Lord Mount Severn. Since the death of her mother when she was 13, she has lived alone with her father (except for a full household of servants). Sweet-natured, trusting and affectionate, she is completely unaware that her father is terribly in debt or that he has failed to make even the slightest financial provision for her. Perhaps luckily for Isabel, her beauty is such that many men will overlook her lack of fortune. She has a light, graceful figure, soft dark eyes that sometimes have a sorrowful expression and dark shining curls that fall on her neck and shoulders. Yet this beauty is something of a double-edged sword since it can incite jealousy in less attractive women.

Isabel is quietly spoken, kind-hearted and occasionally there is an almost fey quality to her character, yet for all her sweetness she does have flaws. She is inexperienced, painfully naïve and is all too susceptible to the charms of a dashing cad. Although she recognises the worth of a kind, decent man he doesn't make her heart beat fast as a scoundrel does and her unworldliness makes her doubt the fidelity of the man who truly loves her. These faults are minor and would in any case rectify themselves as Isabel grows older and wiser, if not for the fact that she throws all her happiness away in a moment of madness. Then she learns that Victorian ladies pay a severe price for their mistakes.

Vane, Emma (Mrs)
From *East Lynne* by Mrs Henry Wood

The wife of Raymond Vane, a distant relative of the Earl of Mount Severn and his heir since the Earl has no son, Emma Vane is a disagreeable woman of 26. Plain-faced, she has an elegant figure which she keeps well-dressed and adorned with precious jewellery. Vain, selfish and cold, she feels intense dislike for her husband's relative, the beautiful and naïve Lady Isabel Vane for whom she is acting as chaperone at the start of the book. Towards her cousin, Captain Francis Levison, she feels more warmly than is wise for a married woman and she makes sure she sees Levison whenever she can, not realising or perhaps not caring that he is a dangerous man for an impressionable young girl like Isabel to be around.

Vane, Raymond
From *East Lynne* by Mrs Henry Wood

Heir presumptive to the earldom of Mount Severn, Mr Vane is a tall, stout man of 43. Although he looks severe and has cold manners, he is a very honourable man who always tries his best to do the right thing in difficult circumstances. Unlike his horrible wife, he is kind to his young relative, Lady Isabel Vane.

Varens, Adèle
From *Jane Eyre* by Charlotte Brontë

Jane Eyre's pupil when she goes to Thornfield Manor as a governess, Adèle Varens is first encountered as a child of about 7 or 8. Lively and engaging, she is petite, with small features and an abundance of long, curly hair. Something of a chatterbox, Adèle is frivolous, rather vain, and fond of presents. Despite the dissimilarities in their temperaments, she and Jane quickly become attached to one another.

The daughter of a French dancer called Céline Varens, Adèle lives at Thornfield with Mr Rochester because her mother, formerly Rochester's mistress, has abandoned her. Although he does not believe Céline's claim that he is the child's father, he looks after her all the same.

Vaugon, Jean Pierre de la
From *Milady Charlotte* by Jean Plaidy

A French aristocrat in the diplomatic service of his country, de la Vaugon is visiting London at the start of the book. A friend of the actress Charlotte Walpole, he is an elegant young man who has impeccable manners and dresses like a dandy. Although he is a supporter of the French monarchy, he is aware of the unrest in his country and fears that the populace will not put up with the status quo much longer.

Vermeer, Catharina   RP
From *Girl With A Pearl Earring* by Tracy Chevalier

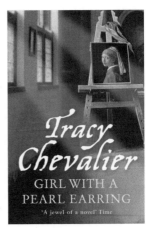

Wife of the painter Johannes Vermeer, Catharina is a tall woman with the rare combination of light brown eyes and blonde hair. When the novel begins she already has five children and is heavily pregnant with another. A clumsy, highly-strung and possessive woman, she lacks the ability to appreciate her husband's work. This failing, coupled with her suspicious nature, creates tension which is felt by all members of the household. With her servants she is an ineffectual mistress, speaking harshly to them but never commanding their respect.

Vermeer, Cornelia   RP
From *Girl With A Pearl Earring* by Tracy Chevalier

Third oldest daughter of Catharina and Johannes Vermeer, Cornelia has bright red hair and the light brown eyes of her mother. Seven years-old when the narrative begins, she is already a cunning, wilful and manipulative child with a decidedly cruel streak.

Vermeer, Johannes   RP
From *Girl With A Pearl Earring* by Tracy Chevalier

A renowned painter in the town of Delft, Vermeer has dark red hair, grey eyes and a long, angular face. He is a quiet man who seems to exist in a world of his own, much of the time oblivious to the comings and goings of his large household. His manner is calm and meticulous and he speaks in a pleasant low-pitched tone. Although he supplements his income by working as an art dealer, his painting is his driving passion and he works with the single-mindedness of the true artist. Even so, his pace is painfully slow and he manages to complete no more than three paintings a year. With only fleeting glimpses of his personality emerging now and then, he remains an enigmatic character throughout the book, yet even so, the author manages to deliver a portrait of a generally well-intentioned man isolated from his family by his art. Should he discover an aesthetic sensibility in an unexpected quarter he is likely to encourage it without stopping to consider the consequences.

Vermeer, Maertge  **RP**
From *Girl With A Pearl Earring* by Tracy Chevalier

The oldest daughter of Catharina and Johannes Vermeer, Maertge is 10-years-old at the start of the story. A merry, friendly girl with dark red hair like her father's, she is old enough to start helping out with domestic chores.

Verus, Decimus Camillus
From the *Falco Series* by Lindsey Davis

A Roman Senator – and therefore by definition a millionaire, but only just - Camillus Verus is a diffident man in his fifties. Married with three grown-up children, Camillus Justinus, Camillus Aelianus and Helena Justina, he lives in a comfortable, but unflashy, freehold mansion in the Capena Gate district of Rome. Although he is of Patrician rank and is on friendly terms with the emperor, he is more down-to-earth and approachable than most of his kind. He becomes acquainted with Marcus Didius Falco when he hires him to investigate a case and although they are far apart in rank, there is genuine liking and respect between them which strengthens over time.

Vespasian, Emperor   **RP**
From the *Falco Series* by Lindsey Davis

Lindsey Davis portrays Vespasian as a solidly built, genial 60-year-old who is ruling his considerable Empire with skill and moderation. Having seized power in AD 69 after eighteen months of upheaval, during which no fewer than four men wore the imperial purple, Vespasian came seemingly from nowhere to restore order and stability. *The Silver Pigs*, the first book of the *Falco Series*, commences in the second year of his reign when his sensible measures are starting to take effect. Although the

Plaster cast of Vespasian in Pushkin museum after original in the Louvre. © Shakko, used under the Creative Commons Attribution-Share Alike 3.0 Unported license.

hero of the series, Marcus Didius Falco is a staunch republican; he likes and respects Vespasian and it seems the feeling is mutual. Vespasian has two sons, Titus Caesar and Domitian Caesar.

Vincy, Fred
From Middlemarch by George Eliot

The son of Walter Vincy, a moderately-successful manufacturer who also happens to be mayor of the town of Middlemarch, Fred is a pleasant enough young man who has been brought up to live beyond his means in the expectation of inheriting a fortune from an elderly relative. A university education, paid for by his parents who are keen to see him climb the social ladder by becoming a clergyman, has failed to turn him from his spendthrift, irresponsible lifestyle. Fred's one saving grace is his genuine love for Mary Garth, his childhood sweetheart, who encourages him to reform by refusing to marry him until he mends his ways and finds a steady job.

Vincy, Lucy
From Middlemarch by George Eliot

The wife of the mayor of Middlemarch, Lucy was born the daughter of an innkeeper and has therefore raised her social standing by marrying Walter Vincy. She is keen for her children – Fred and Rosamund – to advance even further and encourages them to have ideas above their station.

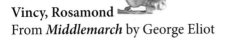

Vincy, Rosamond
From *Middlemarch* by George Eliot

The daughter of Walter Vincy (see below), and his wife Lucy, a relatively low-born innkeeper's daughter, Rosamond is a social climber of the first order. Very beautiful and excessively genteel in her manners, she has a taste for the finer things in life and believes she will get what she wants through her good looks and force of personality. She sets her sights on Tertius Lydgate, the well-born young doctor who arrives in Middlemarch, because she thinks he can raise her socially and give her a life of comfort and ease. Her lack of true affection for him becomes apparent when things go wrong for Lydgate.

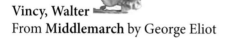

Vincy, Walter
From **Middlemarch** by George Eliot

The mayor of Middlemarch, Walter Vincy is a moderately-successful businessman who has made his money in manufacturing. He has high hopes for the social advancement of his children, Rosamond and Fred. His expectation is that the beautiful Rosamond will make an advantageous marriage and that Fred will become a clergyman. In neither ambition is he destined to be gratified.

W is for Wilkes, Winthrop, Woodville and more

Wales, Prince of **RP**
From *My Last Duchess* by Daisy Goodwin

The heir to the throne, the Prince of Wales is a middle-aged man of average height whose alarming girth has earned him the nickname 'Tum Tum'. He has a florid complexion and cold, heavily-lidded pale blue eyes. Greedy for food and good-looking women, he is easily bored and is a stickler for punctuality. When he speaks he rolls his 'r's in an exaggerated fashion.

Postcard image of the Prince of Wales, later Edward VII.

Walker, Lydia
From *The House at Sunset* by Norah Lofts

A plain girl, Lydia is the only child of a successful, rough-and-ready cattle-dealer and his simple, country-born wife. She grows up at the Old Vine in Baildon, the fine old house her grandfather managed to buy at a bargain price because the owners were in a hurry to sell. Her mother hides away in the kitchen as it is the only room she can feel comfortable in, but Lydia revels in the grandness of her home, soaking up its atmosphere and meeting its ghosts. Determined to be worthy of the house she learns to read and write, develops ladylike airs and recoils from her one suitor because he is not the refined gentleman she dreams of marrying.

Walpole, Charlotte  RP
From *Milady Charlotte* by Jean Plaidy

The daughter of a Norfolk gentleman, Charlotte has shocked her family by swapping her comfortable, dull existence in a large country house for life on the London stage. She first appears in the book as a successful actress with a house of her own in Drury Lane where she enjoys an unconventional yet respectable social life.

Charlotte is very beautiful, with large dark eyes, well-defined brows and curly black hair. She is a warm-hearted, idealistic young woman, kind, generous and always ready to give assistance to those in need. Although her goodness has won her many devoted friends it is not always tempered by wisdom and she has a tendency to imbue people with characteristics they don't necessarily possess.

Warbeck, Captain Davey
From *The Pursuit of Love* and *Love in a Cold Climate* by Nancy Mitford

Second son of a Baron, the Hon. Davey Warbeck is a small, fair man in his forties who enters the life of Fanny Logan, the books' narrator, when he becomes engaged to a member of her family. An affectionate and understanding man, he is knowledgeable about a multitude of subjects and far more cultured than the family he marries into. In his own way, however, he is equally eccentric; obsessed with his health, he is forever taking odd little pills or experimenting with faddish diets. He is fond of Fanny and is devoted to her dazzling cousin, Linda Radlett.

Wareham, Duke of
From *My Last Duchess* by Daisy Goodwin

Ivo Maltravers, the ninth Duke of Wareham, lives quietly at Lulworth, the family's ancient seat in Dorset. A younger brother, he inherited the title eighteen months ago from his brother Guy who died in a riding accident. Now he has a title he never coveted without the means to maintain the aristocratic lifestyle. If he is to save Lulworth his only option is to marry a rich heiress. When the narrative begins he is 30-years-old but looks older because of lines around his mouth and grey flecks in his black hair. He has hooded, dark brown eyes, and a grave face which is considerably lightened by a rare but charming smile. His usually wry and ironic manner fails to mask completely a deep sadness.

Warwick, Earl of   **RP**
From *We Speak No Treason* by Rosemary Hawley Jarman

The most powerful nobleman in the land, Richard Neville, Earl of Warwick has earned himself the sobriquet 'Kingmaker' by helping to win the throne for his young cousin, Edward IV. Adored by the common people for his splendour and largesse as much as for his undoubted skill in battle, Warwick is a proud man who expects much in return for the service he has given and is rankled when his expectations are not met. As a friend he is dedicated and true, as an enemy he is dangerous and deadly.

The Earl of Warwick kneeling before Margaret of Anjou.

Warwick has a regal bearing and clear grey eyes that gaze out of his square, commanding face. He underlines his wealth and status by adorning his costly attire with magnificent jewels and surrounding himself with an extensive retinue that wears his emblem, the Bear and Ragged Staff.

Wentworth, Captain Frederick
From *Persuasion* by Jane Austen

When handsome, gallant Frederick Wentworth makes his first appearance in Persuasion, he is a successful naval captain who has amassed a considerable fortune in the Napoleonic wars and is ready to enjoy his wealth now his country is at peace. Eight years previously, however, he was a more junior officer with no money and only his youth and ambition in his favour. Thus, when he met and fell in love with Anne Elliot he was considered unsuitable by her family and she was persuaded to break off the engagement she had entered into with him. He has spent the intervening years smarting over his hurt feelings and resenting Anne for lacking the backbone to stand up to her family. Intelligent, pleasant and socially adept, Captain Wentworth is now a very eligible bachelor and he is not above enjoying the attention he receives from hopeful young ladies.

C.E. Brock illustration of Frederick Wentworth and Anne Elliot, 1909.

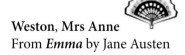

Weston, Mrs Anne
From *Emma* by Jane Austen

Known as Miss Taylor before her marriage to Mr Weston at the start of the book, Anne came to Highbury as governess to Isabella and Emma Woodhouse following the death of their mother. She has been with the family for sixteen years and has become Emma's closest friend and confidante. Her marriage, therefore, leaves Emma feeling somewhat vulnerable, even though her new home, Randalls, is in close enough proximity to Emma's for them to visit every day. She is a good, sensible woman who remains devoted to Emma after her marriage and looks forward to building a relationship with her stepson, Frank Churchill.

Wickham, George
From *Pride and Prejudice* by Jane Austen

Son of the Pemberley estate manager, George Wickham is a good-looking man with 'a fine countenance, a good figure, and very pleasing address'. He arrives in Meryton in order to take up a commission in the local militia. Charming, easy-going and likable, he is the type of man many women, especially the inexperienced, find irresistible. However, all is not what it seems because although Wickham spins a plausible hard luck tale, he is revealed as a thoroughly untrustworthy, wild and unscrupulous character.

C.E. Brock illustration of Mr Wickham meeting the Bennet sisters, 1895.

Wilkes, Ashley
From *Gone With the Wind* by Margaret Mitchell

Handsome, cultured and honourable, Ashley is the heir to the Twelve Oaks plantation which neighbours Tara, the home of the O'Hara family. Where Gerald O'Hara in an Irish immigrant made good, the Wilkes family are products of the Old South with connections to all the best Southern families. Tall, fair and handsome, Ashley is the epitome of the perfect Southern gentleman; he is athletic and an excellent horseman, but is also cultured and refined, taking pleasure

Early hardback edition of *Gone With the Wind*.

in books and intellectual conversation. At the start of the story, with civil war imminent, he is resigned to doing his duty to defend the way of life he loves even though he knows it to be flawed (he intends to free his slaves as soon as he inherits Twelve Oaks). Although he is intelligent enough to know that the South is unlikely to triumph in the coming conflict he nonetheless feels honour bound to fight for the cause. In this he differs from most of the other young bucks in the book who believe, at the start at least, that the South can and will teach the interfering Yankees a lesson they will never forget.

Just as there is conflict between what Ashley believes and what he must stand up for, there is also conflict in his romantic affairs. He loves his sweet, gentle cousin Melanie Hamilton because she is like him in many ways and he knows she will make him a perfect wife. On the other hand, he is drawn to Scarlett O'Hara because she is his opposite – vital, spirited and impulsive with an unladylike lust for life. While his head tells him that Melanie is the woman he must marry, a small corner of his heart finds Scarlett's charms virtually impossible to resist. In due course this weakness for Scarlett will tie him to a life he despises and destroy his self-respect. He is adrift in the new world that emerges after the Civil War and his only hope of recovering his self-esteem is to break with the South and Scarlett once and for all.

Wilkes, Honey
From *Gone With the Wind* by Margaret Mitchell

Known as 'Honey' because of her habit of addressing all and sundry as honey, she is the sister of handsome Ashley and the less attractive India Wilkes. There is an unofficial understanding between Honey and her Atlanta-based cousin, Charles Hamilton.

Wilkes, India
From *Gone With the Wind* by Margaret Mitchell

The plain sister of Ashley and Honey Wilkes, India lives at Twelve Oaks and is engaged to Stuart Tarleton, one half of the dashing, red-headed Tarleton twins. At the start of the book, however, Stuart's affections have been wandering in the direction of the captivating and irrepressibly flirtatious Scarlett O'Hara. Not surprisingly, India dislikes Scarlett intensely. Later on, she is one of the first to suspect that Scarlett has designs on her brother and this further fuels her animosity.

Flyer for musical adaptation of *Gone With the Wind*.

William
From *Frenchman's Creek* by Daphne du Maurier

A servant whose surname is never divulged, William runs Navron, the house on the Helford River owned by Sir Harry St. Columb. As the owner has been absent for a very long time, William has taken it upon himself to dismiss the staff and look after the house entirely on his own. This arrangement ensures there are no prying eyes in the vicinity and allows him to entertain a mysterious 'master' at the house whenever he wants.

   A thin, spare man with a button mouth set in a small, inscrutable face, William has the ability to alter his expression from smiling to solemn in a split second. With an English father and Breton mother, William is fluent in both tongues, and although he is partly foreign he is well-liked by the Cornish villagers. Resourceful and wholly faithful to those he loves, when he first meets Lady St. Columb, wife of Navron's owner, he addresses her in a manner that is overly familiar for a servant. Instead of being outraged, she finds herself curiously delighted by his boldness and soon comes to value him.

Williams, Kat   **RP**
From *Wolf Hall* by Hilary Mantel

The oldest sister of Thomas Cromwell, Kat has taken the place of the mother he can't remember, comforting him when he is beaten by their violent father and, following a particularly vicious attack, giving him money so he can get away. She is married to Morgan Williams, a Welshman with whom she has two sons, Richard and Walter.

Williams, Morgan   **RP**
From *Wolf Hall* by Hilary Mantel

A shrewd, pugnacious little Welshman living and working in London, Morgan Williams is married to Thomas Cromwell's sister Kat. He is an affectionate husband and father, and is fond of his brother-in-law.

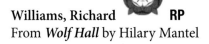

Williams, Richard   **RP**
From *Wolf Hall* by Hilary Mantel

The son of Kat and Morgan Williams, Richard is a sharp, intelligent lad who works for his uncle, Thomas Cromwell. He has strong Protestant leanings.

Willoughby, John
From *Sense and Sensibility* by Jane Austen

John Willoughby is an extremely handsome young man with an estate of his own in Somerset and expectations of inheriting another from an elderly relative in Devon. The very embodiment of manly beauty, grace and elegance, Willoughby has an open and lively personality. He is passionately fond of music and dancing and can read and discuss literature with great sensitivity. In many ways he seems the perfect partner for the romantically-inclined Marianne Dashwood, but beneath his charming disposition lurk some damaging secrets.

Hugh Thomson illustration of Willoughby with Marianne Dashwood.

Williamson, Johane   **RP**
From *Wolf Hall* by Hilary Mantel

The sister of Liz Wykys, Thomas Cromwell's wife, Johane is very like her sister in looks and temperament. She and her husband John have one child, a daughter also called Johane, but known as Jo.

Wilson, Jane
From *The Tenant of Wildfell Hall* by Anne Brontë

The daughter of a wealthy farmer and his narrow-minded wife, Jane is an ambitious and attractive 26-year-old woman who is keen to enhance her social position by marrying a rich gentleman. To this end she has insisted on receiving an expensive boarding school education which has given her many accomplishments, elegant manners and a degree of polish uncommon in a farmer's daughter. Now she has set her sights on Frederick Lawrence, the local squire who owns Wildfell Hall but lives in a larger and more comfortable mansion in a neighbouring parish. Refined and superior, she is devoid of warmth and heartily dislikes the new tenant at Wildfell Hall whom she takes to be a rival for Lawrence's affections.

Wincham, Alfred
From *The Pursuit of Love* and *Love in a Cold Climate* by Nancy Mitford

A young don at the fictitious St Peter's College, Oxford, Alfred becomes engaged and later married to Fanny Logan, narrator of both *The Pursuit of Love* and *Love in a Cold Climate*. Dark-haired like Fanny, he is said to look both serious and clever. An academic with leftish sympathies, Alfred only quite likes Fanny's frivolous and enchanting cousin, Linda Radlett, and is not in the least attracted to her beautiful friend, Polly Hampton. In fact, he doesn't appear to be interested in people at all which seems a pity as Fanny is consumed with interest in the goings on of her friends and relations. However,

Oxford, where Alfred Wincham is a don. Image © Tejvan Pettinger used under the Creative Commons Attribution 2.0 Generic license.

their marriage is apparently happy and in *The Pursuit of Love* Fanny reveals that he is a wonderful lover. Even so, his serious and rather distant nature makes him seem dull in comparison with the many fascinating characters found in both books.

de Winter, Maxim
From *Rebecca* by Daphne du Maurier

The owner of Manderley, a famously beautiful country estate in Cornwall, Maxim de Winter is a 42-year-old widower staying at the Hotel Cote d'Azur in Monte Carlo when the narration of his story begins. Dressed in English tweeds, with an arresting face and an air of quiet mystery, he immediately captures the attention of a young woman who is staying at the hotel in her capacity as paid companion to Mrs Van Hopper, a rich American woman. When Mrs Van Hopper becomes ill de Winter starts taking her young companion out for long drives, most of the time speaking to her with a sort of detached amusement but occasionally wandering off into impenetrable silences, leading her to conclude that he is grieving heavily for his wife who has been dead for just a year.

Maxim de Winter is the type of man women are supposed to find irresistibly attractive. His impeccable breeding, perfect manners and rugged, manly charm disguise a passionate, tormented soul desperately needing the absolving love of a good woman to assuage guilty feelings. In this he is rather like Edward Rochester from Jane Eyre, and like Rochester he hurts the woman he loves by being aloof, dismissive and angry. His silences and evasions breed doubt and his cool reserve inhibits the explicit declarations of affection that he actually craves. Far more vulnerable than his outward persona suggests, de Winter is in danger of losing everything that matters to him if he doesn't open up about his feelings and his past.

de Winter, Mrs
From *Rebecca by* Daphne du Maurier

The reader is never told the name of the second Mrs de Winter, the book's narrator, but early in the story it is described by Maxim de Winter as 'very lovely and unusual'. Aged 21 at the time of the events she describes in her narration, she is working as a paid companion for Mrs Van Hopper, a rich American woman. Her father and mother died within a few weeks of one another and she is alone in the world, obliged to earn a living doing a job she dislikes. Whilst staying at a hotel in Monte Carlo with Mrs Van Hopper, she meets the enigmatic Maxim de Winter and falls headlong in love with him. She has no thought of her love being reciprocated, but just as she and Mrs Van Hopper are due to leave Monte Carlo and travel to New York, de Winter asks her to marry him. After a brief honeymoon they travel to Manderley, his English home, to start their new life together.

With a husband twice her age who, moreover, she barely knows, the odds are already stacked against the second Mrs de Winter finding happiness in her marriage. The extreme reticence of her husband on the subject of his first wife, Rebecca and the hostility of the housekeeper at Manderley only add to her problems. Her biggest enemy, however, is her own insecurity which stems from the knowledge that she is out of her depth in Maxim's world. Unaware that her lack of sophistication is precisely what her husband loves about her, she worries that her straight-bobbed hair, unpowdered face and terrible clothes give her a school-girlish appearance that matches her mannerisms. Diffident, gauche and ill-at-ease with strangers and servants, she blushes too easily and agonises over social blunders. These tendencies make her transition into the role of mistress of

Manderley a nightmare, as does her growing belief that Maxim has never stopped loving Rebecca.

Winthrop, Harry **RP**
From *The Winthrop Woman* by Anya Seton

Handsome, pleasure-loving Harry Winthrop is austere John Winthrop's second son. While very young he is packed off to Barbados to run the family's tobacco plantation but is too lazy to supervise the slaves, preferring to roister with well-connected friends. Returning home under a cloud with massive debts, he further angers his father when he falls in love with his cousin and seduces her, making marriage the only respectable option. Regardless of the disappointment he has caused, he and his wife are welcomed back into the Winthrop family fold and his father attempts to straighten him out by keeping him busy with work. When the family decides to leave England for the Massachusetts Bay Colony, John Winthrop chooses Harry to accompany him as part of the advance party, leaving their wives and the rest of the family to follow later.

Winthrop, Jack **RP**
From *The Winthrop Woman* by Anya Seton

The oldest son of John Winthrop, Jack (real name John) is everything his brother Harry is not – reliable, sensible and godly. Although he shares his father's principles he has a more relaxed attitude to them, and is kinder and more tolerant of people's weaknesses. Nevertheless, he has enormous respect for his father to whom he is devoted. Early in the story he is tempted to form a romantic attachment he knows his father will disapprove of, so instead, he suppresses his feelings and continues to be a model son. Only when it is too late does he realise he has missed a chance of great happiness. In an attempt to assuage his feelings he marries someone he does not love sufficiently. In New England, steadfast Jack becomes a respected figure in the Puritan community and eventually finds a kind of contentment in his personal life. Towards the end of the book he is instrumental in helping his cousin Bess in her greatest hour of need.

Engraving of John Winthrop by Amos Doolittle after John Trumbull.

Winthrop, John   RP
From *The Winthrop Woman* by Anya Seton

Son of minor Suffolk gentry, John Winthrop is a
Cambridge-educated lawyer with strong Puritan beliefs
and a deep rooted conviction that his opinions are the
only ones that matter. Serious and stern with a very strict
moral code which leads him to treat harshly those that
fail to live up to his expectations, he is highly respected
by his fellow Puritans who encourage him to leave
England in order to help establish the Massachusetts Bay
Colony. While he is infuriating in his religious
inflexibility and moral certainties, he is in some ways an
admirable man who loves his wife and children and
attempts to see to the well-being of his extended family
including his wayward niece, Bess.

Statue of John Winthrop by
Richard Saltonstall Greenough.
Photo © Daderot.

Winthrop, Margaret   RP
From *The Winthrop Woman* by Anya Seton

Born Margaret Tyndal, daughter of a knight with a substantial estate in Essex,
Margaret becomes the third wife of John Winthrop and bears him many children.
A kind, gentle lady, she loves her difficult husband and has genuine affection for
his children and extended family. She becomes a kind of substitute mother figure
to Bess, the central character in the book, who she endeavours to protect from
her husband's frequent anger. When the family leaves England for a new life in
the Massachusetts Bay Colony, Margaret is very reluctant to go, but as she is a
dutiful wife she keeps her misgivings to herself.

Wilmot, Annabella
From *The Tenant of Wildfell Hall* by Anne Brontë

Already an heiress at the age of 25 following the death of her father, Annabella
stands to inherit considerably more when her elderly uncle dies. This ought to
mean that the accomplished and attractive young woman can marry for love rather
than advantage, but Annabella is ambitious and wants a title to go with her wealth.
To that end she has set her sights on marrying Lord Lowborough, a reformed

gambler and drunkard who is deeply in debt, even though she despises him. Committed as she is to this path, she is unable or unwilling to resist indulging in light dalliance – or perhaps something more – with the dashing but irresponsible Arthur Huntingdon. Flirtatious, selfish and immoral, Annabella understands how to make men desire her and she uses her knowledge to get what she wants, be that a husband or a lover.

Wolsey, Cardinal Thomas   **RP**
From *Wolf Hall* by Hilary Mantel

Aged 55 at the start of the book, tall, handsome Wolsey is Lord Chancellor of England, Archbishop of York and Henry VIII's right hand man. A brilliant man, early in Henry's reign he took charge of the country while the young king enjoyed himself. Latterly Henry has taken more interest in affairs of state, but Wolsey remains his closest advisor on matters of policy. He is currently attempting to find a solution to the king's dissatisfaction with his marriage to Katherine of Aragon which has failed to produce a living son. A network of spies keeps him informed of everything that happens at Court and beyond.

Wolsey has a subtle, elegant mind, and he enjoys showing off his cleverness, but he dislikes extremism and overt violence. Although as a cleric he is supposed to be celibate, he has two children, a scholarly boy and a girl who has been put in a convent to pray for her

Engraving of Wolsey by N.C. Wilson.

parents. A weakness of the flesh – as evidenced by the existence of his children – is further proven by his large stomach which adds to, rather than detracts from, his impressive appearance. Unlike most men in prominent positions at Court he is not nobly born, his father having been a prosperous Ipswich butcher.

Woodhouse, Emma
From *Emma* by Jane Austen

Eponymous heroine of the fourth Jane Austen novel to be published, Emma Woodhouse is a privileged young woman with many reasons to be thankful. Aged around 21, she is good looking, clever and rich, with a pleasant personality, a comfortable home, Hartfield, situated in the large village of Highbury, and a loving father. But although her circumstances are enviable, life is less perfect for Emma than the facts suggest.

The book begins with the marriage of Miss Taylor, her governess and only close female friend. Since the death of Mrs Woodhouse when Emma and her sister Isabella were aged 5 and 12 respectively, Miss Taylor has been a key figure in her life. Now she is married and since Isabella is also married and living away from home, Emma is left alone with her father. Although she loves him dearly, he makes a poor companion for a spirited young woman as he is a fussy elderly man. Bound to him through duty and affection, Emma is unable to get out into the world and experience much of life.

Perhaps because she can't contemplate leaving her father on his own, Emma claims to have no interest in finding a husband and instead, needing something to occupy her lively mind, she turns to matchmaking for others. Since she has a high opinion of her own abilities and is used to getting her way, she fully expects to succeed in this venture. When Jane Austen started work on *Emma*, she commented that she was going to create 'a heroine whom no one but myself will much like.' Certainly there are occasions when Emma can irritate, and it would be easy to dismiss her as interfering and self-satisfied except that her heart is in the right place, and when she knows she has caused offence she is genuinely mortified. Deep down Emma is a likeable girl who needs to discover some self-awareness if she is to be truly happy.

Woodhouse, Mr Henry
From *Emma* by Jane Austen

The wealthy owner of Hartfield, a neat, comfortable modern house in the village of Highbury, Mr Woodhouse is an elderly widower with two grown-up daughters, Isabella and Emma. Since the marriage of Isabella to John Knightley, he now lives alone with Emma and relies heavily on her companionship. A small, fussy, feeble man, he is obsessively concerned with health, chiefly his own but also that of his children and grandchildren. Hypochondria aside, he is an amiable gentleman, but he is unable to see that her concern for his welfare prevents Emma from living her own life and that she is at risk of suffocating in the overly anxious atmosphere of his house.

Illustration by Chris Hammond of Mr Woodhouse talking to his daughter Emma and Mr Knightley, 1898.

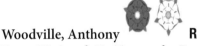

Woodville, Anthony   **RP**
From *We Speak No Treason* by Rosemary Hawley Jarman

The oldest son of Richard Woodville, Earl Rivers and his wife, Jacquetta of Bedford, Anthony is a handsome and erudite young man who is also an accomplished jouster. Since his family supported the losing Lancastrian side during the recent contest for the throne, his prospects for advancement are not great even though he and his father have now pledged allegiance to the Yorkist king, Edward IV. Therefore, he has much to gain from his sister Elizabeth's plot to ensnare the heart of the most influential man in the country. His debonair manner conceals a ruthless ambition and he is not afraid to engage in sinister activities in order to achieve his end.

Wykys Liz   **RP**
From *Wolf Hall* by Hilary Mantel

Liz Wykys was a widow when Thomas Cromwell started working with her father who was involved in the wool trade. She married him because she wanted children and he wanted a wife with connections. The marriage has been a success and love has blossomed between husband and wife. They now have three children, Gregory, Anne and Grace. Although she doesn't like them, Liz has resigned herself to her husband's frequent absences from home as he travels the country on business for his master, Cardinal Wolsey. She keeps busy looking after the children and running a little silk-work business which employs two girl apprentices. Although she has great respect for her husband's intellect she does not share his Protestant leanings. She is not a beauty, but this makes no difference to Cromwell who values her for more than her looks.

X and *Y* are for Xanthos and Yellan

Xanthos
From *The King Must Die* by Mary Renault

Brother of Persephone, Queen of Eleusis, Xanthos is a big man of about 29, with unattractive red hair and russet fox eyes. The commander of the Eleusis troops, he also advises his sister on the rare occasions she seeks a male opinion. His men know him to be greedy when it comes to sharing the spoils of battle.

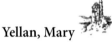

Yellan, Mary
From *Jamaica Inn* by Daphne du Maurier

Daughter of a farming couple from Helford in South
Cornwall, Mary has had a hard life helping her widowed
mother run the family farm. Even though life has
sometimes been a struggle, Mary is reasonably happy
until her mother becomes ill and dies. Now, at the age
of 23, she must leave her home and all that she holds
dear, to live with her Aunt Patience who is the landlady
of an inn on the desolate Bodmin to Launceston road.

Mary is small, with bright 'monkey' eyes and long
brown hair. She is quite pretty but her looks suffer when
she is cross or anxious. Having lived all her life on a
farm, she is tough and hard-working, and she finds
physical exertion a good way to let off steam. She is
courageous, with a spirited nature and a strong sense of familial duty which binds
her to her aunt. Having had little experience of romance, she is inclined to regard
love as a fancy word for what happens in the farmyard. Although she is a moral
individual, despising depravity and violence, she has greater tolerance for some
crimes than for others.

Epilogue 1

Favourite Novels and Characters

The Big Read

Women's historical fiction featured prominently in The Big Read, the BBC's 2003 search for the nation's best-loved novel. Ten of the fifty-plus books mentioned in the A to Z section of this book made it into the Big Read's top one hundred titles as voted for by 750,000 people. The field was open to male and female authors of every nationality, and included books in a wide variety of genres such as fantasy, sci-fi, contemporary and children's. This makes it all the more remarkable that number two on the list was Jane Austen's *Pride and Prejudice*, a book written nearly two hundred years ago and about a very narrow strata of society. Its high ranking in the list is testament to Austen's ability to engage readers with her characters and delight them with her perceptive wit. Interestingly, all the top five titles in the Big Read bar *Pride and Prejudice* were fantasy or sci-fi novels: *Lord of the Rings* took first place, with Philip Pullman's *His Dark Materials*, Douglas Adams' *Hitchhiker's Guide to the Galaxy* and J.K. Rowling's *Harry Potter and the Goblet of Fire* taking third, fourth and fifth place respectively.

The following list shows the A to Z entries together with their Big Read placings.

2. *Pride and Prejudice*
10. *Jane Eyre*
12. *Wuthering Heights*

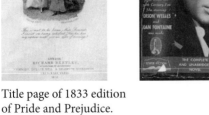

Title page of 1833 edition of Pride and Prejudice.

14. *Rebecca*
21. *Gone with the Wind*
27. *Middlemarch*
38. *Persuasion*
40. *Emma*
82. *I Capture the Castle*
95. *Katherine*

Favourite characters of the literati

A list published in *The Independent* newspaper on 3 March 2005 reveals the hundred favourite fictional characters as chosen by one hundred literary luminaries. Once again, Jane Austen fares well with five of her characters featuring in the list. The presence of Elizabeth Bennet (chosen by Donna Leon) comes as no great surprise, and to a lesser extent, neither does that of Emma Woodhouse (the choice of Diana Wynn Jones), Elinor Dashwood (chosen by Sarah Smyth) and Anne Elliot (chosen by Toby Litt). All are excellent choices; Lizzie Bennet fizzes with wit, Emma is reassuringly human, and gentle Anne Elliot captivates as she suffers in silence. Yet by concentrating on the heroines, Austen's large cast of fabulously awful characters is overlooked. The balance is somewhat redressed by Sally Beauman who nominates hateful Mrs Norris from *Mansfield Park* on the grounds that she 'is Austen's most profound, subtle portrait of the banality of evil'.

Three other characters from the A to Z featured in the list: Jane Eyre (the choice of China Miéville), Uncle Matthew, aka Lord Alconleigh (chosen by Kathleen Tessaro) and Rhett Butler (chosen by Penny Vincenzi). According to Vincenzi, 'He seems to encapsulate every desirable male quality – sophistication, wit, courage and tenderness, too.'

Romantic Reads

Another list published in *The Independent*, this one on 13 February 2009, puts forward the ten best romantic books for Valentine's Day. The list's selection process is not revealed, suggesting the titles may have been editorial choices. Once again, *Pride and Prejudice* makes an appearance, this time at the top of the list. In second place comes *Wuthering Heights*. It is a masterful work of fiction, but with its theme of obsessive love and vengeance, it seems an odd recommendation for Valentine's Day.

Ten recommended reads

The following works all fit The Historical Novel Society's definition of a historical novel in that they were written at least fifty years after the events they describe, or were written by someone who was not alive at the time of those events.

- *The Town House* by Norah Lofts – the first in Norah Loft's famous House trilogy, this spellbinding tale follows a runaway serf's struggle to survive as a free man
- *Katherine* by Anya Seton – charting the progress of Katherine Swynford from penniless nobody to ancestress of our monarchy
- *We Speak No Treason* by Rosemary Hawley Jarman – the story of Richard of Gloucester (later Richard III) through the eyes of three people who loved him
- *Niccolò Rising* by Dorothy Dunnett – a fascinating glimpse of life in fifteenth century Europe
- *Wolf Hall* by Hilary Mantel – Thomas Cromwell's journey from low-born brawling youth to Henry VIII's chief minister
- *Rebels and Traitors* by Lindsey Davis – the English Civil War in vivid, meticulous detail
- *Girl with a Pearl Earring* by Tracy Chevalier – compelling portrait of seventeenth century Dutch domestic life combined with tale of repressed passion
- *Gone With the Wind* by Margaret Mitchell – the American Civil War told from the losing side's point of view
- *My Last Duchess* by Daisy Goodwin – an American heiress struggles to survive amongst the aristocracy in fin-de-siècle Britain
- *The Light Years* (first novel of the Cazalet Chronicle) by Elizabeth Jane Howard – a convincing study of a middle-class English family shortly before the outbreak of World War II

Award winners

Gone With the Wind by Margaret Mitchell, Pulitzer Prize, 1939

Girl With a Pearl Earring by Tracy Chevalier, Barnes & Noble Discover Great New Writers Award, 2000

Wolf Hall by Hilary Mantel, Man Booker prize for fiction, 2009

Epilogue 2

Servants in Women's Historical Fiction

Servants are an important staple of women's historical fiction. Very occasionally a servant is the main character – think of Griet in *Girl with a Pearl Earring* – but more usually they appear in supporting roles as either trusted friends or troublemakers. Trusted friend servants carry messages for their master or mistress, share below stairs gossip with them and proffer sage advice and a shoulder to cry on when things go wrong. Troublemakers may dislike their employers and set out to make their lives difficult, or have an unfortunate habit that renders them bothersome. There are also servants who defy categorisation since they can be warm and friendly one day, huffy and resentful the next. For want of a better word these servants are classified as changeable. Examples of all three types are encountered in the A to Z section of this book, and the list presented below identifies the category into which each of them falls. (Several other characters in the A to Z work as servants at some point but listing them here would constitute a spoiler).

Trusted friend servants

Mammy, *Gone With The Wind*
Ellen Dean, *Wuthering Heights*
William, *Frenchman's Creek*
Bertha, *My Last Duchess*

Hawise Maudelyn, *Katherine*
Telaka, *The Winthrop Woman*
Mrs Fairfax, *Jane Eyre*
Martha, *Cranford*

Troublemaker servants

Mrs Danvers, *Rebecca*
Jeanette Moulin, *Milady Charlotte*
Grace Poole, *Jane Eyre*

Changeable servants

Tanneke, *Girl With A Pearl Earring*
Bessie Lee, *Jane Eyre*

Epilogue 3

From Page to Screen

The public has a seemingly insatiable appetite for adaptations of women's historical fiction. As a result, many well-known characters from the genre have been portrayed over the years on the big and small screen. Some of the most memorable are listed here, as well as a few that are fairly obscure.

Big Screen

East Lynne (1931)
Ann Harding (Lady Isabel Vane); Flora Sheffield (Barbara Hare)

South Riding (1938)
Edna Best (Sarah Burton); Ralph Richardson (Robert Carne)

Gone with the Wind (1939)
Vivien Leigh (Scarlett O'Hara); Clark Gable (Rhett Butler); Olivia de Havilland (Melanie Hamilton); Leslie Howard (Ashley Wilkes)

Wuthering Heights
1939 version
Merle Oberon (Catherine Earnshaw); Laurence Olivier (Heathcliff); David Niven (Edgar Linton)

1970 version
Anna Calder-Marshall (Catherine Earnshaw); Timothy Dalton (Heathcliff)

1992 version
Juliette Binoche (Catherine Earnshaw/Cathy Linton); Ralph Fiennes (Heathcliff)

Jamaica Inn (1939)
Maureen O'Hara (Mary Yellan)

London bus with Pride and Prejudice advertisement. Photo © Arne Koehler used under the Creative Commons Attribution-Share Alike 3.0 Unported license.

Pride and Prejudice
1940 version
Greer Garson (Elizabeth Bennet); Laurence Olivier (Mr Darcy)

2005 version
Keira Knightley (Elizabeth Bennet); Matthew Macfadyen (Mr Darcy); Dame Judi Dench (Lady Catherine de Bourgh); Carey Mulligan (Kitty Bennet)

Rebecca (1940)
Joan Fontaine (Mrs de Winter); Laurence Olivier (Maxim de Winter)

Jane Eyre
1944 version
Joan Fontaine (Jane Eyre); Orson Welles (Mr Rochester)

1996 version
Charlotte Gainsbourg (Jane Eyre); William Hurt (Mr Rochester)

2011 version
Mia Wasikowska (Jane Eyre); Michael Fassbender (Mr Rochester); Jamie Bell (St. John Rivers); Judi Dench (Mrs Fairfax)

Frenchman's Creek (1944)
Joan Fontaine (Dona St. Columb); Arturo de Cordova (Jean-Benoit Aubéry); Basil Rathbone (Lord Rockingham); Nigel Bruce (Lord Godolphin)

Emma (1996)
Gwyneth Paltrow (Emma Woodhouse); Jeremy Northam (George Knightley); Ewan McGregor (Frank Churchill)

Sense and Sensibility (1995)
Emma Thompson (Elinor Dashwood); Kate Winslet (Marianna Dashwood); Hugh Grant (Edward Ferrars); Alan Rickman (Colonel Brandon)

Mansfield Park (1999)
Frances O'Connor (Fanny Price); Jonny Lee Miller (Edmund Bertram);

Girl With a Pearl Earring (2003)
Scarlett Johansson (Griet); Colin Firth (Johannes Vermeer)

I Capture the Castle (2003)
Romola Garai (Cassandra Mortmain); Bill Nighy (James Mortmain); Tara Fitzgerald (Topaz Mortmain)

The Other Boleyn Girl (2008)
Scarlett Johansson (Mary Boleyn); Natalie Portman (Anne Boleyn); Eric Bana (Henry VIII)

Small Screen

Middlemarch
1968 version
Michele Dotrice (Dorothea Brooke); Clive Francis (Fred Vincy); Michael Pennington (Will Ladislaw)

1994 version
Juliet Aubrey (Dorothea Brooke); Douglas Hodge (Tertius Lydgate); Rufus Sewell (Will Ladislaw)

South Riding
1974 version
Dorothy Tutin (Sarah Burton); Hermione Baddeley (Alderman Mrs Beddows); Nigel Davenport (Robert Carne)

2010 version
Anna Maxwell Martin (Sarah Burton); David Morrissey (Robert Carne); Douglas Henshall (Joe Astell); Peter Firth (Alderman Snaith); Penelope Wilton (Alderman Mrs Beddows)

Rebecca
1979 version
Jeremy Brett (Maxim de Winter); Joanna David (Mrs de Winter); Anna Massey (Mrs Danvers)

1997 version
Charles Dance (Maxim de Winter); Diana Rigg (Mrs Danvers); Emilia Fox (Mrs de Winter); Faye Dunaway (Mrs Van Hopper)

Love in a Cold Climate
1980 version
Judi Dench (Lady Alconleigh); Lucy Gutteridge (Linda Radlett); Rosalyn Landor (Polly Hampton); Michael Williams (Capt. Davey Warbeck)

2001 version incorporating The Pursuit of Love
Rosamund Pike (Fanny Logan); Elisabeth Dermot Walsh (Linda Radlett); Megan Dodds (Polly Hampton)

East Lynne (1982)
Lisa Eichhorn (Lady Isabel Vane); Gemma Craven (Barbara Hare)

Jamaica Inn (1985)
Patrick McGoohan (Joss Merlyn); Jane Seymour (Mary Yellan); Trevor Eve (Jem Merlyn); John McEnery (Francis Davey)

Persuasion
1995 version
Amanda Root (Anne Elliot); Ciaran Hinds (Captain Frederick Wenworth)

2007 version
Sally Hawkins (Anne Elliot); Rupert Penry Jones (Captain Frederick Wentworth)

Pride and Prejudice (1995)
Jennifer Ehle (Elizabeth Bennet); Colin Firth (Mr Darcy); Alison Steadman (Mrs Bennet); Julia Sawahla (Lydia Bennet); Benjamin Whitrow (Mr Bennet)

Emma
1996 version
Kate Beckinsale (Emma Woodhouse); Mark Strong (Mr Knightley)

2009 version
Romola Garai (Emma Woodhouse); Jonny Lee Miller (Mr Knightley); Tamsin Greig (Miss Bates)

The Tenant of Wildfell Hall (1996)
Tara Fitzgerald (Helen Graham); Toby Stephens (Gilbert Markham); Rupert Graves (Arthur Huntingdon)

Tilly Trotter (1999)
Carli Norris (Tilly Trotter); Simon Shepherd (Mark Sopwith); Amelia Bullmore (Eileen Sopwith); Gavin Makel (Steve McGrath)

The Cazalets, an adaptation of the first book in the Cazalet Chronicle (2001)
Hugh Bonneville (Hugh Cazalet); Stephen Dillane (Edward Cazalet); Lesley Manville (Villy Cazalet); Joanna Page (Zoe Cazalet); Patsy Rowlands (Miss Milliment)

Jane Eyre (2006)
Ruth Wilson (Jane Eyre); Toby Stephens (Mr Rochester); Georgie Henley (young Jane)

Mansfield Park (2007)
Billie Piper (Fanny Price); Blake Ritson (Edmund Bertram); Douglas Hodge (Sir Thomas Bertram); Maggie O'Neill (Mrs Norris)

Northanger Abbey (2007)
Felicity Jones (Catherine Morland); J.J. Field (Henry Tilney); Carey Mulligan (Isabella Thorpe)

Cranford (2007 & 2009)
Judy Dench (Miss Matty Jenkyns); Eileen Atkins (Miss Jenkyns); Imelda Staunton (Miss Pole); Barbara Flynn (Mrs Jamieson); Jim Carter (Captain Brown)

Sense & Sensibility (2008)
Hattie Morahan (Elinor Dashwood); Charity Wakefield (Marianne Dashwood); Dan Stevens (Edward Ferrars)

Wuthering Heights (2009)
Charlotte Riley (Catherine Earnshaw); Tom Hardy (Heathcliff); Andrew Lincoln (Edgar Linton)